RETRIBUTION

An Angela Masters Detective Novel

By Mike Worley

Dedication

To my wife, Nancy, without whose love and support this project would not have been possible, and to my son, Jaffe, who challenged me to complete this story.

Chapter One

April 15, 1981 - Santa Rosa, California

Butch Agenbroad sat in the old yellow Honda Civic, waiting. The moment he had anticipated for four long years, the moment when he would punish her arrogance, was near. He took another drag on his cigarette and blew smoke at the windshield. Her husband's Chevy pickup turned the corner at the end of the block and left the subdivision. It was time.

"What are you doing here?" Sharon screamed. Her eyes grew wide as Agenbroad strode through her side door. *Why? After all this time. Why now?* she thought.

"Don't worry, Sharon. I just want to talk. I just want to see my daughter."

You lying sack of shit. I can see it in your eyes. Her eyes darted toward the adjoining living room where her three daughters played. She wanted to bolt for the door, to run screaming through the quiet neighborhood. But she could not leave her children with this snake.

Agenbroad's expression never changed. He wore a crooked smile as he approached within two feet of his ex-wife. His eyes narrowed on her face, the face of the one woman who had done the unthinkable. His haughty expression was fixed as his arm whipped out and he backhanded her across the right cheek. Blood spurted from the torn flesh at the corner of her mouth. Her hair, the color of a new penny, flew up as her head snapped to one side. Only then did the crooked smile leave Agenbroad's face.

Maybe if I don't talk, he'll think he's made his point. Please, God, please make him leave.

The crack of hand meeting jaw brought five-year-old Stacy Agenbroad through the partially open door of the kitchen. "Mommy, are you okay?"

"Yes, Stacy. Go back and watch television with your sisters. Mommy will be okay."

"Wait!" the deep voice of the man said.

"Yes, sir," the child said.

"I'm your daddy, Stacy. Your real daddy."

* * *

Who is this stinky man? Stacy reeled. *This isn't my daddy.* She turned to run but the stranger lifted her in his arms and kissed her cheek. She choked when the man held his face close to hers, his nicotine-laden breath assaulting her nostrils.

"No kiss back for your daddy?"

"Put her down, Butch!" Sharon struggled to pull her daughter from his grasp, even as blood flowed from the corner of her mouth and her cheek began to mottle. "She doesn't know you. Don't try to be a father now. Just leave her alone!"

"OK, Sharon. Don't blow a gasket. I was just trying to be nice." Agenbroad smiled as he lowered the child to the floor. "You go back to the television, Honey. I have to talk to your mommy."

"Yes, go into the other room and take care of Jennifer and Kelsey. Mommy will be fine."

Agenbroad was still bent over from setting Stacy on her feet. He watched as the child edged out of the kitchen and out of sight.

Then he jerked up. His swift rise added momentum as he backhanded the left side of Sharon's face, sending a mist of blood spatter across the door of the refrigerator.

"Don't *ever* tell me what to do! I just came here to see Stacy. Now look what you're making me do!"

Sharon's mouth dropped open as he pulled a six-inch Buck knife from his waist. She started to run but he was on her before she took two steps. He hit her again and again until she could no longer fight. With her last glimmer of consciousness she whispered, "Butch, please don't hurt my babies."

* * *

Without a word, Agenbroad jammed a chair under the knob of the door leading to the living room. *I don't need any little brats interrupting me now.* He picked up the limp form of his former wife and dropped her roughly onto a chair. Then he bound her wrists to the chair arms. *Let's see how your sweetie pie husband likes this,* he thought as he ripped the clothes from Sharon's body, leaving her naked. He backhanded her again.

Sharon, jolted to semi consciousness, choked through her sobs. "Please, Butch, please."

For a moment, he toyed with Sharon's naked breasts. She tried to twist away but couldn't escape his pawing hands. Then Butch clasped his left hand over her mouth and whispered in her ear through clenched teeth, "You divorced me, you bitch! And you told them I was abusive. Now, I'm going to show you what abusive really is."

Sharon's eyes widened as she saw the blade shining in his right hand. His movements came to her in agonizing slow motion as the knife arced down, plunging into her left breast. Life left her soft green eyes as he ripped the razor-sharp blade diagonally across her torso, laying her open to the hip.

Agenbroad stepped back and took a long look at Sharon. Her eyes stared blankly at the ceiling as her head, with its long flaming mane, flopped against the chair back. Blood ran down her right thigh and was already pooling on the white linoleum floor.

Agenbroad snorted and spit on the floor at Sharon's feet. He turned toward the door where he had entered. But then he heard the sounds of the children in the next room.

Chapter Two

5:55 p.m.

It had been a long day. Even though Doug McElroy loved his job as a computer systems manager, the demands of integrating new technology into the mainstream of business activities drained his energy. Now, as he entered the subdivision where he and his wife of four years lived, his mind was filled only with thoughts of spending a quiet evening with his girls.

"Sharon. I'm ... ," he called as he entered the side door. He was jolted to silence by the sight in his kitchen. His wife sat strapped to a chair, her skin gray and pale except for the gaping wound on her torso. At the sight, Doug felt vomit surging in his throat. He rushed to the sink and then ... *My God! The girls!* Eleven-month-old Kelsey was in the living room, asleep on the floor but covered with blood. Doug snatched her up and frantically examined her. He could find no injuries. It wasn't unusual for the baby to be out of her crib, playing with her sisters but where were they?

With the baby in his arms, he dashed through the rest of the house. "Stacy! Jennifer! Where are you?" Dread ripped at his heart as he raced next door. *Maybe the girls are at the Johnson's house.*

Mrs. Johnson answered the pounding on her door to find her neighbor and close friend sobbing incoherently. His white dress shirt was covered in blood. She pulled the baby from his arms and checked her, confirming she was unhurt.

"Doug, what happened?"

"Sttt..acy? Jennifer?"

"They're not here. I haven't seen them. What on earth happened?"

The man's heaving sobs were punctuated by one word ... "Sharon."

* * *

Detective Angela Masters had just left home on an early date with a man she considered a friend, a local high school football coach. The night out was a rare occurrence for the 33-year-old. She smiled at him as they waited for a table at one of the nicer restaurants in Santa Rosa. *What a pleasant start.* Then the pager on her hip emitted its insistent *b-zzz.* The date was over.

Fifteen minutes later, she parked her city-issue car next to several marked patrol units in front of a well-kept ranch-style home. The first thing that caught her eye was the color — it wasn't brown in the ordinary sense. The home was more the reddish-brown color of cinnamon.

The front door to the house was guarded by a uniformed officer, a rookie Angi didn't recognize. As she approached, Angi pulled a leather case from her pocket and flipped it open, revealing a shiny gold badge. "Detective Angela Masters, Homicide. What do we have?"

"Sergeant Thomas will brief you, detective." He motioned to the supervisor, standing beside the house with two other uniformed officers and an obviously distressed man in civilian clothes.

Angi Masters was well acquainted with Ray Thomas. He had been a sergeant for several years and her supervisor at one time. It was Thomas who had recommended Masters for her first assignment as a detective, the property crimes investigations unit.

Thomas excused himself from the group and walked with Masters to the center of the lawn, where they could talk with some privacy. "It's bad, Angi, really bad," Thomas said. "The husband — his name is Douglas Charles McElroy — came home and found his wife murdered in the kitchen. She's cut up real bad, but that's about all I know. Looks like she's been there all day. The husband refused to go to the hospital until he could talk to a detective."

"Any ideas on who did it?"

"None. We don't ... we don't have any suspects at this point—no witnesses that we know of."

Angi nodded. She turned to leave but Thomas' shoulders heaved as he struggled to hold his emotions in check.

"Wait, Angi. There's something else. The killer took two of her daughters. The son of a bitch left the youngest in there and the door to the kitchen was open. The baby ..."

Chapter Three

7:15 p.m.

Masters walked toward McElroy. As the husband of the victim, he was a natural suspect. When a person is killed in their home, the killer is, in a high percentage of the cases, the victim's spouse. He was also the person who had discovered the crime, so it was imperative that she lock down his story.

But before she could get to him, she saw another unmarked detective car parked near hers. It was her partner, Detective Devon Anderson's car. She paused at the sidewalk until he joined her. Anderson was an experienced homicide detective, having served in the Santa Rosa Police Department's Violent Crimes Unit for more than a decade.

He was not Masters' 'partner' per se – Santa Rosa did not have enough violent crime to warrant that type of assignment. Normally, all detectives worked alone, only teaming with other detectives when a need arose. Even though he was the senior investigator, Angi had been assigned as the lead investigator. The responsibility for the investigation would lie with her. She felt she was up to the challenge, but was also thankful that Anderson had drawn the assignment as her partner on this case.

"What's up, Ang?" Anderson asked. Anderson was a direct kind of guy. No cordial greetings for him—just cut right to the meat of the reason they were there.

"I don't know a lot yet, Devon. Man came home and found his wife stabbed to death. I understand it's a blood bath and two of her children are missing. I was just about to have a talk with the guy when you drove up."

Doug McElroy visibly struggled to compose himself as the detectives approached.

"Mr. McElroy, I'm Detective Masters and this is Detective Anderson. Let's go over here where we're away from the crowd a bit." A throng of neighbors and media were gathering outside the yellow-and-black police barricade tape.

"I want you to know that you don't have to talk to us, but we'd really appreciate whatever information can think of that might help," Angi said. She wasn't going to give McElroy the *Miranda* warnings against self-incrimination yet. But just in case he turned out to be more than a victim himself, she wanted anything he said to be voluntary.

"I know I don't have to talk to you, Detective. I also know that I am probably a suspect. But I didn't do this, so please ask whatever questions you want. Just please do it so you can get out there and find them!" McElroy looked firmly at Masters as he spoke.

"I was at work all day. You can verify that with my boss. We were working together at the computer center from the time I arrived this morning, about 8:40 a.m. until I left at about 5:05. We even had lunch together." McElroy's adrenaline was now pumping, his voice as steady as the emotion would allow, but he seemed anxious to get his story heard.

"I drove straight home, getting here at about 5:50, as usual. I didn't see anything out of place until I started in the side door. I noticed the door was unlocked but I didn't think much about it. This is a quiet neighborhood and we often don't lock the doors except at night. I walked in and ... and then I saw her ..." He broke into heaving sobs.

Angi would check his alibi, but her gut told her he was telling the truth. "Mr. McElroy, we can finish this later. Let's get you someplace where you can be more comfortable," Anderson said. He started to lead the distraught man toward the waiting supporters and signaled a uniformed officer to summon a nearby paramedic, just in case.

They had walked only a few feet when McElroy suddenly pulled away from Devon's guiding grasp. "No, sir! I can't help you find this bastard and my girls by lying drugged up in some hospital room."

"OK, sir. Go ahead," Angi said when McElroy had composed himself.

McElroy's voice cracked as he told of finding his butchered wife and frantically searching for his two daughters after finding the youngest covered in blood. His eyes again welled with tears as he recounted going to the Johnson's house next door. "God, I left Kelsey with the neighbor. You think she's safe there?"

McElroy stood, as if to retrieve his youngest from the neighbor. "Oh, God, I can't believe he took the girls." The thought seemed to take all the air from his body, and he dropped back onto the concrete wall where he'd been seated.

"Mr. McElroy, can you think of anyone who would want to hurt your wife?" Angi asked.

The man thought for a moment. "The only one I could possibly think of would be her ex-husband, but he hasn't bothered her for years. In fact, I think he's still in jail—almost killed a man in a bar fight or something."

"What's the ex-husband's name, Mr. McElroy?" Anderson asked. "We'll need to check him out just to be sure."

"Agenbroad. A-G-E-N-B-R-O-A-D. He goes by Butch, but his real name is Elwood or something like that."

"OK, sir," Masters said, "we'll check him out. Here's my card, if you think of anything else."

"I guess I should tell you that Stacy is not really my daughter. Sharon divorced Agenbroad before Stacy was born. I met her when Stacy was about six months old and, like I said, there's been no contact from him. So I've raised her like my own."

"That's helpful, Doug. Thank you. We'll talk again, and I will keep you advised of our progress."

McElroy tried to look hopeful but his swollen eyes betrayed his anguish.

Masters and Anderson watched as the man walked silently to a group of waiting friends and relatives.

Chapter Four

Angela Masters

Five foot ten, with long naturally blonde hair, Angela Renee Masters looked every inch the star athlete she once had been. In high school, the Santa Rosa native was an A student and stand-out volleyball player, with a competitive spirit.

Angi attended Cal State Northridge on a volleyball scholarship. A four-year starter as the setter on the Matadors volleyball team, she graduated with honors and a degree in business administration.

At 22, she returned home to Santa Rosa, determined to pursue a career, not in business, but as a police officer. Angi's uncle was a Sonoma County deputy sheriff, and she grew up listening to his stories of manhunts and arresting felons. She took the test for police officer, and was hired as a Santa Rosa city police officer at age 23.

Ten years later, here she was—a homicide detective. But the sight of McElroy being comforted by his friends and family caused her mind to drift. *If only my father had that kind of support so many years ago.*

* * *

Her mind flashed back to that terrible day in 1956, a day which began as a beautiful August day, clear and sunny. As usual, her father had risen early to be at work by 6:30 a.m. He was the general manager of SonomaVita, the largest distributor of milk products in the Santa Rosa area. Don had managed the company since 1948. With only an eighth grade education in his native Kansas, he had taught himself management accounting. This brought him attention from the primary investor, who had named him as manager. Don was capable, but it came at personal cost. He sometimes worked eighteen hours a day to be certain his work was done right.

He did his best to be a father to his two daughters and a good husband. But his Depression-era upbringing put more value on being a provider than on being a nurturer.

At home, Rose Masters was in charge. Everyone knew they could count on the stay-at-home mom. On that beautiful August morning, eight-year-old Angi's friend Nancy had come to play, filling the remaining summer days with fun before school began. Angi's house was popular with her friends. A plastic-lined, corrugated twenty inch deep pool at the Masters home was an August mecca, paradise on a hot summer day.

Rose demanded one rule: No one was allowed in the pool unless Rose was there, with her eagle eyes on the kids. With the temperature already at 84 degrees, at only 10:30 a.m. that day, the kids were ready for the pool. But Rose was busy this morning, and the pool would have to wait. The girls reluctantly came back inside and went to Angi's room. Rose busied herself in the kitchen and checked routinely on four-year-old Karen, who played in the living room.

As she worked, Rose was suddenly overcome by a cold, foreboding chill. She walked to the living room. *Where is Karen?!* Bile surged in her throat as she turned to see that the sliding glass door connecting the family room with the back yard was open. A bowl filled with mashed potatoes dropped from her hands and crashed to the linoleum as she bolted for the open door. Dashing through it, Rose Masters confronted the sight that would permanently torture her mind. Her youngest daughter was floating face down in the pool, lifeless.

Her screams brought Angi and Nancy running downstairs, as well as attracting the attention of several neighbors who ran to help, but it was too late. The four-year-old was gone.

* * *

"I don't understand how she could have gotten that door open," Don said through his tears. "It was heavy and she wasn't tall enough to get good leverage on the handle." But for Rose, the blame for her daughter's death lay squarely with her husband. The sliding door's locking latch had been broken for months, and

13

she had nagged Don to get it fixed. But no one locked their doors and so the latch was not high on Don's weekend to-do list.

Rose saw it another way. Words that spit like nails punctuated her tears, and she put her head in her hands. "Had you been there, you would've seen how much she's grown! Then you might've thought twice about fixing that latch!"

Don could only defend himself by countering, "Why weren't you watching her?"

Blaming each other only escalated the terrible rift and a year later, the couple separated. Don moved to an apartment across town. He still saw Angi on weekends, but it was never the same. Eventually, he sank into depression, blaming himself for everything—the loss of Karen and the loss of his family.

When Angi was 13, she came home from school one day to find two Sonoma County Sheriff's cars parked at her house. One of the deputies was her uncle, her father's brother. He was trying to comfort her sobbing mother. When he saw Angi enter, the uncle turned to her. "Angi, Honey, I'm sorry to have to tell you that your daddy was killed in a car accident last night. His car went off the road and hit a tree. He was killed instantly."

Angi began to cry too, but her tears were accentuated by her own guilt. Her father was always a cautious driver. He would never have been driving 85 miles per hour on a winding mountain road in rural Sonoma County, as her uncle had said. Not unless he wanted to kill himself. She knew he was depressed but didn't know what she could do.

Now she regretted that she had never told anyone. And to make it even worse, her last visit to his apartment had ended badly, thanks to her teen-aged angst. "He tried to hug me and I blew it off. I just pushed past him and out the door," she would later tell close friends. It was a moment she remembered, and regretted, forever.

But even more, she cried with the guilt she had carried since Karen's death. Karen could not have opened the sliding glass door using the handle. Angi knew her sister still wasn't strong enough or tall enough to get enough leverage on it. Karen could, however, open the door if it was left open a crack so that she could get her little hands on the edge of the door. *Did I close the door completely when Nancy and I came in from the back yard that day? I don't think I did!* She would never be certain of the answer but the question played in her mind again and again.

What she did know was that she now had the power to at least try to prevent further tragedy to the McElroy family. It was up to her to bring Stacy and Jennifer back so that Kelsey would not grow up without her sister, as Angi had. She also had to bring them back so that Doug McElroy would not blame himself for something he could not have prevented.

Chapter Five

7:45 p.m.

"Angi, are you with me?" Devon's voice pulled Angi back to the murder scene.

"Sorry, Devon. My mind was somewhere else for a second. Let's go."

They checked in with the officer at the entrance, the same one Masters initially approached. Angi pushed open the mahogany front door and peered inside. The detectives paused before even entering the scene. Their senses were alert for any clues to the all-too-real drama which had played out here. They also took in their impressions of the general lay of the scene. Overturned furniture? Loose clothing lying about? Papers or other items on the floor? Anything which seemed out of place or which might shed even minuscule light on what had happened.

"Nothing jumps out at me right now," Devon said.

"Me, neither," Angi said. She stepped inside the dimly lit living room. As her eyes adjusted to the light, she moved toward the kitchen. She eyed each step before she took it, careful not to step on any evidence. Anderson remained at the doorway, observing Masters' progress and watching for any inadvertent disturbance of evidence. Her objective was merely to get a sense of the murder scene itself. Close examination would wait until later, after the crime lab techs had processed the route to the body and the area around it.

What met her eyes as she peered into the kitchen would be indelibly etched in her mind. Sharon's blood, still moist in many places because of the large amount of it, formed a river down her right thigh and clotted in pools across the white floor.

Angi's eyes followed the bloody stream down the body until, there on the floor; she caught sight of the drag marks. These were not drag marks in the sense that a homicide detective normally encounters — those caused by the victim's body being dragged. Rather, these drag marks were those of tiny hands and legs being pulled through the blood pool, the evidence of a small child crawling in search of the comfort of her mother.

On the woman's left leg, more evidence of horror. Tiny hand prints were cast in drying red blood on the pale flesh. Masters choked back the tears and swallowed hard to hold down the bile roiling in her stomach.

Her sisters gone, the baby crawled through the open kitchen door in search of her mother, and left her tracks in the fresh blood. She then left her tiny hand prints as she touched her lifeless mother's skin.

Focus, girl. Damn it. Focus! I can't let ... The thought was interrupted by a surge of bile in her throat.

The baby was gone now, taken away by the paramedics. Masters searched the kitchen for any clue, but nothing stood out as immediately in need of preservation. Taking one last look at the once-beautiful Sharon, she carefully exited, following as closely as possible the exact path she had taken on her entrance.

* * *

"I didn't see anything that would point me to a suspect," Angi said to Devon after they were both outside. "But one thing is sure. There was a lot of rage in this crime. It screams personal to me."

"OK. How about I get started on checking the husband's alibi. Patrol guys are already canvassing the neighbors for any witnesses."

"Good. And I think my next priority is to look into this Agenbroad character."

As Masters was getting into her beige Chevy Caprice, its red emergency dash light still rotating in the windshield, a uniformed officer she recognized as Toni Burton approached her. "Detective Masters—Angi. I might have something for you."

"What is it, Toni?"

"I found a girl, a neighbor across the street from the McElroy house. She was sick and stayed home from school today. And I think she may have seen the killer."

Chapter Six

The Previous Day -- April 14

Martita had a bad feeling—a touch of dread that niggled at the back of her mind as she thought about the past few days. *What is he up to now?*

She didn't know that she was not the first Mrs. Butch Agenbroad, or even the fourth. She only knew that she loved this charming man.

Certainly, he had been in trouble. As a prison social worker, she met him in 1978 while working at San Sebastian State Prison. Martita was immediately attracted to the prisoner called 'Butch' by his fellow inmates. He was serving a five to seven-year sentence for aggravated battery, having nearly killed a man with a pool cue.

"Honest, Martita. The other guy started it, mad that I beat him in a simple game of pool. He attacked me and I was just defending myself."

Martita had heard similar stories from prisoners before. They were all victims of the 'system,' people who really had done nothing but be in the wrong place at the wrong time and powerless to avoid the court's judgment.

Butch's case had been different. His story was so sincere. She was sure he was wrongly convicted. At the very least, he was the victim of some gung-ho prosecutor trying to make a name for himself at someone else's expense. The fact that his sentence was far more severe than that of other first-time offenders convicted of the same offense did not register with her. She fought to have Butch released after serving the minimum sentence.

After serving only four years and one month, Butch walked out of San Sebastian Prison as a paroled man. Martita had been waiting for him at the gate. She knew how to get things done in the prison system far better than she knew how to pick men.

Within a week, Martita had become Mrs. Butch Agenbroad and he moved into her small but comfortable house in Santa Cruz. *I'm no beauty queen and I'm almost thirty, but he treats me like I'm the only woman alive. I couldn't be happier,* she thought.

"Martita, *mi hija,*" her mother had said, "I do not trust this man. He seems *resbaladiza* — too slick to me. He is like the hustlers in the barrios of East L.A. I am afraid he will hurt you."

"No, Mamá. Butch is a good man who made a mistake. He is honest, a carpenter like Jesús. I will help him get his life back and he will give me love and meaning in my life. I promise it is so, Mamá."

Elena Sandoval had gone along for her daughter's sake.

"Don't worry, Martita, mi amor," Butch had said. "I saved some money from my carpentry work before I got tossed in the can. We'll do fine until I can find work."

Within two weeks, he found work for a contractor building a new subdivision. He had also purchased a new Buick LeSabre. On weekends, he took his new bride on drives along the coast highway.

Once, they went as far north as Santa Rosa, where he drove through a quiet middle class neighborhood, dotted with charming but older ranch-style homes. Martita later remembered seeing a little girl playing in the front yard of a house as she and Butch cruised slowly down the street. She also remembered the unique hue of brown that the house was painted.

* * *

Two days ago, Butch made an announcement. "I have to take care of a family emergency. My cousin in Reno is very sick and I'm the only family he has."

"I understand, Butch. Family is first."

"Just my thought, mi amor. That's why I wonder if your mother would loan me her car. I want you to have the LeSabre while I'm away."

"Butch, that's not necessary. My Volkswagen is just fine. I drive it every day."

"I know you do, but we've had a few problems with it and I wouldn't be here to help you if it broke down. I'd feel much better if you'd ask your mother. Besides, she doesn't use it much and it would get better gas mileage than the Buick. That would help our finances until money starts coming in from my new job."

The yellow Honda Civic, now pushing 80,000 miles, had been purchased almost new by Elena's late husband. She had known many good times in that car, sitting beside her beloved Jorge. With his passing, she strived to keep the car as immaculate as he had. The car had suffered a few dents and the paint was oxidizing, but she did her best. And she kept the inside of the car as clean as she kept her small home.

"Oh, all right," Elena finally said. "But one thing, Butch. Please do not smoke in my car. No one has ever smoked in it and I want to keep it that way."

"Of course, Mama. I'm trying to quit anyway."

Elena hated it when Butch called her 'Mama.'

"*Gracias, Mamá,*" Martita said. "I will check on you every day and I can drive you anywhere you need to go."

Butch tossed his small duffel of clothes in the back and driven the Honda carefully away to the east. As the car disappeared around a corner, Martita was sure she had seen the flicker of a match inside the car.

Chapter Seven

Butch

Agenbroad drove south on Highway 101. The girls sat quietly in the back seat and he was alone with his thoughts—and memories.

Elmont Jacob Agenbroad. What kind of a mother names her son ELMONT? Agenbroad had spit out that question a thousand times in his life. His mother. She was the start of all his troubles in life. And she started it by naming him 'Elmont.'

Then to make matters worse, she insisted on calling him 'Monty.' *That's a name for a game show host.* It was a name for a boy destined to become a great man, a feared man.

His father had run off before he was born, so he was the man of the house. Still, his mother never treated him with the respect due the family leader. She expected him to do chores around the house. He refused, often threatening her until she backed down. Men like him simply didn't do chores.

At school, some kids called him a bully. Even some teachers called him that and worse, but he didn't mind. To him, 'bully' was a title of honor, a title befitting the destiny he saw for himself.

Once—he remembered it clearly—he had seen a tough character named Butch on his mother's old RCA black and white television. *Butch Agenbroad. Perfect!*

His mother still insisted on calling him 'Monty,' and demanded he help around the house. But he had a plan for that, too.

One day, as his mother stood at the pink tiled kitchen counter, Butch slipped up behind her with a butcher knife he pulled from the maple rack on the wall. As she reached forward to rinse some cut vegetables, he plunged the knife between her third and fourth ribs. She screamed as she fell to the floor, but no one in their neighborhood would be rushing to investigate.

Someone might call the seven digit number for the local police, but Butch had more than enough time to finish the job. He had intended to pierce her heart. He missed by a few millimeters, but the damage to her lung was sufficient for her to soon drown in her own blood.

Butch stood over her with a cold stare as she gasped, life ebbing from her. He was two months past his thirteenth birthday.

* * *

His first two wives were easy marks, targeted through singles clubs and bars. Moderately wealthy women with no close relatives, each had been an easy prey for his charms. He wined and dined them, always the perfect gentleman. Only after they married him and signed over all their possessions to his care did the true Butch Agenbroad emerge.

With each of them, he liquidated their assets to provide money for his own vices. When the money ran out, Agenbroad forced the women to prostitute themselves. If they refused, he beat them. Sometimes he beat them anyway. And when he was finished with them, he simply abandoned them. Divorce was not in the cards for Butch Agenbroad or the women who had the misfortune to become his wives. That was, until he met Sharon.

Sharon Kelson was a firebrand, with a constitution to match her long, flaming copper mane. She fell in love almost immediately with the strikingly handsome and gentlemanly carpenter she met in a local tavern.

Butch treated Sharon to breathless nights on the town, nights of dancing and partying until the sun's light was peeking over the Mayacamas Mountains. His intensity and temper matched her own, and she found an intellectual bond as well as a sexual one with this rugged but seemingly gentle man.

At 24, Sharon had never been married, although she had her share of boyfriends and a few intimate, if unsatisfying relationships.

"It has been the same for me," Butch said. "I've never found anyone I wanted to settle down with—until now."

Four months after they met, Butch and Sharon were married in a civil ceremony. Sharon would have preferred a beautiful church wedding. The money she inherited from her late father and mother would have paid for a nice ceremony, but Butch would have none of it.

"A simple ceremony is all we need," he said. "We have each other, and that's all that matters. We don't need the world to affirm what we feel."

Within five months, the fairy tale became a nightmare. Agenbroad demanded she turn over custody of all her inheritance to him. "One thing I've learned over the years is how to manage money," he said.

As his nights at home became more infrequent and her money allowances likewise dwindled, she began to question him. Butch's fiery outbursts were more than matched by Sharon's and an uneasy peace emerged.

Sharon would not be as easy a mark as his previous wives but Butch was determined to break her.

Then, she delivered what was, for Butch, bad news. "I'm pregnant, Butch."

It was the first time he had hit her.

It would be the last, in her mind. The next day, she filed for divorce.

Thirteen months after they were married, the divorce was final. Sharon got sole custody of the yet-unborn child.

"You'll live to regret this!" he told her through clenched teeth as they walked out of the courthouse. *Live to regret it and not one minute more!*

Chapter Eight

April 15 - 10: 45 a.m. - Richmond, California

And I kept my promise, didn't I, Bitch?

"Mister, can we please go home? My little sister is scared. We need our mommy."

Damn! This was a stupid idea. Why did I take these little brats? I can't take them home. Shit, Martita would have a million questions and she knows too damn many people in the system.

"Mister?"

"Soon, Stacy. I'll take you home soon."

I'm stuck with them now. I just need to stash them someplace until I can figure out what to do. I might need them for bargaining with the cops if it comes to that.

Heading south on 101, he crossed the Richmond Bridge, a high span over the southern part of San Pablo Bay. The Richmond Bridge. Richmond! Chamberlain lived there. Agenbroad knew he could trust Chamberlain, a man with a past Agenbroad knew too much about.

* * *

Agenbroad parked the yellow Honda in front of a small house on a quiet street. At 11:00 on a Wednesday morning, the blinds were still drawn. Chamberlain was probably still asleep. He would have been drinking the night before, just as he did every night. Agenbroad pounded on the bare front door, long since stripped of its varnish by the salt air. After some time, Chamberlain stumbled to the door.

"What in the hell do you want, Agenbroad? It's too early for me to be up!"

"Come on, Chamberlain. I have a deal going and I need your help."

Chamberlain peered out the door into the sunlit day and eyed the two little faces peering from the window of the yellow Honda. "Who are they?"

"Those are the deal. I just snatched them off the street in Greenbrae. We can get a lot of money for them, but I need you to hold on to them for a few days." *Better he thinks they came from a wealthy town across the bridge. And I sure as hell won't tell him that Stacy is my own daughter.*

"How in the hell am I supposed to do that?"

"I'm sure you can find a way. Just for a few days."

"All right. Bring the little brats in here, and they better not give me any trouble!"

Chamberlain didn't like the idea at all, but Agenbroad had as much on him as he had on the former San Sebastian inmate, perhaps more. It seemed best to go along for now.

Butch led the girls up the cracked sidewalk and into the dark den Chamberlain called home. Jennifer was crying and Stacy tried to calm her.

"Stacy, I have to go make plans for our trip to the zoo. Little kids aren't allowed at the ticket place, so you have to stay here with Mister Smith until I get back. He'll be nice to you." *I don't want any backtalk from her right now, especially since Chamberlain could still back out on me.*

"Mister Smith? Who in the hell is Mister Smith?" Chamberlain barked from his hangover fog.

"You are!" Agenbroad said through clenched teeth. "Don't forget it."

Agenbroad arrived in Santa Cruz in mid-afternoon. He didn't go home right away, nor did he go to Elena's. He realized he needed to clean the car. There was no need for Butch to get his nosy mother-in-law mad or suspicious. She might be fool enough to call the cops.

Agenbroad drove to a drive-through car wash and wiped the smoke stains from the windshield of the Honda. But after that half-hearted attempt to clean the car, he stopped in a nearby tavern to relax.

Just before 5:30 p.m., Agenbroad called Martita at home. "I'm back, Honey," he said in the cheeriest greeting he could muster. "Pick me up at your mama's house, OK?"

"Why are you home so early, Butch? I thought your cousin was near death. Did something happen?"

Butch had completely forgotten about that story.

"False alarm, Martita. The woman who called me exaggerated the situation."

"Here you go, Mama," Butch said, handing the keys to the yellow Honda to Elena. "It ran fine and I took good care of it for you. Thank you for letting me use it. I even washed it and filled it with gas for you, Mama."

Ugh. That 'mama' crap again. "You're welcome, Butch. Any time."

As Butch and Martita drove away in the Buick, Elena opened her car door and caught a face full of smoky air. *I don't see any ashes or signs that he smoked in my car, but I know that awful smell. And what's that?* It looked like some kind of child's toy on the floor of the back seat.

Chapter Nine

3:00 p.m.

Roy Chamberlain sat at the kitchen table in his small bungalow in Richmond, staring out the window at the narrow street. The shimmering waters of the San Francisco Bay were only a few blocks away, but Chamberlain felt nothing except aggravation as he gazed from his filthy window. What was he going to do with these two brats Agenbroad had dumped on him? *I ain't in no position to take care of two little girls.* And their presence might raise questions from his nosy neighbors.

Chamberlain took a long draw on his cheroot, looking over his shoulder at the adjoining living room. There they were, sitting quietly on the worn couch. The older girl eyed him from time to time, but otherwise they caused him no trouble. The little one complained at first about the quality of the picture on Chamberlain's ancient color TV, but the older one quieted her almost immediately. Since then, except to ask for a drink of water, both had been quiet since Agenbroad dropped them off.

As the nicotine laden smoke, artificially scented with cherry, wafted above his head, Chamberlain cursed his existence. It once seemed he had a chance to get above the miserable life of his father. Once, yes, but that was many years ago. In those years, he'd made some bad choices. His association with Agenbroad was one of the worst.

* * *

Chamberlain grew up in the rough-and-tumble neighborhoods of Chicago's north side. As a boy, he was regaled with tales of the bloody gang wars of the 1930s, fought on the very streets where he played. He and his friends took turns pretending to be streetwise gangsters like Hymie Weiss and Jake McGurn. They spurned the better-known Capone and Dillinger, preferring to emulate the cunning outlaws their elders described as 'businessmen.' His rarely-employed father had long since left, but there was another figure in young Roy's life who tried to steer the impressionable youth in a positive direction.

Tooey O'Banion was a distant cousin of slain mobster Charles 'Dion' O'Banion, gunned down in 1924 in a flower shop that had stood less than two blocks from the tenement where Chamberlain grew up. He used this connection to prove to the kids on his beat that one was not destined to follow a life of crime and failure. Officer O'Banion was a Chicago cop, a relative of mobsters by blood, but an honest policeman in his own right.

O'Banion took the young Chamberlain under his wing and tried his best to encourage the youngster toward an honorable life. For a while, it seemed that he was successful. At age 21, with only a high school diploma and no money to attend college, Chamberlain left the north side and moved to California. There, with a recommendation from Officer O'Banion, Roy Chamberlain got a job as a guard at San Sebastian State Penitentiary.

From his first day, Roy took pride in his light grey and blue prison guard uniform. He enjoyed the respect it gave him in the small community where he settled, a lower-middle class area a few miles from the prison. Neighbors who held jobs as laborers or clerks were impressed with the tall, handsome youth from Chicago.

Deep down, though, he loved something else about his job, something even more than the respect of his neighbors. Roy loved the power over people his position gave him. For the first time in his life, he was in control—in charge, if only of a small group of medium-security inmates. But it was power, nevertheless, and Roy quietly relished in it.

For the first three years, little happened to steer Chamberlain from the honest path. He was sometimes unhappy with his low salary, but assured himself he would advance. Besides, at 24, he still made more money than many of his neighbors, most of whom were much older. He enrolled in night classes as a community college and life was looking good. Even the arrival of a tough-looking thug named Agenbroad was just another minor event in the career of Senior Guard Chamberlain.

The tough-acting 20-year-old had been sentenced to three-to-five years for attempted armed robbery. His rap sheet showed he had attempted to hold up a liquor store in San Jose. He hadn't even gotten the cash drawer open before he was confronted by a beat officer who had been in the back of the store. *This Agenbroad kid might be tough, but he isn't a very good robber*, Chamberlain thought as he scanned the paperwork of the new arrival. Agenbroad was not much younger than himself, and he clicked his tongue at the thought of the wasted life.

Chamberlain walked up to the kid with the forced scowl and pressed the bill of his cap against the prisoner's forehead. "Don't even think of getting wise-ass with me, Agenbroad. For the next five years, on this watch, I'm your momma and your daddy. You don't do anything without my okay. You got that, *Elmont*?" Chamberlain could see the prisoner wince at the mention of his unusual first name, but he didn't care. It was just a piece of information he might be able to use later.

"Yes, sir!" Agenbroad spit out the words.

Shortly after Agenbroad was processed into San Sebastian, he was transferred to another section of the prison. After that, Chamberlain did not see him again, although he did hear from other guards that Agenbroad was considered a troublemaker. Despite that, Agenbroad had been paroled after serving the minimum time on his sentence. By then, Chamberlain was preoccupied with problems of his own.

* * *

It started easily enough, just a friendly game of poker or craps with other guards after work. Before long, though, Chamberlain was contacting loan sharks to shore up his gambling losses. Even his promotion to Guard Sergeant didn't bring in enough money to cover his losses. He dropped out of classes at the community college, unable to pay even the reduced tuition offered to public employees.

Then one day an inmate named Gomez approached Chamberlain. "I hear you've got some money problems, Boss," the gangly prisoner whispered. "If so, I know a way to get you clear of all of your gambling debts in one night."

"I'm listening." *What's this little shit up to?*

"We just need a hand steering a prisoner to a certain place at a certain time. You don't gotta do nothing else but get him sent there and keep your mouth shut."

The con's manner was straightforward enough, and Chamberlain had been inside a prison long enough to know what he was being asked to do. He would send the designated con to the laundry or some other secluded place after normal working hours. The shithead would be beaten by other cons for some violation of the inmates' code. It must have been a pretty serious screw-up on this guy's part for it to be worth clearing all of Chamberlain's debts, but who gave a shit. It was just another asshole con. Still, Chamberlain could wind up behind bars himself if he got caught.

"Get the hell out of here, Gomez. Don't be coming to me with this shit." *I could beef this asshole, but I'll just keep my options open. No sense cutting off a source of income if I need it, and right now, I really need money.* It was just a matter of taking the final step for Chamberlain to turn his back on the legacy of Tooey O'Banion.

"OK, Boss. No harm, no foul." After a quick glance around the yard, Gomez pressed a wadded piece of tissue into Chamberlain's palm. On it was written the name of the prisoner to be targeted. "Just in case, Boss," Gomez whispered before sauntering away across the yard.

That night, at home and safely away from the prying eyes that were everywhere at San Sebastian, Guard Sergeant Roy Chamberlain carefully unfolded the tissue. For a long moment, he gazed at the name written on the thin paper, a real shithead troublemaker. Somehow, that justification made the decision easier. The following day during the afternoon exercise period, Chamberlain walked slowly past Gomez and gave him an almost imperceptible nod. There would be no going back.

Chamberlain ordered the targeted prisoner to the laundry building, just as Gomez had directed him. He then went about his business, responding to the laundry following the general guard call when someone reported the beating. The prisoner was severely beaten, but would survive. Of course, the con knew better than to rat on who had beaten him or how he came to be in the closed laundry building in the first place.

Chamberlain saw his actions as purely for his financial benefit. But from that initial episode, he was drawn deeper and deeper into a criminal web.

By the time Agenbroad returned to San Sebastian five years after his initial release, Chamberlain had achieved the rank of Guard Captain and was in charge of an entire shift. He had also made a few thousand dollars setting up prisoners for beatings at the hands of fellow inmates. His greatest relief was that no one suspected his involvement.

He dealt only with Gomez, which ensured a degree of cover for his actions. When Agenbroad returned, Chamberlain had not participated in any such activity for several months. Gomez was nearly at the end of his sentence and it was unusual for a guard captain to personally order a prisoner to do anything.

Chamberlain's source of extra income dried up coincidentally with his promotion to captain. However, his new salary allowed him to maintain the lifestyle which was previously available to him only with the money from his illicit activity. Chamberlain decided he had enough of the seamy second life he had led. He would soon learn that getting away from criminal complicity was not as easy as he hoped.

Chapter Ten

3:45 p.m.

"Please, Mister Smith. Please take us home. We want to go home."

"I'm sorry, ummm Stacy, is it?" *That asshole Agenbroad isn't coming back. I know it but there's not a damn thing I can do about it but I have to help him or he's sure to screw me.* "Stacy, you take care of your sister and I'll see what I can do to get you some place safe, okay?" Then it struck Chamberlain like the dawning of a new day. Sister. Brother. *Dave*, Chamberlain muttered to himself. His younger brother Dave and Dave's wife, Joyce, would be perfect to dump these kids on. *Dave owes me and having a woman around might keep them quiet.* "Go back and watch TV, Stacy. I'm calling someone to pick you up soon."

"OK, Mister Smith, but please, we want to go home."

"I know. Soon." Maybe there was something left of Tooey O'Banion in him after all. Setting up some douche-bag for a beating was one thing. Kids ... well kids were another matter altogether.

He ambled to the refrigerator and tugged on the chrome handle. The old-fashioned solid latch popped open and Chamberlain stared inside at his paltry fare. Besides his ever-present beer, there were the remnants of a bucket of fried chicken from two nights before and half a pound of cheddar cheese.

He scraped the mold from the cheese, sliced two wedges from the block, and placed each on a paper plate. He then pulled two pieces of chicken from the bucket and likewise plopped them on respective plates. Finally he filled two scratched and faded plastic drinking glasses with water and delivered the makeshift meal to his young charges.

"Here, Stacy. I'm sorry it's all I have to feed you, but there's a little more if you want it."

"Thank you, Mister Smith. But please, can't we just go home?"

Chamberlain looked into her soft eyes, turned on his heel without responding, and walked back to the kitchen to make a telephone call. As soon as he replaced the receiver, he felt distinct relief. Dave and Joyce Chamberlain would be there within the hour, albeit reluctantly.

Chamberlain returned to the kitchen table and lit another cheroot. After a drag on the smoke, he took a long pull from the half-empty beer bottle and again stared out the window. "If only it could have stopped there," he said aloud. "If only."

* * *

Shortly after his return to San Sebastian, Agenbroad spotted the captain standing with a small group of guards. He sauntered across the yard to the group. "Speak to you, Cap'n, Sir?" Agenbroad asked in the most subservient tone he could muster.

Chamberlain excused himself from the group and approached the now hardened con. *I remember this shithead from years ago, but what does he want with me now?* "What in the hell do you want, Agenbroad?" Chamberlain growled. Guard captains did not have to speak civilly to prisoners and he made no attempt to hide his contempt for this jerk.

"Sir, I just thought you'd like to know that I'm taking over for Gomez. Sir!"

Chamberlain flushed at the mention of Gomez' name. He hoped that his deeds for Gomez had been discretely handled. No such luck. He was at the mercy of the informal leadership structure inside the prison. To defy Agenbroad, or any of them, would mean he very well could become a prisoner himself.

"I just have a little job for you, Boss." Agenbroad glanced around the yard. Seeing no one paying particular attention to them, he passed a folded scrap of paper to Chamberlain. On the paper was the name of a prisoner who, Chamberlain knew, had informed the guards on illegal activity of some inmates.

"Get him to the infirmary tonight after 8:00. I don't care how you do it, just be sure he's there." Agenbroad smiled at the guard captain, brushed an imaginary particle of lint from the taller man's shiny silver captain's bars, and shuffled away. Chamberlain stood transfixed for a long moment, then dropped his head and slowly returned to his office.

That evening, he called the duty sergeant to his office. "Lenny, I got a sick call slip for London, 57239, a while ago. I don't know what the hell his problem is, but get him to the infirmary." The sergeant also knew of London's informing, so he thought nothing of the special attention the captain was giving him.

Normally, a prisoner wouldn't be transferred to the infirmary after regular hours, except in dire emergency. In this case, London's cooperation was apparently being repaid with a small favor, the sort granted to some prisoners to encourage their cooperation with the guards. Sergeant Lenny Carstensen handled the transfer personally, ignorant of the deadly plot which was unfolding.

London didn't know why he was being moved, but assumed it had something to do with protecting him. "The captain personally issued the order," he was told.

Two hours later, during a routine bed check of the infirmary, a guard found Mark London, prisoner number 57239, dead in his hospital bed. The official cause was an apparent prescription error. London had somehow been given a large dose of digitalis, which was meant for a nearby prisoner.

The final ruling, certified by Guard Captain Roy Chamberlain and the warden, was accidental death. Chamberlain's hand trembled as he signed the death certification form. His career would surely be over as soon as the state attorney general's investigators began their routine investigation of London's death.

Miraculously, the investigators did not question Chamberlain's actions in transferring London during unusual hours. They, too, understood the informal reward structure inside the walls. The attorney general's official report found the death of prisoner London to be accidental although a footnote did pose the possibility that unnamed prisoners had retaliated against London after learning of his transfer to the infirmary.

During the next two years, Chamberlain issued seemingly innocuous transfer orders regarding three other prisoners who later were found dead under questionable circumstances. During the investigation that followed the third, the investigator seemed to question the guard captain's actions more intensely than anyone had previously.

Chamberlain would not stand by idly and be subjected to more scrutiny. Four days later, he announced that he had accepted a position with a private security firm at a significant increase in pay. Fellow guards of all ranks congratulated Chamberlain on his good fortune to get out of the repressive atmosphere of the prison, with a salary increase to boot.

Chamberlain took their congratulations well, but there was no private security job. He couldn't stay and take a chance that some nosy investigator would one day uncover his secret. He would wind up in a cage and probably not live long.

* * *

More than a year later, the former guard captain, who now existed on meager earnings from odd jobs, glanced at the young kidnap victims in the adjoining room. He was powerless to do anything but help. Agenbroad knew all about Chamberlain's activities in prison and wouldn't hesitate to rat him out.

"Damn!" Chamberlain cursed, just as Dave Chamberlain knocked on the bare wood door. Roy nearly bolted for the door, ecstatic that his brother had actually come.

"Dave, I need your help, man. A guy from the old days at San Sebastian dropped these kids off here and ain't come back. He says they're kidnapped, and I believe him, but I can't keep them here. Take 'em for me for a while, will ya?" Roy was begging and he knew Dave loved it. *Dave likes feeling superior to me and thinks I'm weak, but I need him now.*

"Sure, Roy, we'll take them for you. One thing though, we get half your cut of the ransom."

"Sure, sure—you got it, man." *I'm not going to tell him I'm not sure if there even is a ransom.* "Come on, girls. This is your Daddy's brother. His wife is outside and they are going to take you home with them until they can get you back to your Mommy."

Jennifer was wailing and Stacy broke into tears. "Mister Smith, please take us home!"

"Stacy, it's dark and a very long way to your house. Uncle Dave will get you home as soon as he can. Until then, he and Aunt Joyce will take good care of you."

Stacy clearly didn't believe the dirty man, but this 'Uncle Dave' at least looked a little nicer. "Come on, Jenni." Stacy knew that none of this was right, but the options available to her five-year-old mind were limited. She had no idea where they were or how to get home. She also sensed that it would not be good to make these people mad. So, she did what she had to do—she bravely took her sister's hand and stood next to 'Uncle Dave.'

"Thanks, man, I owe you"

"Oh, you bet you do, big brother. Come on, girls. It's almost your bed time, I bet." Dave led his two charges to the Toyota running outside. Joyce Chamberlain gazed out the car window at the two children, then she looked up and her eyes met Dave's. But he knew she wouldn't ask any questions, at least not then. In a moment, they were driving back toward Berkeley.

Roy Chamberlain let out an audible sigh of relief as the gray four-door drove away. He would have some explaining to do to Agenbroad, but he could handle that, if—and it was a big *if*—Agenbroad even came back for them. *I hope to hell that Agenbroad doesn't have any close ties to these kids.*

Chapter Eleven

8:50 p.m.

Officer Toni Burton led Angi to a house across the street from the McElroy's home. It was built in the same style as the McElroy house, as were most of the houses in the neighborhood. It was a little more run down than the rest, but the potential witness's information was more important than the look of the place.

Burton knocked on the door. As she waited, she noted that the faded yellow paint on the house was peeling. The yard also needed tending and the flowerbeds were overgrown—a stark contrast to the home that was now a crime scene. The same woman Burton had spoken to earlier, a Mrs. Leedy, answered the door. Burton introduced Masters.

"I understand from Officer Burton that your daughter may have seen something that could help us," Angi said.

The weary looking woman nodded and led the officers inside. "Chelsea is in the family room, there," Mrs. Leedy said, pointing toward the adjoining room. "You may talk to her alone if you wish."

Unusual for a parent to allow the police to talk to their child without being present, but I won't argue with her, Angi thought.

A red-haired girl sat on a love seat in a semi reclining position, three large pillows propping her upper body. She muted the television with a remote control as the women entered.

"Hello, Chelsea—may I call you Chelsea? I'm Angela Masters and this is Toni Burton." Masters extended her hand, which was met by the girl's.

"I'm sorry I didn't get up. I'm not feeling well."

Very well mannered, especially for a girl her age. "We understand, Chelsea. We'll try not to take too long, so you can get some rest. Your mother told Toni that you might have seen something this morning, which might help us. Can you tell me what happened and what you saw?"

"Sure. Do you want me to just tell you or do you want to ask me questions?"

"Why don't you just tell us what you saw. Then if we have any questions, we can ask, OK?" *She seems pretty bright.*

"OK. Well, about 9:00 or so this morning—I'm not sure of the exact time—I was in the kitchen taking some medicine. I was looking out the kitchen window and I saw an old car that I hadn't seen around here before. It was kind of parked in front of Mrs. McElroy's house, only a little further down the street."

"You know Mrs. McElroy, then," Burton said.

"Yes, Ma'am. I babysit for her sometimes."

Masters glanced at Burton. Toni realized it was a warning not to interrupt Chelsea's story again.

"Please go on, Chelsea," Masters said.

"OK, well, I was looking at the strange car, when I saw a man come out of the McElroy's house. He had Stacy and Jennifer—that's Mrs. McElroy's two oldest daughters—with him. He was leading them to the old car. They didn't seem to be fighting him or anything but I think Jennifer was crying. He was about my dad's age and had dark hair, but I really didn't look at him very closely. They got in the car and just drove away. That's all I saw until I heard all the sirens a while ago. I looked out then and saw all the cop, er um, police cars out there."

Masters smiled. "That's okay, Chelsea. Sometimes I call them 'cop cars' too. Can I ask you some questions now?"

"Yes, ma'am. I want to help."

"Can you describe the car for me? Do you know what kind of car, the color, things like that?"

The girl closed her eyes. After a few moments, she opened them again and looked straight at Masters. "No, ma'am, I'm sorry. I don't know what kind of car it was. I know it was kind of yellowish and kind of beat-up, but not real bad. Do you know what I mean?"

Masters smiled and touched Chelsea's hand. "It's okay, Honey. Just take your time."

After another thoughtful pause, Chelsea sighed. "I can't remember any more about it, except it was kind of like our car, a little one, but maybe a little smaller than ours. I really wish I could help more, but I just can't remember."

"It's okay, Chelsea," Angi said. "You've done fine. You get some rest now, and I'll call you tomorrow, okay?" The girl looked physically drained and Angi didn't want to push her only witness too hard.

"Was she able to help you, detective?" Mrs. Leedy asked as the investigators left the family room.

"Yes, ma'am. I really appreciate you letting us talk to her. She seemed a little tired, so I thought it best to quit for now. Is it okay with you if I call tomorrow?"

"Yes, of course."

"I do have a couple of questions for you. Chelsea said the man she saw was about your husband's age. She also said his car was like yours only a little smaller."

"Oh, I see where you're going. Well, my husband is 35, although people say he looks a little older. Our car is a Honda Accord, a 1978 model, I think."

* * *

"I'm sorry we didn't get more, Angi," Burton said after they had left the house.

41

"No, Toni. It was a good lead. She gave us a description of the car. More importantly, we know that the suspect was alone. And from her statement that the girls left with him willingly, or at least not under physical force, we can be pretty sure Mrs. McElroy knew him. That's where we'll start."

Chapter Twelve

10:15 p.m.

The Violent Crimes office at the Santa Rosa Police building was a bustle of activity when Angi returned later that evening. Several detectives and clerical support people were working overtime to run down basic background information, since the investigators lacked specific leads on the homicide.

Because they had a kidnapping, Angi placed a call to the FBI Santa Rosa resident agency. "Any indication they were taken across state lines or do you have a ransom demand?" the agent who took her call asked.

"No, to either at this time. We're looking at the victim's ex-husband."

"So it appears to me to be a simple custodial interference case. You guys will be working hard on the homicide, I presume, so we'll just let you work the whole thing. We'll open a file on the kidnapping but just keep us informed on anything you learn." In other words, finding the girls, as well as the murderer, would be the responsibility of Detective Angela Masters and the Santa Rosa Police Department.

While waiting for Angi's return, Devon ordered a records check on the victim's ex-husband. Even though Doug McElroy believed he was in jail, it was imperative that the detectives confirm his whereabouts. McElroy had only known that Sharon's ex-husband went by the nickname 'Butch' and that his last name was Agenbroad. With an unusual name like that, it took Anderson less than an hour to narrow the list of convicts and ex-convicts of the California system to the correct one.

"Angi," Anderson said as she entered the work bay, "I've found the info on the ex-husband. Elmont Jacob Agenbroad, and he's out of San Sebastian since last month."

"Thanks, Devon. 'Elmont?' I'd probably go by 'Butch' too." At least they now had a potentially viable suspect to work on. Before they could confront him, they would have to locate him and determine if there was any additional evidence tying him to the scene.

A quick call to the crime lab dampened hopes for that.

"Not a print, not a thread that we can tie to anyone other than the victim or her family," Senior Lab Technician Kim Williams said. "The only possibility left is on the door knob and we're still working on that. There are some smudges that have possibilities. But it looks like anything useful might have been smeared by the victim's husband turning the knob when he first came home. I'll give you a call if we turn up anything. We should know in an hour or so."

"Thanks, Kim," Angi said. "If you do uncover anything at all, check it against the prints on file for an Elmont Agenbroad. He's in the state system."

Hanging up, Angi turned her attention back to Devon. "Have you found an address for this Agenbroad guy yet?"

"Just got it," Anderson said as he ripped a page from the clattering state-wide teletype link. "He was paroled to an address in Santa Cruz — lives with his wife there."

"OK, it looks like that's about all we have now," Masters told the assembled detectives. "Let's all knock off for the night. Devon and I will drive down to Santa Cruz in the morning."

* * *

As she did on most nights, Angi returned home alone. It wasn't that she preferred the single life, but that was her fate at that point in her life. It hadn't always been that way.

Shortly after joining the police department, Angi married a man she had known since high school. Roger was a man she remembered as always happy and friendly, and they dated only a short time before the wedding. He was the manager of a shoe store in the mall, and they both thought of themselves as professionals in their respective fields.

It wasn't long, however, before Angi's decisive nature, more evident to Roger now that they were living together, overwhelmed the more meek man. He had been raised to believe that women should be protected by their men. Angi's strong nature and self-sufficiency was foreign to his being. Eight months after they were married, Roger and Angi divorced. It was an amenable parting and they remained friends.

Angi's house, a ranch-style in a quiet subdivision not far from the McElroy house, was always immaculate. Angi's attention to detail carried into her personal life equally well as in her business life. She loved spending her off-hours working on home projects. Tonight, however, the house seemed almost oppressively closed in, as it sometimes did when she was working on a big case. Since this case was shaping up to be the biggest she had ever encountered, she forced herself to relax.

Rather than settle into the darkened house, Angi walked through the living room into the kitchen, where she poured a glass of her favorite wine, V. Sattui's Gamay Rouge. Kicking off her shoes, she walked through the adjoining family room and out the sliding glass doors onto an open redwood deck. Ignoring the comfortable chaise with its thick weatherproof cushion inviting her to a corner of the deck, she strolled down the two short steps to the back lawn.

She walked slowly through the well-trimmed perennial ryegrass, the same grass used on the fairways at Pebble Beach. She ambled toward the place she jokingly called her 'fortress of solitude,' a name she adopted from Superman's icy retreat. *I certainly don't feel like superwoman tonight.*

The fortress was one of the crowning additions to Angi's residence. Nestled in a back corner of her yard, the fortress appeared to be a flowered island at the edge of a sea of green. The prominent features were roses of varying sizes and varieties, just beginning to bud in the spring sunshine. Concealed among the rose bushes and other greenery was a meandering path of stepping stones, cross-sections of a California redwood tree.

The path led to the 'solitude' portion of her fortress, where a hammock swing sat next to a four foot high water feature, complete with a flagstone waterfall and a bubbling pond. Even though her house was visible from the swing, the place still gave her refuge and she relished it. Angi designed the fortress herself and had done most of the work to create it. And it was hers alone. She never invited guests to enter the path. On this night, she would spend nearly two hours listening to the soothing flow and splash of the water before returning to the house to sleep.

Despite her time in the fortress, Angi Masters didn't sleep well that night. Her mind raced with thoughts of possible ways to solve this puzzling case. *If it is the ex-husband, why did he kidnap the girls? Even if he wanted to take the oldest, his own daughter, why take the younger girl? What questions would be best to ask this character when I talk to him tomorrow? Surely, he's con-wise and probably won't cooperate.* Still, he represented their best current lead and it was her job to make the most of it.

Chapter Thirteen

April 16, 1981 - 10:15 a.m.

At 10:15 the following morning, Masters and Anderson knocked on the door of a green bungalow on the outskirts of Santa Cruz. They were anxious to meet the only suspect they had in the murder case, now barely 24 hours old.

After a few moments, a plain woman who appeared to be of Hispanic decent answered the door. "Yes, can I help you?" Martita Sandoval Agenbroad asked.

Masters displayed her badge. "We're from the Santa Rosa Police Department. Is Butch here?"

Anderson touched her arm. "I'm Detective Anderson and this is Detective Masters, ma'am. We are following up on a case in our city and think that Butch might be able to help us. May we speak to him?" Anderson was usually the brash one, but this time he recognized the need to move slowly.

"He didn't do anything," Martita said. "He was here with me." She prayed he had really gone to Reno.

"We're not accusing him of anything, ma'am. We just think he may know some of the people involved. Are you Mrs. Agenbroad?" Anderson asked.

"Well, OK. I'm sorry, but my husband has had problems with the law before. He is going straight now and I don't want anyone messing that up for him. Won't you please come in?"

"Butch, Honey," she called, just as the man the detectives had come to see stepped into the room.

"Yes, what is it, Martita?" Butch asked, wiping his hands with a damp chamois.

"Mr. Agenbroad, I'm Detective Masters and this is Detective Anderson. We're from Santa Rosa, and we need to ask you a few questions."

Butch glanced at Martita with a wry smile. "Of course. Please sit down."

Martita looked into her husband's eyes and then turned to the detectives. "If you don't need me, I have some things to do in the kitchen."

"Certainly, ma'am," Anderson said. "We may want to talk to you before we leave but it can wait." He was glad she was leaving them alone with Butch. As an ex-con's wife, she knew that they would find a way to get her out of the room anyway.

"How can I help you, officers?"

"Butch—may I call you Butch?" Masters said. "How long has it been since you saw your ex-wife, Sharon?"

A lifetime of living on the edge, of conning the cons, of the game of mastery of wits, now served Agenbroad well. Without a hesitation, he looked Masters in the eye and answered, "It's been several years, Detective Masters. I'm sure you know I spent some time in the joint and was just recently released. I really have no reason to see her, or even want to."

"What about your daughter, Butch? Haven't you wanted to see her since you got out?" Masters said. She would play the gentle woman who wanted to believe Agenbroad's story. It might give him a chance to slip up.

"Well, Detective, I think it's better that Stacy not know about me right now. I've had some problems in the past and I don't want to hurt her. I'm working on getting my life straightened out. Someday, maybe I'll contact her, but not now. I've heard that Sharon was remarried and has a good life. I don't want to screw that up for her or for Stacy."

Masters seemed to buy it. "Mr. Agenbroad, we're sorry to have to tell you that something has happened. Sharon is dead."

Agenbroad, of course, knew the statement was coming, and was prepared for it. He played his part well, reacting with just the right amount of shock and surprise. "No. When? How did it happen?" Agenbroad looked from Masters' eyes to Anderson's and back again. His eyes opened wide.

Anderson was quietly watching Agenbroad. He knew the con was trying to play Masters but hadn't seen a flaw in the performance that he could exploit — yet.

"Sharon was murdered yesterday," Masters said. She looked hard into Agenbroad's eyes.

"Murdered? Why would anyone kill Sharon? She was one of the kindest people I've ever known."

"We were hoping that perhaps you could tell us something about it, Butch. We've heard that the divorce was not really amicable."

The wily Agenbroad didn't skip a beat. "No, it wasn't at the time. In prison, though, I had some time to think about it. I came to see that I wasn't the best husband to her. I know that now. And with my wife's love and help, I can be a better man. I can't fix the past with Sharon, but I certainly would have no reason to harm her, and I don't know anyone who would."

"Well, Butch, you know the drill. We have to ask where you were yesterday," Masters said. She knew something wasn't right but couldn't put her finger on it.

"Well, I'm a little embarrassed to tell you, but I lied to my wife. I told her I was going to Reno to visit a sick relative. I really just wanted to spend some time at the tables. I didn't get to gamble much in San Sebastian." Agenbroad lowered his head and grinned sheepishly. "So, I just drove over to Reno for a couple of days and had a little fun. You understand."

Both Masters and Anderson noted the discrepancy immediately. Martita had said that Butch had been home all day the day before. For now, they would let that pass.

"That's fine, Butch," Masters said. "We won't tell her, but we will need the name of the place you stayed. You did say you were there for a couple of days, right? If you can just tell us where you were gambling, that would help too. You understand why we have to ask these questions."

"I'd like to help you, Detective Masters, but the truth is I didn't do very well at the tables the first day. I wanted to have money to play the second day, so I slept in my car. I just parked on a little side road in that valley between Reno and Carson City. I don't know if anyone saw me, but no one bothered me all night.

"As for the places I played, I was in several casinos downtown. I really wish I'd been a big winner, so that someone would remember me, but that wasn't the case. Unfortunately for me, the second day wasn't any better. I couldn't even afford to stop for dinner on the drive back home. I had just enough cash for gas."

"Butch, we need to tell you something else," Masters spoke in a low tone.

He had been waiting for the 'big news' to drop, surprised that she had taken so long to spring it.

"We think that whoever killed Sharon also kidnapped your daughter. Stacy is missing."

"Oh, God, no! Not precious Stacy! Why would anyone take her? She's just a little girl."

"Do you know anyone who would have reason to take her, Butch? Maybe someone who has something against you?" Masters asked. Maybe he would bite on the 'victim card.'

"No, no. My old cronies in the joint don't even know about her. Like I told you, I didn't want my problems to hurt her. Please, please do what you have to do to find her." Real tears flowed down Butch's cheeks. Quiet sobs punctuated his speech.

Hearing Butch's sobs, Martita rushed into the room. "What is it, Butch? What have they done to you?"

Turning to Masters, she said, "Why don't you leave now? We don't know anything about whatever it is that brought you here. We're just trying to get on with our lives the best way we know how. We don't need cops harassing us every time they need a patsy." Martita's anger was real.

"Yes, ma'am, we understand. It's just something we have to do," Masters said. She looked again as Agenbroad, still hunched over in quiet sobs. "We'll let you know if we hear anything else, Butch."

As they reached the door, Anderson turned back. It was the first time he had spoken since the interview began. "Just one more thing, Butch. What kind of car do you have?"

Martita started to speak, but Agenbroad interrupted, "We have two cars, a Buick LeSabre and a Volkswagen. They're both in the driveway. It was the Buick that I took to Reno. Now, if there's nothing else, please leave us alone."

"Thank you, both," Masters said. "We'll be in touch."

Why did Butch lie about the car? Martita wondered. *Did he have something to do with whatever the detectives are investigating? He seems to be in so much grief over whatever it was, and yet, why did he lie?* "Butch, Honey." She touched his shoulder.

Agenbroad's grief abruptly ended. "You don't know nothing, Martita. Just keep it that way and nothing will happen—to either of us."

Chapter Fourteen

April 17, 1981

Berkeley, California, is remembered by many as the scene of frequent and sometimes violent clashes during the era of anti-Vietnam War protests. It is also a serene town, not unlike hundreds of other university towns across America. Dave and Joyce Chamberlain loved Berkeley, with its eclectic population. They could easily blend in there. No one looked twice at a neighbor who might display an occasional quirk.

The Chamberlains lived in one of the city's most diverse neighborhoods. Their small frame house on a quiet street was only a few blocks from the university. It was populated by students, professors, laborers, poets, artists, clerks, and writers. The makeup of the neighborhood was in constant transition. Yet things always remained the same. There was an easy familiarity about the place, an area where everyone was friendly but no one asked too many questions. Thus, a couple who suddenly had two young girls in their house raised no cause for alarm in anyone.

There had better be some good money in this, Dave thought as he sat at the kitchen table. The night before, the strange call for help from his older brother left him with the two youngsters, almost babies. *Why in the hell did I agree to this?* Sure, Roy said they were kidnapped and said Dave would get half the ransom. But the girls didn't look like they come from a wealthy family. If anything, they were ordinary middle class kids. And the older girl was very polite and deferent to adults. Dave hadn't heard of that in many rich kids.

"Dave," Joyce said as she sat beside her husband at the table. "I know you don't like me to pry into your business, but what's with these kids? You didn't say a word driving home last night, but I could tell you weren't happy with Roy. Is he in some kind of trouble? Are these girls part of it?"

"Damn it, Joyce. Don't worry about it! They're the kids of some girlfriend of Roy's that got killed in a car wreck. He got the cops to give them to him by saying they were his kids. But we both know that he can't take care of himself, let alone a couple of kids. So we're going to hang on to them. Maybe one of your sisters can take them—just for a while until Roy figures out what to do to stay out of trouble for taking them." It was the story Roy and Dave had concocted to keep Joyce in the dark. *She ain't blind to my past but it's better for everyone if she don't know too much.*

At that moment, a small girl appeared in the kitchen doorway. Her soft brown eyes masked fear and sorrow. "Ma'am? May my sister and I have something to eat?"

"Of course, Honey," Joyce said. "You both come in here and we'll have a good breakfast." As the girls entered, Dave grimaced and walked out of the kitchen without a word.

* * *

Two days later, Dave pounded on his brother's front door. Once inside, he wasted no time. "I've had enough, Roy. You get over to my place this afternoon and get those kids. I don't care what you do with them, but I'm not babysitting anymore. I'm finished with it. You got that? Besides, you stupid idiot, didn't you see the news?"

Roy was still half asleep, his usual condition on any day before 11:00 a.m. "What news? You know I don't watch that old TV." In his still-groggy state, Roy sounded like a whining child.

"Those kids aren't just kidnapped. Your buddy, whoever the hell he is, killed their mother. And he was damn nasty about it. The whole damned world is out looking for them. Hell, I'm still on probation. I don't need this shit!"

"Damn it!" This was bigger than Roy had imagined. He knew Agenbroad was a killer, but killing his mother had happened so long ago. Butch's more recent crimes revolved around money. If Butch had killed to kidnap these kids, there had to be money in it somewhere. The Butch Agenbroad he knew would never do anything that didn't have money in it. "OK, OK, Dave. I'll get in touch with the man and have them out of your place today. I swear, brother."

* * *

"Put Butch on the line ... now!" Chamberlain said when Martita answered the telephone.

The abruptness of the demand startled her and Martita dropped the phone without a word of acknowledgment. "Butch, I don't know who it is, but he's very rude and angry."

Butch knew who it was and had no desire to talk to him.

The night before, Butch had barely managed to get the television turned off as Martita walked into the living room. He wanted to hear what they were saying about the murder, but he was afraid Martita might put things together. He could only speculate as to how close the detectives might be.

"Don't give me the cheery hello, Butch," Chamberlain said. "This is way too deep and I'm out of it. Either pick those kids up today or I'm dropping them off with the cops." Chamberlain was angry and Butch knew it. Of course, he was not going to go anywhere near a police station. He just hoped Butch didn't know that. He was wrong.

"Now listen, Roy. Calm down. You know that's not a smart thing to do. The cops will probably figure you're involved, no matter what you say. Besides, I wouldn't want to have to tell them you are involved, or about the shit you did in San Sebastian. Now, I have a few things to take care of here. You take good care of those girls and I'll call you back later. And don't ever call here again!"

Now Chamberlain knew he was going to have to deal with the girls, and with Dave, in some other way. "OK, Butch, you know you can count on me." The prospect of easy money had bit him in the ass in San Sebastian and now it was doing it again.

The following day, Roy drove to Dave's home. He was prepared for a confrontation and had no plan to handle it. *Maybe I can convince him to keep the girls for at least a few more days until I can*

54

come up with a plan. He probably won't buy it, but I gotta try. No choice.

Dave opened the door as his brother walked up the broken walkway. He glanced around to be sure Roy hadn't been followed. "I don't know why I'm doing this," Dave said through clenched teeth before Roy could say a word. "I don't need this, but you are my brother and I can't let your stupidity get you the gas chamber."

Roy's eyes widened at the thought. *Yeah, prison would be bad but if I get tied to this — to a murder — I might get gassed right along with Butch.*

"Joyce and I have talked it over, Roy. She doesn't want to see anything happen to you, either. She still thinks those girls are your girlfriend's kids. Her main worry is that nothing happen to them. I don't care one way or the other, but they might be useful later. Besides, there was never any ransom."

That fact dawned on Roy at the same moment Dave said it. "Yeah, I know. And Butch ain't coming back for them, either."

Roy was amazed that Dave would have a soft spot for a couple of kids, strangers even. Dave was four years younger than his brother and had grown up in the same neighborhood with the same temptations. The difference was that Dave met Tooey O'Banion one time and hated the experience. At 14, he was already an accomplished burglar and part-time numbers runner. He saw the back side of the law as his ticket out of Chicago, or at least into the big time there. No cop, even if he was related to a famous mobster, was going to talk him out of it. Dave loved life in the criminal world. Even a couple of stretches in state prisons had been primarily an educational experience for him. Certainly, this new revelation of his character came as a complete surprise to his older sibling.

"OK, little brother. Thanks for taking care of this for me. I owe you."

"Oh, you're damn right you do, Roy. Don't forget that. Now get the hell out of here and leave it to me."

* * *

Joyce had gone to Wal-Mart earlier where she bought new clothes for each of the girls. Now, she assured them that things would be fine. Stacy asked again to be taken home, but Joyce had an answer to quiet her. "Stacy, Honey, I don't know how to tell you this, but you're a big girl so I'll just be honest. Your mother and daddy were killed in a bad car wreck. We have been afraid to tell you until now, but it's better that you know. Don't worry, though. I'm kind of like an aunt to you and I will do everything I can to take care of both of you."

Joyce sat for a long time with Stacy and Jennifer as the girls grieved over the loss of their parents. Then Stacy asked, "What about Kelsey, my other little sister?"

There's another kid in the family? Where is she? "I don't know, Stacy, but I will find out. But for now, you're going to stay with us. We will do our best to take care of you just like you were our own children. And I have two sisters who both have kids about your age. Maybe we'll take you to visit them someday soon and you can make new friends."

Chapter Fifteen

June 23, 1981

Two months had passed since Sharon McElroy was murdered, and Angi was no closer to finding her killer. Nor did she have a clue of the whereabouts of Sharon's two children. A bullish city councilman had proposed that a special fund to be allocated to the police department to allow the detectives to pursue the case wherever it might take them. The city council unanimously approved the idea. A crime this horrendous in their city would not go unsolved solely due to budgetary limitations or disinterest from the feds.

A follow-up interview with Doug McElroy produced no new useful information. The husband simply did not know why the terrible crime had happened. Angi believed him. His alibi for the day of the murder fully checked out. And neighbors and friends described the McElroys as a warm and loving couple with no known conflicts or enemies.

Forensic examination of the scene produced nothing that would directly help to identify the killer. "I found three hairs near the victim's body which didn't match any family members," Lab Technician Williams said. "They're not enough to point to an unknown suspect, but we might be able to at least get a blood type match if you come up with a suspect."

Angi also re-interviewed the young witness who saw a man leading the two children away from the McElroy house that day. She was obviously trying to help, but could provide no new information. The canvass of the surrounding neighborhood produced little of value.

Neither Angi nor Devon felt good about Butch Agenbroad. His answers had come across as rehearsed, his shock at hearing of the crime just a little too dramatic. However, they had nothing to tie him to the crime and didn't want to risk tipping their hand until they had something solid. Angi even sent his prison photograph to the Reno Police Department on the long shot that they might confirm his alibi.

She received a report back, but it was less than encouraging. 'A pit boss in a small casino on South Virginia Street identified Agenbroad from your photograph. However, the employee could only state that he had been in his place and had been a big loser at the tables. Whether it was three weeks or three months before, he claimed not to recall,' the report said.

Angi circulated a flyer with photographs of Stacy and Jennifer throughout the Bay Area. All local newspapers and television stations ran stories on the case. So far, nothing had come of it.

It was in this atmosphere that Sergeant Garrison called Angi and Devon into his office. "I'm not telling you anything that you don't know, but if there's nothing promising on the McElroy case, I've got to get you two back in the rotation."

Both detectives nodded. Since Sharon's murder, there had been another homicide in Santa Rosa. It was a straight-forward case, though, and another detective had made an arrest within 24 hours. However, there were also robberies, rapes, and assaults that required the continuing attention of the small staff of the Violent Crimes Unit.

"Put it on the back burner for now," Garrison said. "Of course, Angi, if something comes to light on it, you have the go-ahead to pursue it immediately. Just keep me in the loop."

Angi nodded and headed outside for her car. Doug had a right to know that the efforts to find his wife's killer and to locate his daughters was being scaled back.

* * *

He took the news as well as she could expect. She assured him that they were not dropping the case and that she would immediately check any leads that came in.

"I understand," the unwilling widower said as he looked Angi squarely in the eye. "I know you are doing your best, and I also know you won't let this case fall through the cracks."

It was as much a request for assurance as a statement, and Angi answered him directly. "No, Doug, it will not drop through the cracks — not as long as I have anything to say about it."

As the detective turned to leave, Doug called after her. "Have you thought about hypnosis for Chelsea? I've read where it can sometimes help a witness recall facts they don't consciously remember. She's our only witness. I just wondered if it might be feasible."

Angi had no experience with the use of hypnosis beyond a sideshow at the county fair and held little hope for anything positive to result. Still, she promised Doug that she would consider the idea and discuss it with her supervisor.

* * *

When she dropped the idea on him, Devon immediately embraced it, despite Angi's doubts. He had read of cases where hypnosis had been used to help a witness recall facts. "I don't have any personal experience with the concept, but it might give us a break. We sorely need that." But Devon also had read that there were risks in hypnotizing a criminal witness. Trial courts generally frowned on the practice because of the possibility that improper techniques could suggest facts to a witness rather than enhance recall of what they already knew. Hypnosis might not even work on some people.

Sergeant Garrison put the idea in perspective. "What else do you have? Chelsea Leedy can be an important witness. But right now, she really hasn't given you much to work with. She's a willing witness and her mother is supportive of her helping us. Give it a try. I'll call Dr. Tim Breckenridge in San Francisco for you. I know his work. He's a certified forensic hypnotist so, if we can do this, he'll do it right."

Dr. Timothy Breckenridge, in addition to having a thriving practice in psychology, had conducted more than a hundred forensic hypnosis sessions.

"I was the lead investigator on one of those cases, a particularly nasty rape," Garrison told Angi. "Dr. Breckenridge's work with the victim gave me new and critical information which led me to the suspect. The guy was ultimately convicted, and I gained an appreciation of the doctor and his work."

Angi remained skeptical.

* * *

Tim Breckenridge loved his involvement with law enforcement. It gave him a chance to do something extra for society. Certainly, his medical work helped hundreds of individual patients and their families. Forensic hypnosis, on the other hand, gave him what he viewed as an opportunity to give back to society.

"It's my calling," he often said. He never charged for his services beyond basic expenses for travel and the like. Santa Rosa, only fifty-eight miles from his office, wouldn't even require an expense billing.

"She's young, Doc," Garrison told the psychologist on the phone. "But she's eager to help and she seems to me to have a good grasp of the importance of truthful testimony. Maybe she's got nothing else, but we're stuck right now."

"It sounds like there may be a possibility," Breckenridge said. "I can drive up to Santa Rosa the day after tomorrow, if the young lady and her mother agree."

"They do." Garrison said. "I'll have Detective Devon Anderson set it up."

Chapter Sixteen

June 27, 1981

Four days later, shortly before 10:00 a.m., Anderson walked slowly up to Angi's army-surplus grey steel desk at one side of the Santa Rosa detective squad room. In his hand was a written report from Dr. Breckenridge.

"Well," Anderson said, "Chelsea was unable to recall any more detail about the man she saw with Stacy and Jennifer. The description is pretty much the same as we already have. It could fit 700,000 men in California alone."

Angi's heart sank. "Damn! But I really didn't expect much anyway."

"She did give us some more detail on the car. It was a faded yellow, and I think it was probably an older Honda Civic, judging from her description." Anderson watched Angi closely, gauging her reaction.

She barely moved, but raised her eyes slowly. "Great, Devon. There are probably only a few thousand of those in the Bay Area."

Devon dropped the report on her desk. "Well, I thought you should know." He turned to walk away but a few feet from her desk, he spoke over his shoulder. "Oh, by the way, did I mention that she did recall the license number on the suspect's car?"

The impact of what she had just been told didn't hit Angi immediately. When it did, she looked up suddenly to see Devon's broad grin. "Yes, Angi, the license number — all of it."

"Really funny, asshole!" But she was smiling as she jumped from her chair and hurled the first thing she could get her hands on, her appointment book, at Anderson. "God, that's great, Devon. I won't ever doubt you again."

"Angi, it gets better. The license number that Chelsea recalled is listed on a Honda Civic, to Elena Sandoval. She has an address in Soquel, California."

Angi's mind raced. "Sandoval, that sounds like a Hispanic name. Our suspect was described as white. Still, that doesn't mean that he might not have a name like Sandoval. "Where did you say she lives, Devon?"

"Soquel, Angi. Do you know where that is?"

"I've heard of it, but can't place it. But I'm sure you'll tell me. What are you grinning about?"

"Soquel is a small town outside Santa Cruz.

"My God, Devon. Agenbroad's wife was Hispanic. Do you think ... ?"

"I certainly think it's worth checking out. Shall we go?"

* * *

Just after 1:00 p.m., Angi parked in front of the address listed for Elena Sandoval. The house was small, but appeared to be well kept, as did the yard and flower garden in front.

"There's the car," Devon said. In the driveway sat a faded yellow Honda Civic that matched the description given by Chelsea Leedy during her first interview. The license number matched the one Chelsea had given during her interview with Dr. Breckenridge.

The detectives approached the door carefully. They had worked out a cover story to shield their real interest in the car and the Sandoval house, in case they met someone who matched the killer's description. Even though this house was not far from the place where they had interviewed Agenbroad only a few weeks before, it was still possible that the car owner wasn't connected to him at all. It was also possible that someone other than Agenbroad was the killer. That person might be in the house they now approached.

Each took a position at the side of the front door, and Anderson rang the doorbell. After only a few seconds, a short woman who appeared to be in her late 50s answered the door.

"Elena Sandoval?" Angi asked.

"Yes, ma'am. May I help you?"

She doesn't look like a threat, Angi thought. Still, they needed to proceed with caution.

"Mrs. Sandoval, we are detectives," said Angi, displaying her police identification. "Please step outside."

"Of course, Detective," Sandoval said. "I've been expecting you." She walked out onto the front yard of the house she shared with Jorge for twenty-one years before his death. She prayed that God would give her the strength to do the right thing.

"Is there anyone else in the house, Mrs. Sandoval?" Angi asked.

Elena noticed that the male detective had not yet spoken nor really looked at her, but kept his eyes on the door and interior of the house. "No, ma'am. I live here alone, but you are welcome to check the house for yourselves, if you'd like."

"Thank you, Ma'am," Angi replied. "Detective Anderson will just take a quick look around, OK?"

Elena nodded.

"All clear," Devon said a few minutes later.

Angi extended her hand to Elena. "I apologize for the way we approached you, Mrs. Sandoval, but we have reason to believe your car was used in a major crime. I'm Detective Angela Masters from Santa Rosa and this is Detective Devon Anderson."

"I understand and I'm pleased to meet both of you. Won't you come inside? May I offer you some coffee?"

Once inside, Elena said, "As I said, I've been expecting you, or at least someone from the police. I think I know what you've come for." Elena stepped into a side room and returned a moment later, holding a small stuffed kangaroo. "Is this what you are looking for, detectives?"

Angi and Devon glanced at each other.

"Mrs. Sandoval, why don't you tell us why you think we are here?" Angi said. It was possible that the woman had no idea what had brought them to her home.

"*Bueno.*" Elena said as she sat in a chair opposite the detectives. "I think it has something to do with my daughter's husband. He is a terrible man, but she loved him, at least at first."

"What is his name, Mrs. Sandoval?" Angi asked. Anticipation was unmistakable in her voice.

"His name is Elmont Agenbroad, but everyone calls him Butch."

"Please go on, Mrs. Sandoval," Devon said.

"A couple of months ago, Butch borrowed my car, the yellow one in the driveway. I felt it was strange at the time, since he had a beautiful new car of his own. He insisted and my daughter convinced me to let him take it. He said he was driving to Reno, but he came back the next day. After he dropped my car off, I found this stuffed toy in the back seat. I don't know what he was up to, but it didn't seem right. And he didn't go to Reno."

Elena's last statement was made with such conviction that it took the detectives a moment to comprehend its meaning.

"You say he didn't go to Reno, Mrs. Sandoval. How can you be sure?" Angi asked.

"I know he didn't, Detective Masters. Jorge — that was my late husband — taught me to keep close track of the car's mileage to be certain the oil is changed regularly. I just had it done before Butch took the car. When he returned it, it had only been driven 291 miles since the oil change. Jorge used to love to take me to the shows at the clubs in Reno. I know it's almost 600 miles round trip from here to Reno. I don't know where Butch went, but it wasn't to Reno."

"Have you noticed any changes in the way Butch acts since then, Mrs. Sandoval?"

"Well, none lately, but that's because he's gone. A day or so after two detectives talked to him—was that you two?—he left in a hurry. I have not seen him since. Neither has my daughter as far as I know. Good riddance as far as I'm concerned."

Devon looked at Angi. Their prime suspect apparently now had a six-week head start.

Angi thanked Mrs. Sandoval for her help and took the stuffed kangaroo. If Doug McElroy could identify it, it would be another link connecting Agenbroad to Sharon's murder.

* * *

The detectives drove back to Martita Sandoval Agenbroad's Santa Cruz home. Martita's mother had already called to alert her daughter that they were on the way.

"I know I should have called you," Martita said, "but I was so afraid. After I questioned Butch about why he lied to you about taking his Buick to Reno, he told me to keep my mouth shut. I knew what he was capable of, and I was afraid to tell anyone, even my mother."

"We understand, Mrs. Agenbroad," Angi said. "No one is blaming you"

"Detective Masters, please don't call me 'Mrs. Agenbroad.' I mean, I know that legally we are still married, but I don't want to be reminded of a major mistake in my life. I thought he was such a good man, just a slightly misguided man ..." Her voice trailed off into quiet sobs. She felt like a fool for letting the man mislead her so badly.

"Martita, we need your help. Can you tell us anything that would help us find Butch or the two girls?"

"Two girls? What are you talking about? I've never heard anything about two girls until just now. Detective Masters, I don't know what Butch may have done. He never told me anything. It's just that I know in my heart it was something horrible. I'll never forget the way he looked at me when he told me to keep my mouth shut. I really thought he could kill me at that moment. But I don't know what he did or where he went. The morning after you were here, he packed his things in the Buick and drove away. I haven't seen or heard from him since."

There was some logic to what she said. Even though there was significant media interest in the case in the Bay Area, Santa Cruz is 125 miles south of Santa Rosa. Given the amount of crime in the San Francisco metropolitan area, a single murder that far away might not have generated much news coverage in Martita's city on the south bay. Even the added notoriety of the kidnapping may have merited only a small segment on an interior page of the newspaper, especially since there was never a ransom demand.

Masters and Anderson now knew for sure that Agenbroad was their primary suspect, but they had almost nothing more to go on than they had a week prior. As Angi steered her car northward, her mind raced with the possibilities affecting the two girls. *Are they even in the Bay Area anymore? The flyers and news stories had produced nothing. Are they with Butch?* Angi doubted it, but didn't know where to begin to look. *Are they even still alive? God, I don't even want to think about that possibility.*

Chapter Seventeen

January 1983

Celeste Campbell sat on the porch of her lakeside home in Carlisle, Idaho, admiring the view across the still waters of Lake Crystal. It was an idyllic setting she could only have dreamed of just a few short months before.

At 26, after an unhappy marriage and contentious divorce, Celeste borrowed money from her older brother and drove to Carlisle, a resort town in the beautiful mountains of Idaho's River of No Return Wilderness Area. There she got a job as a desk clerk in the town's leading hotel. She rented a room from a store owner and his wife because she couldn't afford a place of her own in the inflated resort market.

Three months after she moved to Carlisle, a man with an outgoing and charming way about him checked into the hotel.

"My name is Tom Mason," the man said. "I'm a carpenter and I hear the housing market is booming here. I'm hoping to make some money building homes for the rich people from Boise who vacation here."

Before long, the carpenter and the desk clerk were seen together regularly around town.

Celeste was enamored with the charming Mason. *He has an eye for other women, but I'm sure he's just looking. Otherwise, he wouldn't treat me so well.*

For his part, Celeste was just what Mason needed at that point in his life—a stable companion who didn't ask questions, questions that Mason, alias Butch Agenbroad, could not answer. For a few months, the two were nearly inseparable. In time, however, Mason's old habits returned. Although attractive, intelligent, and attentive to him, Celeste had no material possessions that he could exploit. Something inside Mason demanded more from a woman than mere love and attention.

More and more, Tom's eye roved to more eligible women, or at least wealthier ones. Then, just as he began giving serious thought to abandoning Celeste, she experienced a magical stroke of luck—Celeste won the lottery.

It wasn't the largest jackpot in the history of lotteries, and she would have to share it with a man from Alabama, who also picked the winning numbers. Still, Celeste's share was $3.7 million. Even with the payoff being spread over twenty years, Celeste would still receive nearly $115,000 a year after taxes. Celeste was ecstatic.

So was Tom Mason.

* * *

Celeste moved from her rented room to a small but elegant home she purchased on the lakeshore. Her new home was tastefully furnished, yet not ostentatious, a testament to her rural upbringing. *A beautiful home, enough money to live comfortably, and a man who genuinely cares for me – my life really has turned around.* Still, she kept her job at the hotel. Celeste loved to interact with people.

The change in Celeste's life could not have been more fortuitous for the man who called himself Tom Mason. In this mind, it could not have worked out better. He already had a relationship with the woman before she had money, so she would never suspect what was coming. *I'm just damned glad she won that money before I dumped her ass.*

For Celeste's part, she had a man who truly loved her. *Wasn't he here for me when I had nothing? And now that I have a little money, nothing has changed. He still supports me in whatever I do, and he has never asked me for anything.*

Celeste noticed that Tom's eye for the ladies seemed to disappear. To her that was a good thing.

For the next four months, Celeste's life could not have been better. Her boyfriend—Tom Mason was officially her boyfriend as everyone in town knew — treated her with a level of respect and understanding that she had never known before. He was never prying, but was always there with advice if she asked for it. He was always there to encourage her when she felt any doubt. Most importantly, he never showed the slightest interest in her money.

Even though her winnings made her income greater than his, he always insisted on paying for their frequent dates. "I fell in love with you long before you won the lottery. I still love you, not your money. Besides, I am making a good living in construction. I can afford to treat my lady to the best."

'My lady.' That sounded so refined to Celeste.

Thanksgiving season arrived in the Idaho mountains and Carlisle was blanketed with eighteen inches of snow, not an unusual amount for that time of year. The snow did nothing to dampen the enthusiasm of the small town's residents for the holiday season. This was one of the best times of the year. The summer tourists had gone, the wealthy summer homeowners had returned to the city and the skiers who came in hoards to the nearby ski resort had not yet arrived.

Most of the permanent residents came out for the annual Thanksgiving presentation put on by the high school drama club. Following the play, everyone joined for a traditional Thanksgiving meal in the gymnasium. Many had finished their dinner of turkey, dressing, sweet potatoes, and pumpkin pie and had begun conversations with their neighbors. Then, the amiable carpenter most knew as Tom Mason rose and took the microphone.

"Friends, the last year here has been one of the best of my life. This town has been good to me. I can count many wonderful friendships among you all here. My work has been satisfying. Most of all, for the first time in my life, I have found someone that I really want to share my life with." He held out his hand to the brunette beauty seated next to him. "Celeste Campbell, will you marry me?"

Celeste had known the question might be coming, although she was a bit surprised that it would come in such a public forum.

Still, there was only one answer for her. "Yes, Tom, I will." The gymnasium erupted into applause for the popular couple.

Two days before Christmas, in a simple ceremony in the Baptist Church, Celeste Campbell became Mrs. Tom Mason. Tom moved into Celeste's lakefront home and they began what Celeste believed would be a fairytale life.

Chapter Eighteen

April 1983

Many detectives keep photos on their desks. It's usually done as a way of reminding themselves that there is a world out there separate from the world of crime and evil that they encounter in their daily jobs. Not surprisingly, photos of family and children occupy many desks, along with an occasional photo of a memorable fishing expedition or a favored woodworking project.

Angi's desk contained a prominent photo of two young girls. But the girls weren't family, at least in the traditional sense. The photo was one of Stacy Agenbroad and Jennifer McElroy. The photo of the two little girls, sitting together on a staged set at a photographer's studio, had been taken a few weeks before they were abducted.

Almost a year previously, Doug McElroy had given the photo to Angi. "I know you will have to work on other cases, probably others where people's lives are at risk or have been taken. Those cases will maybe have better leads than our case has, and I understand what you have to do. But please take this picture as a reminder never to forget my wife or my beautiful girls. No matter how long it takes, I have to believe that you will find Sharon's killer and, God willing, you will bring my girls home to me."

"Doug, I will never stop working on this case until Stacy and Jennifer are home safe. And if you think of anything new, or just want to talk, you call me anytime."

On that day, Angi left Doug in the lobby, turned on her heel and re-entered the secure area of detective office. Silently, with her head down, she hurried to the ladies room, where she entered a stall and sat down. Staring at the photo of the two little girls, Angi wept in the quiet confines of the metal booth.

* * *

In the months after the police department released what information they had about the case to police departments across the country, few leads trickled in. No one had seen Butch Agenbroad since the day he drove away from Martita's house in Santa Cruz.

Police departments in Las Vegas, Phoenix, Dallas, Little Rock, Topeka, and even Boston had called saying someone had reported seeing the girls, as a result of the case being profiled in *Real Detectives* magazine. However, each of those leads had turned out to be false, usually a case of mistaken identity by well-meaning citizens.

Angi and Devon had even traveled to Topeka with the blessing of the police chief when leads in that city looked especially promising. They also planned to go to a Phoenix suburb called Chandler, but police there assured them that they had thoroughly checked out the lead they had been given.

Given the amount of time that had passed, along with Agenbroad's known violent streak, there was a high likelihood that the girls could be dead, perhaps never to be found. *Damn it, Angi. Don't think that way,* she ordered herself. *I have to believe that the girls will be found, alive. That's what keeps me going. Besides, I promised Doug, and myself, that I would hunt that dog Agenbroad down no matter what.*

To make matters worse, almost two years after Sharon's murder, Sergeant Garrison called her and Anderson into his office and closed the door. "Another bullshit roadblock for the McElroy case, I'm afraid," Garrison said as he dropped a sheaf of paper on the desk in front of them. Angi and Devon stared at the white paper brick.

"You can read it if you want but here's the essence of it. Our wonderful state supreme court had a case where they decided that testimony from witnesses who have been hypnotized is unreliable and therefore inadmissible. This means the girl across the street from McElroy's house can't testify even if we do catch Agenbroad. It's all out. The DA also told me that we won't be able to use anything resulting from the information we got while she was hypnotized.

"All of the stuff linking the car in Soquel to the murder is out, too. So now you have to find Agenbroad and get him to admit something. That, or find the girls alive and hope they can give you something to tie Agenbroad to the crime despite their ages. It's bullshit, guys, I know, but that's the way it is. Now get out there and find some evidence that's not tainted."

Garrison left no room for questions, and the detectives knew it. As they left he office, Angi turned to Devon. "Where in the hell do we turn now?"

Chapter Nineteen

Spring 1983

At first, it seemed that Celeste's fairytale vision of life had finally come to her. Tom was as attentive as he had been before the wedding and still called her 'my lady.' By Memorial Day however, Tom returned to a life filled with late night binges at the Carlisle Brewing Company, the fanciest bar in town. There, he entertained a variety of women, although never becoming intimate, while the faithful Celeste remained at home.

Celeste's previous experience with marriage had hardened her to life's disappointments. *I hate that he's gone back to partying all the time, but at least he's never done the one thing I can never forgive. He's never hit me.*

In fact, when he was home, he was still attentive and caring toward her. "It doesn't mean anything, Celeste. You have to believe me. It's just the result of years of living a rough-and-tumble life of a carpenter. It has nothing to do with you. You know I love you more than anything. If you want me to stop going out with the boys, I will. It's just part of the life I've had."

Never mind that the 'boys' were mostly female. Celeste always assured Tom that she understood. After all, she enjoyed a night out with her girlfriends from time to time, and Tom never denied her that opportunity. So, for the time being, Tom and Celeste Mason settled into a comfortable, small-town existence.

* * *

In many ways, Celeste was a tougher mark than the others had been. Her hard-scrabble life taught her a degree of self-sufficiency that Butch's previous conquests, other than Sharon, had not mastered. As time went on, Butch tried numerous tactics to win control of Celeste's small fortune. Even though they were now married, her assets prior to the marriage did not become part of the community property.

He was always careful to avoid pressing Celeste too hard on this matter, opting instead to try to charm her into ceding control of her finances.

"I love you and trust you but that's not the issue," she said. "I just feel like I need to take some control of my own. The little bit of money I have seems perfect for me to manage." She also assured him, "I will always be willing to provide any money that we need to improve our life, but I don't want to interfere with you. You're still the man of our house and the bread-winner to me."

To most men, such concern about their 'masculine' role in the marriage might have been welcome. To Tom, it was a slap in the face from a woman who deserved no mercy.

* * *

Earlier in the spring, Tom had insisted that they employ a maid for the routine housekeeping chores. After all, they could afford it. Celeste wanted to hire a woman she had known from the hotel, a woman who was known as a hard-working maid there. However, Tom wouldn't have it. *I don't want some bitch that she knows to be around for her to whine to.* Ultimately they hired another local woman. Celeste had not known this woman previously, except in passing as people in any small town know each other. However, the woman performed her duties well and Celeste became comfortable with her.

Finally, Butch's frustrations came to a boiling point. *I've tried everything I can think of and she just mocks me. 'Oh, Tom, honey, you know I'll use my money to help us get anything we need but it's just something I have to do — to decide my own destiny,' she keeps saying. Just something you have to do, huh? Well, now I'm going to show you what I have to do! And that time I spent with that jackass, Yamashita, in prison learning that karate bullshit might just pay off now.*

The next morning, Tom surprised Celeste with an announcement. "Great news, darling. I've been asked to bid on a big construction job in Spokane. If I get it, it would not only give me—us—a big windfall, but it would help me get jobs around here. Only thing is, I have to go there and submit the bid personally and do some kind of interview."

"Of course, Tom. Go for it!"

There was no construction job in Spokane, but there was a man called 'the scribe.' Few knew his real name, and no one wanted to—at least no one outside law enforcement. 'The scribe' was a master forger.

"So you want a power of attorney which gives you total control of this woman's finances. Idaho notary seal and notary signature?"

"Yeah. How much?"

"For you, Butch, five hundred. Special deal for my friends. You want me to put her signature on it, too?"

"Wish I could but I don't have anything with her signature in her married name. Just make it up and date it for June 30, and I'll get her to sign it."

'The scribe' knew better than to ask. If the woman was going to sign, why didn't Agenbroad just get a legitimate power of attorney.

Just before the July 4th holiday weekend, Butch was ready to execute his plan. All he needed to do was get her signature. Then he would execute her option for a final payout of the remainder of her winnings and transfer the money to his hidden account and get the hell out of the hellhole in the wilderness. *I'll get the signature today and then keep darling little Celeste locked up while I take it to the bank. The money will transfer tomorrow, Friday. Then since Monday is a holiday, it will give me extra time with the bank closed to get the hell out of here.* It was a perfect plan.

When Celeste returned home from a short shopping trip on the morning of June 30, Butch greeted her at the door.

"You look so happy, honey," she said. "Did you hear back from Spokane? You got the contract, didn't you?"

"No," Butch said, smiling. "But I got something better for you from Spokane." Suddenly, his face took on an angry mottled scowl. He grabbed Celeste's left arm and flipped her body across the room in a practiced, if less than perfect, karate move. She crashed into two tables in the living room and crumpled to the floor, unconscious.

Whether it was from her head striking one of the heavy wooded end tables, from the pain of four spiral fractures in her arm, or the pain of her dislocated left shoulder didn't matter. She was out cold and wouldn't be signing anything for a while.

"Damn!" Butch said. "I just wanted you to understand that you needed to sign this damned paper without an argument." He knelt over the unmoving form on the floor. *She's not dead but probably won't be waking up soon.* He would take a little walk down to the *Ram's Horn* and grab a beer. Then when he came back and woke her up, she'd sign. *She'd better!*

Chapter Twenty

June 6, 1983

Now, two months after Garrison's bombshell and no new leads, Angi sat at her desk, staring at the pile of new case folders on the left corner. Slowly, her eyes wandered to the photo of Stacy and Jennifer. "Damn it!"

Her thoughts were suddenly interrupted by the jangle of her telephone. *Great! Probably notice of some other new crime that will take me further from finding the girls!*

"This is Berry in communications. I have a call for you that came in on the non-emergency line. This guy says he has information for you on the kidnapping case, but won't give us his name or any details. The call looks like it's coming from a phone booth in the Napa Valley."

"Go ahead and put him through, Steve. I'll see what he has to say."

* * *

It had taken months for Antonio Aurelio Gomez de Lopez to get up the courage to make this phone call. He had started a dozen times, but always hung up before anyone at the Santa Rosa Police Department answered.

After he had been released from San Sebastian, his first thought was to return to the life of crime and easy money — his life since he was 11 years old. But with that life came violence. Despite his deep involvement in setting up other inmates for retribution inside San Sebastian, Gomez did not view himself as a violent man.

But more than that, he liked children. He had never, nor would he ever harm a child. So, when he read a story in the *San*

Francisco Chronicle about a murder and the kidnapping of two young girls in Santa Rosa, he was mad. And he became even more pissed when he saw that a guy named Elmont Agenbroad was being sought as a suspect in the case.

Gomez knew he had to do something about it, but what? *With an uncommon name like Agenbroad, the suspect has to be that asshole from San Sebastian, Butch Agenbroad, or at least some relative of his.*

Still, he had think of his own life. He had come so far in turning it around. Shortly after his release from San Sebastian, he resolved to try to go straight. Gomez had never really made an honest dollar in his life, but this time he felt it was at least worth trying. His decision was helped immensely by his Aunt Sofia.

Tía Sofia had always looked out for him, even in his darkest days in the gangs. She never preached to him, but tried only to provide positive guidance. In his younger days, Gomez had rejected her help, but she was the first person he went to see after his release.

Gomez had spilled his heart to *Tía* Sofia and she was convinced her nephew really did want to go straight. Sofia worked in a small family-owned winery in the Napa Valley and she approached the owners about a job for her nephew.

Sofia was completely honest about Gomez' criminal past, to the extent she knew of it. But the winery owners were willing to take a chance on the young man based on the recommendation of one of their most reliable and hardest working employees.

Gomez soon came to enjoy his work at the Keltner Family Winery and began to feel good about himself. *Life is so good when you do not have to always look over your shoulder.* In a short time, he gained the trust of the winery owners. They always treated him well, never mentioning or even hinting about his past.

But Gomez could not forget the two little girls he had read about. *I can do nothing about the murder. But perhaps I can somehow help to find the children, if they are still alive. If they are with Agenbroad, then I might be the only chance they have.*

Still, he had done many things in San Sebastian for which he was never held accountable. Although he had never personally participated in the beatings of inmates, he was the go-between with Roy Chamberlain to set up many inmates to suffer for violating the prison code. *I do not know about the statute of limitations, especially for criminal acts in the prison. But I have made a good life for myself now. I do not want to go back to prison.*

Still, there were those *niñas. My own little sisters were so innocent in their First Communion dresses when they were only slightly older than those girls. No. I cannot sit by. I know what I must do no matter what happens to me.*

* * *

Gomez drove to a pay phone in Calistoga, many miles from the winery. Inserting quarters into the slot, he called the number of the Santa Rosa Police Department, a number he had memorized from previous aborted call attempts. This time, Gomez stayed on the line.

The call was connected to Angi's desk. On the other end of the line, a male voice with a definite Spanish accent, although the caller was obviously trying to mask his voice, said, "I hear you are looking for a guy named Agenbroad."

"Yes, we are. Do you know where he is?"

"Well, if it is Butch Agenbroad you want, I ... I might be able to help you."

The voice was still hesitant and Angi forced herself to remain calm. *Don't push this guy too quickly, Angi. This is our first new lead in months. Don't blow it.*

"Do you know where Butch is now, sir?"

"No, but I might know someone who does."

"How do you know Butch, sir?" Immediately, she thought, *Shit, I shouldn't have asked that. Of course this guy probably has a record and knows Butch that way. But that doesn't matter if he has good info.*

"I'm sorry, Detective. I would rather not say. I have done some things in my life that I am not proud of. But now I have a good life. I do not want to be involved. I just want to give you a little information that might help."

He's almost pleading with me not to ask him too much. I'll go along as long as he gives me something concrete. "OK, you said you might know someone who knows where Butch is. Just tell me as much as you can, OK?"

"*Sí.*" The caller sounded a little more relaxed. "When Butch was in San Sebastian, he was pretty close to a guard named Roy Chamberlain." Gomez omitted the details of how the two were 'close.' "Butch has no family, at least that I know about. But if anyone would know where he is, it would be Chamberlain. I think he is still a guard at the prison. That is all I can tell you. I hope it will help."

"Thank you, sir, but in order for me to act on this information, I need to have some idea of how you know Butch and how you know about him and this guard. I believe you, but I have to have a little more information for my boss, so he won't think you are just another crank caller. How do you know this?"

Angi felt safe in pushing the caller a little more now. Dispatcher Berry dropped a note on her desk that the call was coming from a pay phone in Calistoga. Not that it mattered at that moment. By the time they could get anyone there, the caller would be gone. *I really have more than enough information to look into the prison guard. But let's see if he'll give me a little more while I have him on the line.*

"I'm sorry. I cannot say more. I hope I have helped you and I pray for those *niñas.*" The line went dead.

Angi sat momentarily still, the telephone receiver still buzzing in her ear, before she hung up. She started scribbling notes of the conversation she had just finished. The caller was most likely someone who had been an inmate at San Sebastian. Otherwise, how would he have known about a relationship between Butch and a guard? She also noted her thoughts. The guy's identity wasn't important at that point. But finding out about a connection between Agenbroad and the guard, Chamberlain, was.

Chapter Twenty-One

10:20 a.m.

Royce Crowder had spent most of his adult life in prisons of one kind or another. His prison experience began as an inmate, or more precisely as a prisoner of war. Staff Sergeant Crowder had taken part in the rush across France following the Normandy invasion in World War II as a tank commander in Patton's Third Army. He saw considerable action during the war and was lucky to have escaped harm.

But on December 23, 1944, as the Third Army moved to relieve the defenders of the besieged city of Bastogne, Crowder's tank ran out of fuel. While waiting for a supply truck to reach them, Crowder and his crew were captured by a roving German patrol. They spent most of the remainder of the war in a POW camp in western Germany.

When he returned to the United States after the war, Crowder was uncertain about his future. One day, he noticed an advertisement for prison guards in a small state prison near his hometown of Bakersfield, California. He thought it might be an interesting job, at least until he could decide on what to do with his life.

He applied and was accepted almost immediately. Thus began what would become a life-long career inside a prison. Now, after nearly 37 years in the corrections field, Crowder was the warden at one of California's highest security prisons, San Sebastian.

* * *

Crowder answered the phone on the first ring, as was his habit. The clerk whose job it was to answer all incoming calls to the administrative wing of San Sebastian announced that there

83

was a call for the warden from a detective in Santa Rosa. *I hope this detective isn't calling with some sort of news that turns a good day bad.*

"Warden, I am working on a murder kidnapping case where a suspect is Elmont Jacob Agenbroad, alias Butch." Angi said after introducing herself. "He was an inmate in your facility until a couple of years ago. He was on parole but has skipped and we haven't been able to locate him."

"Yes, Detective, I think I read about your case in the papers. What do you need from us?"

"We have information that Agenbroad had some sort of connection to a guard named Roy Chamberlain while he was in San Sebastian. My feeling is that the information comes from another former inmate, although I'm not certain of that. I am hoping that you can put me in touch with this Chamberlain to see if he can help."

"Hold on one minute while I pull the files, please." Crowder buzzed the clerk in the adjoining office area.

Within a few minutes, Crowder was back on the line. "Detective Masters, I'm looking at Agenbroad's file now. We don't really have anything on him that's current. He had a few yard beefs early on, but seemed to settle down after a couple of years. About that time, he was getting regular visits from a woman named Martita Sandoval. She was a social worker here at the prison. I have an address for her, if that would help."

"No, thanks on that, Warden. We've spoken to her. In fact, she was the last person we know of that has seen him."

"OK, I'm looking at Chamberlain's file now. He was a bit of an unusual guy."

"Was?"

"Yes. He no longer works here. He actually had a pretty good career as a guard, rising to a captain's rank. However, a couple of years ago, he apparently got a high paying job with some security outfit in San Francisco and quit. I have his address, at least the forwarding address he gave when he left us."

"Thank you, Warden. You said Chamberlain had a pretty good career but was an unusual guy. Can you tell me anything else about him? Do you think he would be cooperative in helping us locate Agenbroad?"

"Well, I can tell you that I knew him slightly. He was a captain when I took the warden's job here. He seemed to have a pretty good handle on what was going on in the prison and the yard. He could be a bit of a hard-ass with some inmates, never violent or anything like that. He just didn't take any sass from any of them."

There's something the warden isn't telling me. She waited for him to continue rather than acknowledging his statement and risk breaking his train of thought.

After a long pause, the warden said, "One thing I should tell you. Over a period of several years, San Sebastian had a number of incidents where inmates were in locations they weren't supposed to be. They wound up getting assaulted, some pretty badly. We even had a couple of cases where a prisoner died. We always suspected that a guard was in on it because in most of the cases, a guard would have had to approve the inmate going to the place where he was assaulted. But we never could develop enough information to even confront anyone.

"Shortly after Chamberlain quit and Agenbroad was paroled, the assaults dropped significantly. We looked at the possibility that those two were somehow involved, but the assaults had followed a similar pattern back to a time before Agenbroad arrived. And we could never develop anything beyond mere suspicion on Chamberlain.

"But when you told me that your information indicated there was some type of relationship between Chamberlain and Agenbroad, that set off some alarm bells. It's not enough for us to act on but still, it raises interesting questions.

"As for your question about Chamberlain helping you, yesterday, I would have told you that he probably didn't know Agenbroad as more than a name but that he would help you as much as he could. Now, I'm not so sure. Sorry, Detective, that's about all I can tell you."

"Thank you, Warden. That's been very helpful, all of it. I'll let you know if we develop any information that might help your case if we can locate Chamberlain or Agenbroad."

"One more thing, Detective. I see from the file that on his original application, Chamberlain listed a brother, David Lazarus Chamberlain, as his contact. That information is pretty old, but it might help." Crowder gave Angi the address and phone number Chamberlain had listed for his brother, an address on Chicago's Near North Side.

"Thanks again, Warden. I'll let you know if we find anything that can help you." Angi hung up the telephone handset and leaned forward, resting her head in her arms on her desk. *So much to think about, but will this lead us to those girls?*

Chapter Twenty-Two

June 30, 1983 - Carlisle, Idaho

Agenbroad, alias 'Tom Mason,' sat on a barstool in the *Ram's Horn* bar, staring into his vodka tonic. *Well, that did not go like I wanted, but maybe it might work out better this way. When she wakes up, she'll know that I could have killed her or hurt her a hell of a lot worse. That might just work to get her to sign the damned paper without any more bullshit. After all, my dear, it's better to be poor and alive than poor and dead, because I'm gonna get that money either way.*

Butch had gone back to the house once about 30 minutes previously to check on her. She was still unconscious. He decided to finish one drink—and maybe one more—and then go wake her up. It was now too late to get to the bank that day, but he could still get the transfer the first thing on Friday morning. *Until then, my darling little Celeste will just have to wait with me in the house—and wonder.* Butch snickered and finished the drink.

* * *

Rosa Martinez, the woman Butch had hired as a housekeeper to help Celeste, was not, by nature, a nosy person. She had learned to keep her thoughts to herself through a variety of life experiences, both occupational and personal. Rosa was born in Texas into a large family of migrant farm workers. Each summer, her family traveled from Texas to Idaho or Oregon to work in the fields, planting, tending, and eventually harvesting crops of all varieties. Then in the late fall, the family returned to Texas to work the winter crops there. It was a lonely existence and Rosa made few friends outside the other migrant families that traveled more or less with hers.

That changed when Rosa's family decided to locate permanently in Idaho when she was fifteen. The stability allowed Rosa to attend the same high school for the entire school year and she made friends quickly. After high school, she moved to Carlisle hoping to find well-paying work in the resort community. She found her niche as a maid for some of Carlisle's wealthy permanent residents. She was highly recommended for her hard work and for the discretion she displayed in dealing with some very private people. Butch learned about her through the owner of a construction project. When he determined that Celeste did not know her, he hired Rosa to come to the Mason house once a week to help with the housekeeping.

Rosa was discreet, but that did not mean that she did not see and hear things that were going on in her clients' homes. She knew details of some important business dealings before they happened or details of marital problems. Her clients were comfortable with her to the extent that they almost forgot she was around. *Señor* Mason was different. He was more quiet than most of the men she saw in their homes. But years of observing people told Rosa that he was not the loving husband he pretended to be. Celeste, on the other hand, was very friendly and outgoing. The women developed a friendship bond.

* * *

June 30 was not Rosa's regularly scheduled day to work for the Masons. However, she had a last minute cancellation from another client. She had almost an hour to spare before her next appointment. Her next job was in Celeste's neighborhood so she decided to stop by. Maybe she could just help tidy up a bit, and pass the time talking with her friend.

It was shortly after noon when Rosa Martinez knocked on the Masons' door. No one answered. She was about to leave when she thought she heard a faint call for help from inside the house. She cautiously looked through the window and gasped when she saw Celeste sitting on the floor. There was a nasty gash on the woman's head and her left arm was sitting at a very unnatural angle, obviously broken. Rosa knew she had to help the kindly woman, her friend as well as a client, and her first instinct was to break a window to get inside.

No, if I break the window, I might get in trouble. I have never destroyed anyone's property before. Perhaps if I try the front door.

To her surprise, the door was unlocked. That was suspicious because Señor Mason was very strict about keeping the house locked at all times.

As Rosa slowly opened the door, Celeste cringed and attempted to move back into a corner. Pain shot through her arm and head and she nearly passed out again, but she tried to focus on the figure entering the house. "No, Tom. Please don't hurt me again." She knew she was too weak to even put up a fight, and couldn't understand why he had done this to her. It was the first time he had ever struck her. In fact he had never even raised his voice. A thousand thoughts, none of them pleasant, raced through Celeste's head.

Then through the fog that surrounded her consciousness, she recognized that the figure was not Tom but her friend. "Oh, thank God, Rosa. It's you. Help me please. I've got to get out of here before Tom comes back."

"Miss Celeste, what happened?" Rosa looked for the phone to call for help, but it had been ripped from the wall.

"I'll tell you later, Rosa. Just help me out of here before Tom comes back and does something terrible to both of us." The panic in Celeste's voice was palpable and Rosa quickly helped her friend to stand. Celeste bumped her arm against a table and let out an involuntary scream.

"Maybe we should do something for your arm before we move, Celeste. I do not want to hurt you more."

"No, Rosa, I can make it. We have to get away from here fast."

With Rosa bracing the younger and taller Celeste as well as she could, the two women stumbled out of the house and onto the sidewalk. As they moved toward a neighboring house where Celeste knew family members were likely to be home, a dark figure staggered down the sidewalk toward them.

"Where in the hell do you think you're going?"

Fortunately for the women, Butch had stayed at the *Ram's Horn* a little too long and had more than a little too much to drink. His movements were slow and halting. Still he was coming toward them, looking more menacing than either woman had ever seen.

Rosa looked toward the house across the street. *There is no way we can get there and get inside before he gets us.* Quickly, she looked around and considered her options. She was sure several people would be home, but which house to choose? If she picked one where the family wasn't home, Tom could cut off any other options. Standing on the sidewalk in the quiet resort neighborhood and supporting the nearly unconscious Celeste, Rosa's mind raced. There was only one option with a chance of saving them.

"Rape! Murder!! Help us! Rape, murder!" The usually quiet Hispanic lady screamed at the top of her lungs. She had no idea how long her voice would hold out, but she resolved to keep screaming until help arrived or ... she wouldn't even contemplate the unthinkable.

* * *

Within seconds, six people were looking out their windows at the events unfolding on their quiet street. At least two of the people had telephone handsets to their ears. Within another second or two, doors of two houses on the street flew open. Two men, both of whom worked nights, strode out onto their front porches. Each man cradled a shotgun in a manner leaving no doubt he knew how to use the weapon effectively.

Oh shit! Butch thought. The *money will have to wait.* Adrenaline cleared some of the alcohol-induced fog from his brain and legs. This was no place to be! He turned to run as fast as he throbbing heart would allow.

Butch had gone no more than ten steps when a thunderous *Kaboom* echoed through the buildings. He stumbled as two hot pellets of #4 buckshot entered the back of his left leg. Fortunately for Butch, the distance between him and the scattergun was sufficient that the shot pattern had greatly expanded. Most of the

21 pellets contained in the hunting shell missed him. The two that found their mark penetrated his skin after puncturing his pants.

The air seemed alive with sirens. Carlisle had no police department, so law enforcement was handled by the sheriff's office. But the sprawling rural county required little regular patrol outside the small resort area. So the four frantic calls from the same area of town that came into the sheriff's dispatch center, all reporting a possible rape in progress or even a murder, brought an emergency response from every deputy on duty. That included Sheriff Jay Ulmen himself.

Agenbroad was like a cornered animal. He was free on the street for the moment but the noose was tightening and he had nowhere to run. He tried to hide in a small shed behind a nearby house but several residents pointed out his hiding place to the first arriving deputies. Within minutes of Rosa and Celeste's exit from the house, Agenbroad was in custody.

Chapter Twenty-Three

11:00 a.m. - Richmond, California

While Butch was biding his time in the *Ram's Horn*, Anderson was driving south on U.S. Highway 101. He then turned east to follow Interstate 580 across the bridge between San Pablo Bay and San Francisco Bay. He couldn't know that this was the same route taken by Agenbroad more than two years earlier as he left Sharon's mutilated body.

Devon was focused on contacting the former prison guard. According to what the warden had told Angi, Anderson could expect that Chamberlain would be cooperative. But there was also the nagging piece of information that Chamberlain may have been involved in criminal activity while employed as a guard. Anderson's cop instinct raised concerns of the mere fact that this prison guard was considered by the anonymous informant to be 'close' to Agenbroad, a two-time convicted felon. Of course, the informant could be lying for some unknown reason, but so far his information about the two men had checked out.

Devon parked a few doors away from the address the warden had given to Angi for Roy Chamberlain. He didn't want to telegraph his arrival, even if Chamberlain was on the up-and-up. But the place looked like it had been abandoned a long time ago. Even from 75 feet away, he could see that several of the front windows were broken. The screen door at the entrance hung precariously by the bottom hinge alone. Leaves and dirt littered the walkway from the street. It didn't look like anyone had even walked up to the front door of the dump in ages.

Anderson looked around for any residents that appeared to be in view in the surrounding area but saw none. So he began the methodical task of attempting to contact someone in every house that had a view of Chamberlain's former address. Perhaps someone had seen something and could remember it, even though if Agenbroad had been there, it was probably at a considerable time in the past.

After ringing five doorbells and finding no one home, Anderson located residents in two other houses with good views of the suspect house. However, neither had seen anything suspicious at Chamberlain's house. Both people, although cooperative, told Anderson that Chamberlain was very reclusive. Neither person had ever actually met the man, although they had seen him come and go from time to time. Anderson showed photos of the missing girls and Agenbroad to the residents, but neither could say that they had seen either girl at the Chamberlain house or in the neighborhood.

As Devon sat in his car completing notes of his investigative actions, he noticed an elderly couple approaching on the sidewalk. Both were dressed in old but clean jogging suits. Anderson stepped from his car as they approached and displayed his police ID, "Excuse me. May I talk to you a moment?"

"Yes, officer?" the man asked.

"I'm Detective Anderson from Santa Rosa and I'm investigating a murder and a kidnapping. Do you live on this street?"

"No, sir," the man said. "We live two streets over and are just out for a walk. Good for our health, you know."

"Good for you. I should spend more time exercising, myself. Do you walk this way often?"

"Almost every day, if the weather cooperates. It's good that, at our age, we can get out for a good walk together."

"By any chance, have you ever seen any of these people around that house when you've been on your walks?" Anderson asked as he showed them the photos and pointed out the house where Chamberlain had lived.

"No, we haven't. Sorry, officer. Can we go now?" the man said.

"Now just a minute, George," the woman said. "Officer, can I see those pictures again?" The woman looked carefully at the photos of the girls and handed them back to the detective.

"Now, I can't be sure, but quite a while ago—must have been a couple of years ago now—we were walking by here and there was a couple of girls sitting in an old yellow car. You remember that, George?" The man shook his head. "Sure you do, George! It was a warm day and two little girls was sitting in this car alone. They looked like they had been crying. At first, I was going to make George stop because I worried about their safety, but then we saw two men talking on the porch of that house you pointed out. I don't know if that man in the picture was one of them 'cause the porch was pretty shaded. But I remember those girls, especially the older one. You remember, George?"

This time the man nodded. "Yes, dear, I do now that you mention it. I remember you were worried but I saw the two men and we figured they were watching the girls."

"You figured they were with the girls, George!" I wasn't so sure, Officer. The older girl looked at me like she was so scared, but then George insisted everything was okay and we continued our walk. When we came back by a while later, the car was gone."

"Thank you for your help. I really appreciate it. Is there anything else you can tell me about the men or the car?"

"Well, the car was a Honda. If Rita says it was yellow, then it probably was," George said. "But it was for sure a Honda, an early 70s model. It was a little beat up but actually in pretty good condition for its age. I remember thinking that the owner must have tried to take care of the car but didn't have the know-how to do it. I know because I was a mechanic all of my life."

Anderson noted the couple's names, George and Rita Camarello, and their address. They had no telephone, the couple told the detective.

As Anderson was about to let them go on their way, Rita Camarello asked, "Did you talk to Helen Bernstein? She lives in that house right over there, across the street. She's always home and keeps pretty good tabs on her neighbors."

"Yes, ma'am. I rang her doorbell but no one was home."

"Oh, for goodness sake! She's home, unless she's dead, and even then she would be in there. She never goes out. The furthest she goes from that house is out to the sidewalk, and then only if she needs a better look at something going on in the neighborhood. She even has her nephew bring her groceries. Follow me, young man." George gave Anderson a slight smile and shrugged his shoulders, as if to say there was no stopping Rita Camarello if she was on a mission.

Chapter Twenty-Four

11:40 a.m.

"Helen!" Rita called out as she banged her fist on the front door. She ignored the doorbell button, which Devon had pressed three times without a response only a short time before. "Helen, I know you're in there! It's Rita. Open this door! We need to talk and it's important."

Helen Bernstein slowly cracked her front door. "I see you out there, Rita Camarello, and I see that cop with you too. What do you want?"

"Open this door, Helen! This is important." Helen opened the door about half way and stood in the opening.

"What is it, Rita?" Helen's face showed a mixture of irritation and intrigue.

"Well, let us in, Helen. We need to talk and to be comfortable doing it." Helen shrugged her shoulders and opened the door for her friend and the men.

Rita made introductions. Anderson noted that Bernstein was well dressed, including wearing a dress and low-heeled pumps, but that the house was dark. Every blind or curtain in the visible parts of the house was closed. *I'm sure that the rest of the house is just as dark, from her demeanor.*

"Please have a seat." Helen motioned her guests into a small living room just off the entry area.

"Thank you, Helen," said Rita. "Let's have a little light in here!" Rita peeled open the blinds on the front picture window and turned on three table lamps in the living room. Anderson noticed a grimace from Helen but she made no comment.

"Go ahead, Officer Anderson," Rita said as they were all seated. Anderson briefly explained to Mrs. Bernstein who he was and why he was in their neighborhood. As he showed her the three photos, Anderson started to explain who the persons in the photos were and why he was asking about them.

However, Rita interrupted. "Helen, remember we talked about the girls George and I saw in the car that day a couple of years ago — the yellow car. Remember? You told me you had seen them too."

I should ask her to let me ask the questions, but she got us in here, Devon thought. Besides, Rita Camarello didn't strike him as the type of person who would sit quietly anyway.

"Yes, I remember that, and yes, officer, I did see these girls more than once at that house," Helen said.

"Well, tell him about it, Helen!"

Helen glared at her friend. "Rita, you just be quiet and let me tell the story. You came banging on my door, remember. Now, I'm going to tell my story. So just be quiet!"

OK, Anderson thought. *Two strong willed women as my best witnesses so far. This is good.*

"Alright, Officer," Helen said, "This is what I remember. Now mind you, I keep to myself and I'm not a nosy neighbor but sometimes I just happen to see things."

"Of course, ma'am, I understand. Please go on."

"Well, this one day — I don't remember the date, but it was in the spring and it was a nice day and I think in April sometime — I looked out my window and saw this little yellow car pull up in front of the house across the street. There was a rough looking man driving the car, but mostly I remember these two precious little girls in the back seat. The youngest one seemed like she was crying and the older one seemed to be trying to comfort her. I noticed that the man didn't even try to do anything to soothe them. In fact, it seemed like he didn't care about them at all."

Devon started to speak, but Helen held up her blue-veined hand and gave him a stern look. "Don't interrupt me, young man. I have to get this all out and if you interrupt me, I might forget something." He smiled and sat back, focused on taking notes. "But, in answer to your obvious question, I can't be one hundred percent sure, but I'm pretty sure those girls were the ones in your pictures, especially the older one. The man in your picture was definitely the driver. I'd remember that ugly mug anywhere."

Anderson nodded and continued his note taking.

"The man left the girls in the car while he went up to talk to that awful man across the street. Awful man. He would never speak to you when he came out of his house, which was almost never. I think the man must have slept until noon every day. Awful man he was."

Anderson and the others stared at Helen.

"Sorry. I was rambling, wasn't I?" she said. "Anyway, after the men went inside and talked for a while, the driver came out and got the girls. He carried the little one and led the older one by the hand and took them inside. Then after about five minutes, he came out and got back into the car and left. I never saw him again."

Helen paused and closed her eyes.

Did she fall asleep on me? Anderson thought after a few minutes.

Suddenly the elderly woman opened her eyes. "I need some tea. Would any of you care for tea?" Helen rose and started for her kitchen.

She's got more to say, I know it, Anderson thought. But it would definitely come on her schedule, and it looked like teatime came first. But so far, the woman had provided good info, so better to just go along with her.

As Helen began to move, Rita started to get up to help. "Sit back down and relax, Rita. I can do this. It will take only a minute." 'A minute' turned into twenty and more, for there was no such thing as instant tea or a pre-made tea bag in Helen Bernstein's house.

After the tea was steeped in hot water, she pulled down four small teacups and matching saucers from their place on the lower shelf of her cupboard. She poured the cups three-quarters full, straining the hot liquid through a paper coffee filter to ensure that no tiny particle of tea leaf entered a cup. Helen delivered the cups on their saucers to her guests and then took her seat.

"Now, where was I?" Helen asked.

The look on her face is like she's only been gone for a few seconds, rather than almost thirty-five minutes. Anderson sighed to himself.

"Oh yes, so after the man left in the yellow car, I didn't see the girls or that awful man across the street until the next day. Maybe it was the next day, or maybe it was that night ... well, I don't know but it was getting dark when I saw the girls again. This time, another car stopped in front of the house. I just happened to be looking out the window at the time. You know, I'm not nosy but sometimes I notice things." Helen looked at Devon, "Officer, what did you say their names were? I'm sure you told me but it has slipped my mind."

"The older girl is Stacy and the younger one is Jennifer."

"Oh yes, Stacy," Helen sighed. "Did I mention that my great-granddaughter's name is Stacy? That's a very pretty name. She is my son, Julian's granddaughter and ... well, as I was saying, this other car pulled up in front of that house. It was a smaller gray car that kind of looked like the yellow car but was different. I don't know about cars, but they weren't the same. Anyway, there were a man and woman in the car. The man got out and went to the door while the woman stayed in the car. A few minutes later, the man came out with those two girls and he put them into the back seat of the car. He got back in the car and drove away. After that, I never saw those girls again until you showed me their pictures just now."

Anderson smiled. Bernstein would be good on the stand if it came to that.

"I know that awful man across the street—he really was an awful man, you know—was still around until he moved out about six months later, but I never saw those girls or any of the adults again. After that man moved out, the guy who owns the house—he lives in San Jose and thinks he's a real big shot but he's just a bum—just let it go to pot. I never saw that awful man again, thank God."

Devon scribbled notes for a few minutes. *So Agenbroad brought the girls to Chamberlain almost immediately after kidnapping them and killing their mother. Chamberlain kept the girls for a short time, perhaps less than a day, after which a man and woman had come and taken them away. The girls had not returned to Chamberlain's house and he was now in the wind.*

After thanking the three, Anderson headed back to Santa Rosa, his mind swirling with the new information. He had come to talk to a likely cooperative witness. But now, it looked like Chamberlain was up to his eyeballs in the case. He was the one who transferred the girls. Now the question is—two damned years later—who got them and where are they now?

Chapter Twenty-Five

2:15 p.m. - Carlisle, Idaho

Dr. J. Frank Wilcox had been practicing medicine for more than fifty-five years. In that time, he had seen all manner of gunshot wounds. The two small piercings in this man's left upper thigh and left buttock were almost superficial but had penetrated into his flesh.

Deputies brought Agenbroad to Dr. Wilcox's clinic because it was on the way from the scene of the arrest to the county jail. The wounds weren't serious enough to require that the prisoner be transported to the county hospital emergency room. However, the deputies couldn't book an injured prisoner, particularly one with gunshot wounds, into the jail without clearance from a medical professional.

Dr. Wilcox spent most of his career as an emergency room physician at Good Samaritan Hospital in Los Angeles. The location afforded him the opportunity to treat people from across the spectrum of economics and ethnicity. He was a first-rate caregiver who had little tolerance for those who preyed on others. He had moved to the mountains of Idaho two years before and his mindset fit with that of most others in the central mountains.

Dr. Wilcox provided excellent care to his patients and he was known by all as a gentle and caring man. Fortunately, in this community, he had almost no call to deal with the predator mentality. That was, until Butch Agenbroad was helped into his clinic by two deputies.

"What have we here?" the doctor, now almost 83 years old, asked.

"We just arrested his guy for aggravated assault on his wife. I think you know Celeste Mason. Broke her arm in several places,

101

and I don't know what else. They took her to the hospital. Anyway, as this guy was fleeing the scene, one of the neighbors—you know Jerry Dentinger—let him have it with his shotgun. Mason here has a couple of pellets that probably need to be removed or at least looked at before we can book him into jail."

"Mason? Tom Mason?" The doctor hadn't looked closely at the man's face in the moments since he had come in. Dr. Wilcox had never seen Mason as a patient but knew of the man and had seen him around town. "Well, drop your pants and put yourself face down on that table. We'll have a look."

"Hmm," Wilcox mused as he inspected the two wounds, "Yes, it would be best if we got those pellets out of there. Lie still."

As Dr. Wilcox picked up a set of forceps and spread the first wound open with his fingers, Agenbroad's head snapped to look at the physician. "Doc, what about anesthetic?"

"Aw, Tom, you're a tough guy. Takes a real tough guy to beat up on a woman and to break her bones." Wilcox inserted the forceps tips into the open wound on Agenbroad's buttock, twisted the tip, and pulled the BB out of his flesh.

Butch wanted to scream but wasn't going to let these dumb yokels see him sweat.

"There. That didn't hurt did it, tough guy?" Wilcox said as the pellet clanged into a metal basin. The doctor then plunged the forceps tips into the second wound on Agenbroad's thigh, deeper this time, and extracted a second pellet.

Agenbroad winced but didn't make a sound beyond a labored exhalation of breath.

"Now we wouldn't want those wounds to get infected. You might die. I'm just a poor country doctor so isopropyl is all I have in stock right now. I'll just cleanse those with a Q-tip and you'll be ready to go." The sting of the raw antiseptic—rubbing alcohol to most people—coupled with the cotton-tipped swab inserted into each pellet hole was almost more than Butch could stand. But he gritted his teeth and remained stoic, betrayed only by the river of sweat running down his forehead.

The deputies stared at Wilcox. This was a whole new side of the gentle doctor.

"All yours, boys. The tough guy is cleared for jail." Wilcox tossed the forceps into an autoclave tray and walked out of the room. *Will this guy complain to the medical board? Probably not, but what the hell. As this point, I don't care. I can just close the clinic and play golf.* Wilcox had helped a lot of people over the years, but few cases gave him the satisfaction he got from his small part in helping Celeste Mason.

* * *

Agenbroad was booked into the county jail under the name Tom Mason, the name by which everyone in the area knew him. He was charged with aggravated assault for the attack on Celeste. When he was searched, deputies found the forged financial transfer in his back pocket. This raised suspicion of the man to a new level.

"Fax his prints to the state crime lab in Boise," Sheriff Ulmen said. *Something tells me this isn't a run-of-the-mill domestic case.*

Two hours later, Ulmen received a phone call from the technician at the lab. "Sheriff, of course we can't make a positive ID based on a faxed print comparison. But it looks like your 'Tom Mason' is really Elmont Jacob Agenbroad, AKA 'Butch.' He's a two time convicted felon, currently wanted for parole violation in California. He's also wanted for questioning in a homicide and kidnapping in California. We'll have to wait for the original fingerprint cards to arrive in the mail to confirm, but this looks pretty good."

"Thank you. I'll have a deputy leave immediately to drive the cards down to you. I have a feeling that his might be a big deal, far bigger than we know now."

Chapter Twenty-Six

July 1, 1983

Sheriff Ulmen called Jerry Rogers, his most junior deputy, into the office. "Jerry, I have a really big job for you. Take these cards and drive them to Boise and deliver them to the state crime lab. I know it's a long drive and you'll get there after they close, but they said to call this number when you arrive. The technician will come in to make the comparison check right away. Call me at home as soon as you have the results."

Ulmen's home phone rang at 2:27 a.m. The state lab had confirmed it. The man in custody was Butch Agenbroad.

The sheriff was in the office by 6:30 a.m. The teletype from the FBI's National Crime Information Center contained a contact name of Detective Angela Masters in Santa Rosa, California, along with the detective's phone number. It also contained the name and contact information for Agenbroad's parole officer in San Leandro. Ulmen decided to call the detective first. He paced his office waiting for 9:00 a.m. — 8:00 a.m. in California — to arrive.

* * *

Angi had barely sat down at her desk and hadn't looked at a piece of paper nor retrieved her morning cup of tea when the phone jangled. "Angi, I think you're going to like this," the dispatcher said. "I have a sheriff in Idaho on the line for you. They have Agenbroad in custody on a local charge there."

"Put him through, Steve. Put him through!"

Ulmen explained the circumstances of their arrest of Agenbroad. "Since he was arrested for a felony, he will be held in the county jail without bond until he can be arraigned. That's the way our state law works. Normally that would have happened this morning but the only judge in our county took the day off for a long weekend. And since Monday is July 4th, the arraignment won't be until Tuesday morning. He hasn't lawyered up yet, so you have until then to come up and interview him if you want."

"Yes, I definitely want to do that, Sheriff! I'll be on the first plane out today." She hoped Garrison and the chief would approve the expenditure for a flight on short notice.

"The best option is to fly into Boise and then rent a car for the drive to Carlisle," the sheriff said. "It's not an easy trip, but we make it several times a year. And since it's summer, the mountain roads will be clear."

Angi hung up the phone and headed directly for Sergeant Garrison's office.

Like the others, Garrison was just getting settled in when Masters rapped on the frame of his open doorway. "Mike," Angi said without even a 'good morning'. "Agenbroad is in custody in some backwoods county in Idaho!"

"That's great news, Angi. What do we need to do now?" Garrison leaned forward in his chair and grinned.

"The sheriff up there says they are holding him without bond pending an arraignment on Tuesday. I want to get up there and try to question him before that. If he makes bail, he'll be in the wind again." Angi explained the steps she would have to take to get to the small resort town.

"I agree, Angi," Garrison said. "Let me talk to the lieutenant and probably the chief about it. I'll get back to you but in the meantime, go get your bag packed."

An hour later, Angi was back in the office, her travel bag in the trunk of her car. Garrison beckoned her into his office as soon as she entered the work bay.

"Well, you can go to Idaho, Angi. However, the chief has some concerns about your travel plans," Garrison said. Angi started to argue, but Garrison held up his hand and said, "Just hear me out. The chief felt your idea of flying to Boise and renting a car for the drive to Carlisle might be pretty fatiguing. We all want to you be sharp when you talk to Agenbroad, so this is how it will go."

Angi held her breath. *Shit! The chief wants some kind of delay, maybe for me to stay overnight in Boise before driving to Carlisle. If that's it, he's got to know I'll never get any sleep sitting in some hotel room. I want to get at Agenbroad the first chance I can.*

"The chief called the police chief in Boise. Seems they know each other from some chiefs' conference. Then they got on a three way call with the sheriff you've been talking to."

God, I love you like a brother, Mike, but sometimes your methodical approach is nerve-wracking. Just spit it out so I can argue.

"The chief's secretary has booked you on a flight leaving in four hours out of Oakland. When you arrive, you will be met at the gate by a Boise police officer who will escort you across the tarmac. The Boise chief has arranged for a helicopter to fly you directly to Carlisle. Sheriff Ulmen will be waiting for you to drive you to the jail as soon as you land."

The cooperation across agencies continued to amaze her. *This case is finally coming together*, she thought.

Chapter Twenty-Seven

10:30 a.m.

Angi was on the road for the one-hour drive from Santa Rosa to the Oakland International Airport. She wished she had been able to talk to Devon about his trip to Richmond, but he was testifying in court on another case that morning.

She had packed light—only a carry-on bag and a notebook, which she would use to draft her interview questions for Agenbroad while she was flying to Boise. She also carried the authorization paperwork that United Airlines had faxed from their corporate office to the Santa Rosa Police Department, authorizing her to carry a concealed firearm on-board their aircraft.

Angi arrived at the airport an hour before her flight was to depart and parked her car in a special section of the parking garage reserved for visiting police officers. She went straight to the airport police office, located on the second floor of the main building. There she met the duty sergeant, showed him her police identification and firearms permit. She also completed a form that requested information such as her name, department, destination, airline and flight number, and the type of case which required her to travel.

Once the paperwork was completed, she was escorted to the security checkpoint by an airport police officer. He led her through a security corridor that bypassed the checkpoint to avoid having her firearm set off the metal detector. Once past the security checkpoint, the airport officer escorted Angi to her departure gate, where he introduced her to the gate agent for United Airlines.

She would be pre-boarded but would need to obtain the pilot's permission to carry her firearm on the plane, even though permission had already been granted by the company. Pilots almost never refused permission to a sworn law enforcement officer on official business, but regulations required that the captain give his authorization. The head flight attendant made a cryptic notation on the seating chart, indicating for other flight crew members that the passenger in seat 12C was armed.

The one hour and thirty-three minute flight to Boise was uneventful and Angi had time to complete her outline of questions for Agenbroad. As she sketched her outline, she wondered if the fact that she had met Agenbroad before would impact the interview. After a moment, she decided that it didn't matter. She would confront Butch with the discrepancies the investigators had uncovered since that meeting. Whether the suspect tried to explain them away or gave a plausible answer, she would learn something about him.

As promised, as soon as her flight landed and she deplaned, Angi was met by an officer from the Boise Police Department. He escorted her through a secure door off the jetway and down to the tarmac. There, a police cruiser drove her across the airport to a waiting helicopter. When the officer noticed Angi's quizzical look at the lettering on the side of the aircraft, *Emmett McCall Corporation*, he smiled and said, "Don't worry, Detective. Our department isn't big enough for us to have our own helicopter like your California departments."

More than a little sarcasm there, officer, Angi thought as he almost spat out the word 'California.' She was unaware of the disdain Idaho natives held against those who had moved to their pristine area from the Golden State.

She dismissed any slight. "I'm from Santa Rosa, which is just about the size of Boise. We don't have a helicopter either, but this is really nice of you guys to help us like this."

"Well," the officer said, "the chief talked to the mayor, who talked to the head of one of our largest local companies, and they donated the use of their helicopter and pilot to you. Must be a big case for them to do that."

"Yes, it is," she said. Maybe she would tell the officer about the case, if she saw him again later. Right now, she needed to concentrate on the coming encounter.

The officer helped Angi board the Bell Jet Ranger helicopter. He loaded her carry-on bag as she fastened her seatbelt and then gave a thumbs-up to the pilot.

The pilot smiled and turned to Angi, "Hi, I'm John Tuning. Have you ever flown in a helicopter before?"

"No, I haven't," Angi said. "But I'm looking forward to it. I'm ready. Let's go."

"OK, ma'am. You'll find some of the sensations a bit different from flying in an airplane because we can do so many different things, but I'm sure you'll get used to it easily." The white and blue aircraft lifted off the tarmac, rotated 50 degrees to the right, and began to climb as it headed north.

* * *

Angi gripped her seat tightly during the unfamiliar rotation after takeoff. But she was soon lost in her thoughts, recalling every detail of the investigation that had consumed her time and her thoughts for more than two years. *I'm ready to confront the monster,* she assured herself, but checked her notes and planned questions just to be sure.

She had been in such deep concentration that she was surprised when the pilot said, an hour into the flight, "There's Carlisle. We're landing in that parking lot by the high school." Carlisle didn't have an airport, although there were a couple of back-country dirt strips in the nearby mountains. Sheriff Ulmen directed the helicopter to land in the school parking lot since it would be an easy landmark for him to pick out and was gated for the summer.

The skids had hardly touched the ground when Angi unbuckled her seatbelt and slid back the left passenger door. As the rotors slowed to a stop, she hopped to the ground in time to greet a silver-haired bear of a man approaching her from a nearby SUV. The Ford Explorer was painted a beige tone with the word

'Sheriff' emblazoned in dark brown letters on the vehicle's side. An old Federal light-bar was attached to the roof with the red and blue rotating lights flashing.

It was 6:42 p.m., eerily dusk-like as the sun settled below the peaks of the Idaho mountains. Angi shivered. She left Santa Rosa in 80 degree weather. In the rushed planning to confront Agenbroad, it hadn't crossed her mind to consider the temperature difference. The evening temperatures in Carlisle, even in early July, were closer to the low 40s than the middle 50s of Santa Rosa. But the approaching man in a brown sheriff's uniform reminded her of why she was here and the chill of the air disappeared from her mind.

"Detective Masters? I'm Jay Ulmen. Glad to meet you."

"Please call me Angi, Sheriff. Thank you so much for all your help." Ulmen picked up her carry-on as she turned to the pilot to thank him.

"Don't worry, Detective," he said. "I'll be staying here for as long as you need. My company has arranged a place for me to stay and the sheriff has the number. Just call when you are ready to go back."

I can't believe the amount of cooperation I'm getting from everyone involved on this end of the matter. I thought California agencies cooperated pretty well, but this is amazing. Now, if only Agenbroad will cooperate.

"What's your plan, Angi?" the Sheriff asked as they climbed into the Explorer. "We can go to the jail now or I've arranged a room for you at the resort hotel if you'd like to rest and talk to Agenbroad tomorrow. I'm sure you've had a long day."

"Thanks, Sheriff, but this family has been waiting for two years for the answers I hope to get here. I'm ready to have a go at him." Angi's adrenaline level rose at the thought of the impending second face-to-face meeting with Agenbroad, especially now that she knew she had him caught in several lies from their first meeting.

The county sheriff's department was located in a modern building near the center of town, one block north of the main street. While much smaller than its counterpart in Santa Rosa, this law enforcement facility had everything needed by a rural department, including a state-accredited jail. The jail was small—only three cells—but it had modern electronic locking systems. At least two deputies were assigned to monitor the jail at any time one or more prisoners were housed there.

A small café three doors west of the sheriff's building held the county contract to feed prisoners. Many deputies tried to get jail duty, since those on jail assignment got to eat the same 'jail food' as the prisoners. It was several steps above what they could find at one of the local fast food joints while on patrol.

Reminds me of Mayberry, Angi thought. The contrast between the idyllic setting and the hardened criminal she was about to confront did not escape her thoughts.

Chapter Twenty-Eight

7:10 p.m.

Sheriff Ulmen led Angi to the tiny room that served as the department's investigative office. The small agency had no specifically designated detective. Every deputy was expected to conduct his or her own investigations, or to ask for help if the case was outside their expertise.

Angi waited only a few minutes before Agenbroad was brought into the room by one of the jail deputies. The deputy directed Agenbroad into a chair across the desk from Angi and then stepped back a few feet. He discretely positioned himself directly behind the prisoner, where he stayed throughout the interview. Agenbroad's hands remained shackled with a pair of Peerless chain handcuffs.

Not an ideal interview situation but I'll make the best of it, Angi thought.

Agenbroad spoke almost as soon as he was seated. "I remember you. Masters, right? Are you here to give me some good news about the SOB who kidnapped my children? Are they okay?" *Eat it up, lady. I'm just a concerned and caring father.*

Interesting that he has 'adopted' Jennifer into his realm of concern. She's no relation to him. "No, Butch, but I think you can help me find that person. I have some concerns about the story you told us when we talked in Santa Cruz. Some things just don't add up," Angi said. "But first, you understand I have to advise you of your rights since I'm talking to you while you are in custody."

"Sure. Sure. I know them but go ahead and read your little card. I just want to help you find those poor babies."

I'm not buying this 'poor father' bullshit, but let's try to follow it before I try direct confromtation. "Butch, tell me again about your trip to Reno, the one you told me about last time we talked?"

Agenbroad repeated the story he told the detectives two years before. He had rehearsed it well enough then. Even today, he remembered the details almost as perfectly as he had when he concocted the story.

"OK, Butch, thanks." Angi jotted some notes which had little to do with the lie she was sure Butch was telling her. "Now, do you know a man named Roy Chamberlain?" she asked, not raising her eyes from the paper.

Butch began to fidget. He clasped his hands to hide his clammy palms. *How much do they know about Chamberlain?* "Well, there was a guard at San Sebastian named Chamberlain, but I don't know his first name. I only know him from there. Haven't seen him since I got out." *That should be safe enough.*

"Hm, OK," Angi said. *I'll go along with this crap for the moment.* The morning has been a whirl getting to the flight to Boise. Because of his court appearance, she had not had a chance to sit down with Devon to see what he might have learned from Chamberlain, if anything. She might try a bluff on that, but it would wait for now.

"Please, Detective," Butch said, "can't you just tell me what's going on? Where are my little girls?" This time, Butch went so heavy with the 'concerned father' theatrics that even the jail deputy winced and rolled his eyes in Angi's direction.

"That's what I'm trying to do, Butch!" Agenbroad was surprised at the edge in the woman's voice.

Then, as easily as she had shown her ire, she calmly said, "Here's a problem I see, Butch. Maybe you can help me with it." Angi's eyes locked with Butch's in an unflinching glare.

"Of course," Butch said. His mind was racing. *I know I can outwit this bitch detective. I just have to figure out how much she really knows and how much she might be bluffing.*

"Great. I'm sure we can clear up the issues and get on with finding whoever did this. First, you told me you had driven to Reno. But the round trip to Reno from your mother-in-law's house is at least 600 miles. We checked the records since she had an oil change only a day or two before. The car had been driven less than 300 miles. I'm confused about that. Can you help clear that up?"

Damn! That biddy Elena must have tipped the cops to the mileage. How else would they know about it? "Sorry, Detective, I can't explain that. Maybe there was something wrong with the speedometer or maybe Elena's records were wrong. I just know I went to Reno that day like I said." *Does she believe me? Probably not, but I've got no good story for the mileage difference. Shit! I should have thought of that and had a story ready. But who would think that a woman, especially an old crone like Elena, would actually check the mileage on a car?*

"OK, we can come back to that later. Would you like to tell me why you disappeared right after we talked to you last time? I have to tell you that it looks really suspicious, not to mention violating your parole."

"No, I don't think I need to get into that!"

"Of course." Angi made a flourish of noting his deception in her notes. "So, do you think Roy Chamberlain might know something about the girls?"

"Yeah, maybe he had something to do with it. I don't know. Like I said, I barely remember the guy from prison and I never had anything to do with him." *I just hope the hammer I have over Chamberlain's head will be enough to keep that asshole quiet about me or the girls. I wonder what he did with them. He doesn't have the balls to actually get rid of them, but I'm pretty sure he doesn't have them anymore. My bet is he dumped them on someone else as quick as he could.*

Angi asked a few more questions which she had prepared in advance, but Butch either claimed ignorance of the issue or dodged the question completely. *Guess I'll re-visit the mileage issue. Maybe he'll get flustered and let something useful slip if I press harder.*

"OK, listen up, Butch! The story about going to Reno is horseshit and we both know it. The mileage thing doesn't add up and we've checked for mechanical problems. That's not it. The car didn't go to Reno—period. So stop wasting both our time and tell me where you really were that day!" *A calculated risk here to approach a convicted felon this way, but I'm getting nowhere with him anyway, so I've got little to lose.*

"I told you where I went! Maybe that bitch Elena is trying to set me up, just like Celeste did. That damn Celeste falls and breaks her arm and then tells the cops I did it. She knows I'm an ex-con and she wants to get my money by sending me back to the joint. And Elena never liked me even though I treated her whiny daughter like a queen. I'm the victim here and you people are trying to hang that thing with Sharon and this bullshit charge with Celeste on me. I'm done talking!"

This isn't helping me, but right now, I don't give a shit. If they know about Chamberlain, then they might find the girls and I'm screwed. I'm already dangling for the parole violation and kicking Celeste's ass. What do I have to lose by putting the fear of God into this bitch? She obviously doesn't realize that she is nothing compared to me, and she will always be nothing. She needs to be put in her place – hard!

Butch lunged across the desk at Angi. But before his knees had even extended, he was grabbed from behind and slammed to the floor. His face struck the cold concrete with a thud. Butch hadn't realized the deputy was still standing behind him, and the strength of the skinny kid in the ill-fitting brown uniform completely surprised him.

"Well, I guess that means we're done here, Butch," Angi said, never moving from her seat at the desk. "You'll probably need to get that cut looked at. It looks pretty bad."

"Yeah," the deputy said. "Doc Wilcox will be happy to stitch that up."

"I'm not hurt!" *I got no interest in seeing that asshole doctor again.* "Take me back to my cell. I ain't talking anymore. I tried to help you and this is what I get."

Chapter Twenty-Nine

8:15 p.m.

Back in the sheriff's office, Ulmen and Angi went over the confrontation with Agenbroad. "I'm sorry you made this trip for nothing, Angi," the sheriff said.

"Oh, it wasn't for nothing. In fact, Butch pretty well convinced me that he's our guy, more from what he didn't say and how he acted. Unfortunately, I'm also sure now that he doesn't have the kids somewhere. I'm guessing he hasn't had custody of them for a long time, and probably has no idea where they are. We'll have to concentrate on his associates if we are going to find them. But I'm glad he will be in your state prison for awhile."

"Well, there's some bad news on that. I didn't want to say anything to you before you took a crack at interviewing him so I wouldn't break your concentration."

"What is it?" *Shit. I hope these guys didn't screw up their case here. If he gets released, he'll be in the wind — until he hurts someone else.*

"Understand that we are a sparsely populated county. To add to that, most of the land in the county is national forest, owned by the federal government and they don't pay taxes to the county or the state. Under Idaho law, each county is responsible for the costs of prosecuting any crime that occurs in the county, including providing a public defender if necessary. We get no money from the state for prosecutions."

The sheriff paused a moment to let the information sink in. "The county prosecutor told me last night that he will probably offer a plea deal to Agenbroad's public defender here. He agreed to hold off until we contacted you folks to see what you might want to do. But now that you've had a chance to talk to him, and don't have enough to arrest him on your case, the prosecutor will likely make the offer before the arraignment on Tuesday.

"Most likely, he will let Butch plead to misdemeanor assault at his arraignment, or sometime shortly after that. We just don't have the money in this county to go for a full blown jury trial on a felony assault case. I think our victim has already agreed as long as Agenbroad is ordered to stay away from her permanently as a condition of sentencing."

What kind of a horse shit operation is this? Butch hasn't even been arraigned yet. True, it's highly unlikely he will plead guilty to the felony charge at his arraignment, but really? — a plea deal is almost cemented already. She was hoping this charge would keep Butch in one place where they could find him for a while. But it was pretty clear that a California case, even murder and kidnapping, didn't mean crap to a local prosecutor's decision. And there was not a damned thing she could do about it. Angi's weak smile said it all.

"I'm sorry, Angi. We'll do what we can to get him the maximum, but that's only a year in the county jail. You've had a long day. Let's get you over to the hotel so you can get some sleep. The helicopter can't fly safely at night in these mountains anyway. The pilot will be ready to take you back to Boise as soon as you're ready in the morning. Here's his contact number."

"Thank you, Sheriff," Angi said as he dropped her off at the hotel. "Please keep me informed on the status of your case and Butch's location."

"You can count on that. I'm really sorry we can't do more, but we'll do our best with what we have. Please call me if we can help you in any way."

Angi believed him, but that didn't help her frustration. The clock was tolling like Big Ben, ticking off the time to find the girls before Butch walked as a free man again.

* * *

Angi was exhausted from the stresses of the previous two days and thankful that the next day was July 4th. She was anxious to find out what Devon had learned in Richmond, but due to flight delays, she hadn't gotten back to Santa Rosa until nearly 7:45 p.m. *I'll call him as soon as I eat something.* She hadn't eaten since having a bagel at the hotel in Carlisle, nearly twelve hours earlier. She fixed a quick dinner of sliced turkey and Gruyere on wheat toast with a light spread of herbed mayonnaise. She also poured a glass of her favorite wine, V.Sattui's *Gamay Rouge*. Then, she collapsed on the couch, phone in hand, and slept soundly until 5:00 a.m.

At 8:00 a.m., she called Devon's house. "Devon, I'm sorry to bother you on the holiday, but ..."

"Angi, it's fine. I would have called you soon. I'll bet you want to hear about Richmond."

"Yeah, I do. And I have some things to tell you about my interview with Agenbroad."

After each had briefed the other on their investigations, Devon said, "I'm planning to spend the day with my family, and — I know this might fall on deaf ears — but I think you should unwind a little too."

Angi laughed. "You know me too well, Anderson. But I agree. I think it's time for a wine tour. I'll see you in the office tomorrow morning."

She hung up the phone, had a light breakfast and took a short run. She then spent the day touring some of the area's many fine wineries, returning to Santa Rosa to watch the holiday fireworks show at dusk. Her mind drifted from time to time to the helicopter pilot.

Chapter Thirty

July 5, 1983

Tuesday morning at 7:10 a.m., Angi was at the office and anxious to plan the next move in their investigation. Devon had arrived at 7:00 a.m. They were sitting in the two chairs on either side of Sergeant Garrison's office door when he arrived thirty minutes later. "I'm guessing you two want to see me," Garrison said through a knowing grin.

The two detectives briefed their sergeant on their activities of the past few days.

"I have to agree with your assessment, Angi. He doesn't sound like the kind of guy to haul two kids around for this long. You're probably right that he doesn't even know, or care, where they are. But even if he pleads to a misdemeanor like your sheriff said, he'll at least be in jail for a few months. So that's our time frame to build a 187 case on him."

Both detectives nodded. 187, the California Penal Code designation for murder, was their goal as far as Agenbroad was concerned.

"But the girls' welfare comes first," Garrison said. He didn't say what all of them knew—hope for their safe return was waning.

"I don't think Chamberlain has them either," Devon said. "The witness in Richmond put them there but only for a couple of days at most. The best lead, to me, seems to be to find the man and woman who took the girls from Chamberlain's house. And I think I know who they might be."

Angi's mouth dropped open. "You do?!"

"Maybe. Although the information from the warden at San Sebastian placed Chamberlain's brother in the Chicago area, I took a chance and searched California records for a David Lazarus Chamberlain, certainly not a common name. I found an address for that name and a Joyce Marie Chamberlain in Benicia. That's only a few dozen miles from Roy Chamberlain's former residence and it gets better. They have been at their current address only since last summer. They moved to Benicia from Berkeley, practically next door to Roy Chamberlain. And the clincher—they own a light gray Toyota Tercel."

"How does that fit in?" Garrison asked.

"Wait!" Angi said. "Devon, you told me that your witness described the car of the couple who picked up the girls from Chamberlain's house as being gray and looking similar to the car that dropped them off. If the first car was Elena Sandoval's yellow Honda driven by Agenbroad, then a Toyota Tercel certainly fits the bill of looking similar to the Honda Civic!"

"Exactly! But I also found that David Chamberlain has a criminal record in at least five states—mostly property crimes, burglary and larceny. But his record also shows a smattering of violent crimes including assaults. In one case, he beat the shit out of a guy with a baseball bat in a dispute over who had arrived first at a gas pump. That netted him his longest sentence, five years in the Nevada State Prison in Carson City. But there might be an in. I couldn't find anything on Joyce Chamberlain, not even a speeding ticket."

"Sounds like the Chamberlains are your best lead to finding the girls," Garrison said.

"I'll put together a photo lineup for each of them." Each lineup consisted of six photos, in this case the driver's license photo for the subject—Dave or Joyce—and five other driver's license photos of people with similar physical characteristics.

As soon as he finished with his briefing, Devon was on the road for a familiar house in Richmond.

* * *

Anderson drove directly to Helen Bernstein's house. This time, he knocked on the door rather than ringing the bell, and called out his name. Helen opened the door almost immediately.

I'll bet she just 'happened' to be looking out her window when I arrived, Anderson thought, smiling.

After repeating her excruciatingly long tea ritual, Helen sat down. She turned on a light beside her glider rocker and looked carefully at the photos. "Yes, I'm sure that's the man that picked up the girls, Officer. No doubt in my mind!" Helen said after a few seconds, pointing to the photo labeled '#4.'

Devon didn't comment but smiled to himself. Photo #4 was the driver's license picture of David Lazarus Chamberlain.

"I'm not sure about the woman. I'm sorry but I didn't really get a good look at her."

"That's fine, Mrs. Bernstein. We don't want you to pick out someone unless you're sure."

Devon finished his tea as graciously as possible and thanked Mrs. Bernstein. Rather than return to Santa Rosa with the news, he stopped at the Richmond Police Department and identified himself. In the detective offices, he called Angi. "The witness positively identified Dave Chamberlain as the man who picked up the girls in Richmond. Can you meet me in Benicia and we can go talk to them?"

"On my way!" said Angi. She almost missed the phone cradle as she hung up the receiver and bolted for the parking lot.

* * *

Angi and Devon met at the Benicia Police Department headquarters. There they met with the patrol lieutenant in charge of the currently on-duty shift. After the Santa Rosa detectives outlined their case and their reason for being in his city, Lieutenant Miles Scott said, "No problem. I'll give you whatever backup you need. Are you sure one patrol car is enough? I can probably spare one or two more."

"I think one will be enough, Lieutenant, but thanks," Devon said. "We don't have anything certain to go on. At best, these people may have picked our girls up from a location in Richmond a couple of years ago."

"Well, as you requested," Miles said, "I had an officer drive by the house a while ago. She didn't see any indication of kids at the house now, but no way to tell if they had been there in the past."

"These people just moved to Benicia a few months ago," Devon said. "We'll just keep it low-key for now. Just having a couple of uniforms and a car standing by would be helpful if we get lucky and find the girls there."

"No problem, and if you do find that you need more help, just signal my guys. They'll be just down the block watching your approach to the house. We're a small city so we can have more cars there before you know it."

* * *

That afternoon, a teletype message from Sheriff Ulmen was delivered to Garrison. It confirmed what the sheriff had told Angi. At his arraignment, Agenbroad pled guilty to misdemeanor assault in connection with the case involving Celeste. He was also given a permanent order to stay away from her. The judge also ordered the marriage annulled. Agenbroad would be transferred to the more secure Ada County jail in Boise to serve his sentence. With 'good time credit' if he obeyed jail rules, he would be released in a little more than nine months. Garrison knew he could still face charges on the California parole violation, but that decision wouldn't be made until shortly before his release in Idaho.

Garrison stared at the yellow paper and massaged his temples. *When Agenbroad is released, he most certainly will see the girls as a liability if they are still alive. Sounds like he would have no compunction against having them killed to keep them linking him directly to Sharon's murder. Time is running out.*

Chapter Thirty-One

3:45 p.m.

When Joyce Chamberlain saw the pair walking toward her front door, she knew immediately they meant trouble. She also guessed the reason they were there. Even though Joyce herself had never actively participated in any criminal activity, she knew the look of police officers from the times they had come to her door looking for Dave. *These two, a man and a woman, look every inch to be cops. No doubt in my mind that they are coming to talk about the girls that me and Dave picked up from Roy's in Richmond. How long ago was it? Two years ago, I think.*

She had been suspicious of the whole affair when they went to Roy's house. But Dave assured her that there was nothing wrong. *In my heart, I've always known that whole story about their mother being killed in a car wreck was a crock.* But she still had no idea where the girls had come from. She told Stacy her parents were killed just to keep her from asking to go home all the time.

Perhaps the story about the traffic accident was true, but she doubted it. Joyce resolved that she would raise these girls like her own daughters until she had an idea as to who they might really be. The option to contact the police or Child Protective Services was out of the question. The only emotion which would override her concern for the children was her concern for her husband.

I just couldn't bear to see Dave go back to prison, even if it meant keeping those two little girls from their family. But now, ...

* * *

Joyce opened the door at the first knock and greeted the officers, trying to remain as calm. *Maybe this has nothing to do with the girls or with Dave. In any case, it's best not to show any concern that we have anything to hide.* She invited the detectives inside.

"Is there anyone else in the house now, Mrs. Chamberlain?" Angi asked.

"No, ma'am." *Be polite, Joyce. They're cops, but be polite.* "My husband is at work and it's just the two of us."

Joyce's hope that the police visit did not involve the girls quickly evaporated when the female, who identified herself as Detective Masters, showed Joyce two color photos of young girls.

"Have you ever seen these girls," Masters asked.

There was no use denying it. The cops must have known about them going to Richmond and picking up the girls. Otherwise, how could they have found them? "Why, yes, I've seen them," Joyce said. "They are the daughters of my brother-in-law's girlfriend. She was killed in a traffic accident and he had been raising them with her. But he couldn't take care of them on his own after she was killed." Joyce was embellishing the story Dave told her originally, but only enough that she hoped the detectives would not question her.

"Good. We appreciate your honesty," Angi said. "Are they here now? We need to see them."

"No, I'm sorry, Detective. We tried to take care of them for a while, and certainly did a better job than my brother-in-law would have done. But you see, we never had children and it was pretty hard on us having little ones around."

"So where are they now?" Anderson asked. There was an edge of irritation in his voice.

Good cop/bad cop. Joyce had seen the routine before. *Let it slide, Joyce. You're innocent. Or at least they have to believe you are.* "As I said, detective," Joyce directed her comment to the 'good cop' female. "They were just too much for us to handle, so we took them to live with my sister in Salem, Oregon, for a while. She owns a daycare there and is great with kids. She has two of her own, both in elementary school now. I can give you her name and address if you like. I'm sure the girls are well taken care of there."

* * *

Joyce didn't mention what had happened the previous summer, an event she was only partially aware of.

She and Dave had taken the girls to visit her sister, Kathy, at her home in Chandler, Arizona. They were considering moving out of Berkeley, and Dave agreed that the change of scenery might be good for the girls. They could stay with 'Aunt Kathy' for a couple of months and thus not be under foot during a move out of the Berkeley house. Kathy agreed to look after the girls while Dave and Joyce moved. She embraced the well-behaved children as did almost everyone who met them.

Three months later, Dave and Joyce had moved into a house in Benicia. It was in a slightly better neighborhood than they occupied in Berkeley. Still, the neighbors were of a type not willing to place a call to the police unless it was about something that affected them personally. After they settled in, Dave and Joyce returned to Arizona to get the girls.

What was not in Joyce's thoughts, because she didn't know, was that Dave didn't trust his sister-in-law to keep her mouth shut. But he also didn't want to alarm Joyce to the point where she might turn on him. Joyce knew too much about his past. Thankfully, Kathy knew nothing of it. After spending only two nights with Kathy and her husband, Dave and Joyce were ready to take the long drive back to central California.

The evening before they left, Kathy mentioned a strange thing that had happened just a month after the girls arrived. "The cops, about five carloads of them, went to a house across the street and a couple of doors down. At first, I thought it was some kind of drug raid or something. That didn't really make sense because the people who live in that house seem really nice. I don't know them well, though, and these days you never know.

"Anyway, after a little while, the cops all got in their cars and left. They didn't arrest anybody. A few days later, I saw the woman who lives there and it was the strangest thing. She said the cops told her that they had a tip that two little girls who had been kidnapped were at that house. Of course, that wasn't true.

They have two girls about Stacy and Jennifer's ages, but everyone knows those girls live there. It was just bizarre." Everyone nodded at the strange story.

What Kathy did not know was that the clerk who took the initial tip was cursed with sloppy handwriting. His note stated that an informant reported seeing two little girls who resembled children he had read about in *Real Detectives* magazine while he was making a delivery in an area he usually didn't visit. The clerk noted the address, but a dispatcher misread his scribble as 2205 rather than the house number of 2208, Kathy's address.

Thus, by a cruel twist of fate, police were sent to a house occupied by two girls who lived there with their law-abiding parents. Police took it as a case of mistaken identity and reported it that way on their call log. That was also what a Chandler detective would report to Detective Angi Masters, who was considering making a trip to Arizona.

Kathy and her visitors all laughed about the incident, and Kathy noted, "It's certainly a good thing to know that my sister and brother-in-law are on the up and up." Dave and Joyce laughed along with the others. Dave never let a hint of concern show, even to Joyce, but his stomach churned at the thought of such a close call.

* * *

We purposely didn't tell her why were looking for these girls, Angi thought. *Strangely, she didn't ask. Maybe she really doesn't know the truth about the girls' history. But she knows something. Her husband's past and now a visit from detectives make that almost a given.* An almost imperceptible eye roll from Devon told her he felt the same way.

"Do you mind if we take a look around?" Angi asked.

Joyce silently nodded and stepped to one side.

The search yielded a few toys and children's clothes which likely belonged to young girls. But, since Joyce did not deny that the girls had been there at one time, the detectives had little reason to suspect the woman had any guilty knowledge.

126

They thanked Joyce and Angi left her business card, telling her they might be back. "In any case, I'd like you to call me immediately if you hear anything from your sister about the girls.

Joyce smiled as she showed the detectives out. *Fooled them! Dumb flatfeet, just like all cops.*

She had not only 'forgotten' to mention the trips to Arizona, but had also withheld the fact that Dave, at that very moment, was in Salem to bring the girls back to Benicia.

* * *

"I think she knows more than she's telling us, Devon," Angi said as they walked to their cars.

"I agree, but let's check out the Salem thing right away. I'd say let's call the locals and have them go to the daycare this afternoon and not wait until we can get up to Salem. We can come back here tomorrow if this doesn't check out."

"Good plan. I'll thank the uniformed cops who were on standby and meet you at Benicia PD. We can make a phone call to Salem from there," Angi said. *Maybe at last we're getting close!*

Chapter Thirty-Two

6:00 p.m. - Salem, Oregon

It was nearly 6:00 p.m. when the phone on Detective Joe Hayes' desk rang. Hayes, a 17-year veteran of the Salem Police Department, was normally gone at this time of day but paperwork kept him late. His partner, Detective Mike Allison, had already left for the day.

"Investigations, Hayes." he said as the phone jangled for the third time, "Can I help you?"

"Hello, Detective, this is Detective Angela Masters from Santa Rosa, California. We need some help from you guys on one of our cases." Angi outlined the case's high points, especially the factors surrounding the girls. "We have current information that the girls may be with a couple named Alan and Darlene Cramer in your city. We can fax you photos of the girls. We'd appreciate it if someone from your agency could contact the Cramers as soon as possible to see if the girls are there. If you find them, we'd like you to take them into protective custody. We can expedite the paperwork for you to hold them for us."

"Sure, Detective Masters, I can do that for you. Give me the address and the girls' names and descriptions as you think they might be now."

Angi provided the address that Joyce had given her and Anderson. "The fax is on the way now."

"OK. That address is in an older but fairly nice middle class neighborhood. I don't know these people but I used to work that area when I was in patrol. It's definitely not a high-crime area."

"Our information is that Darlene Cramer runs a daycare from her home. The husband, Alan, reportedly works for an electronics firm there," Angi said. "From the information we have, I don't believe these people are directly implicated in the crime at all. In fact, my gut feeling is that they probably have no idea that the girls are kidnapped. Probably they just took them in as a favor to Darlene's sister. Of course, I could be wrong, but I just want you to know the score. Also, the guy we think did the murder and kidnapping is in jail in Idaho, so you won't have to worry about him being there."

"OK. I'll go right out there as soon as I receive your fax. It's probably in records by now."

"Great. I'm actually calling you from another city where my partner and I were getting this information, but I wanted to get things moving there ASAP. As soon as we hang up, we'll be on our way back to Santa Rosa." Angi gave Hayes the direct number to the Santa Rosa detective office as well as the dispatch number.

"I'll call you the minute I finish with them, either way."

* * *

Before Detective Hayes left the office, he ran a check on the Cramers' names and checked the daycare center license file. Neither of the Cramers had any criminal history, nor even a traffic ticket. The daycare center, in business for the past four years, had passed every inspection with ease and had not received a single complaint.

There had never been a police call for service to the Cramers' address. It seemed likely that, if the girls were there, it would be as Masters had speculated—the Cramers were merely innocent participants.

It was shortly after 7:00 p.m. when Joe knocked on the door of a well-maintained home. The front yard contained a few toys and a small but professionally created sign reading 'Darlene's Day Dream for Kids.'

He pressed the doorbell button and the door was opened almost immediately by a dark-haired woman who greeted him warmly before he could say a word. "Hi, there. I'm Darlene. How can I help you?" the woman said as she extended her hand.

129

Hayes introduced himself and said "May I come in and ask you a few questions?" His face was friendly but there was a sense of directness in his voice. After inspecting Hayes' badge and identification card, Darlene opened the door wider and invited the detective inside. Hayes detected a slight look of concern on her face, not an unusual reaction when the police come to one's door, although her smile remained.

"Please sit down," Darlene said, as she motioned to a living room chair.

At that moment, Alan walked into the living room from the kitchen. "What's going on?" he asked. His tone was more of curiosity rather than concern.

"Honey, this is Detective Hayes from the police. He wants to ask us some questions." Darlene took a seat opposite Hayes across a coffee table. Alan sat beside her.

Hayes could see that Cramer appeared more concerned than his wife, but wasn't showing the nervousness that he would expect from someone on the wrong side of the law. A direct and truthful approach seemed best with this couple. All the indicators were saying that, if they were involved at all in the California crime, it was inadvertent. "I've been asked to talk to you by some detectives in California." The statement didn't produce any indication of concern in either of the subjects. "We are looking for these two girls," he said, pulling the faxed photos sent by Masters from his portfolio. He laid them on the coffee table facing the Cramers. "Have you seen them or are they here now?"

"Yes, that's Stacy and that's Jennifer," Darlene said immediately, correctly pointing to each photo as she identified the two names. Alan nodded his head in agreement as his wife made the identification. "They have been here but are gone now. They were very sweet and well behaved little girls and we enjoyed caring for them," she said.

"Do you know where they are now?"

"My wife's brother-in-law left with them this morning," Alan said. There was not a hint of concern in his voice. "We actually thought we were going to have them for the whole summer, but Dave — that's my brother-in-law — showed up here a couple of days ago and said he needed to take them home."

"You said 'Dave'?" Hayes asked. "What's his full name?"

"David Chamberlain," Darlene said. "I don't know his middle name. He's married to my older sister, Joyce. They live in a city kind of north of San Francisco but I don't remember the name of it. I can look it up on our Christmas list, though, if you need me to."

Hayes already knew the name and where the Chamberlains resided from Angi's briefing, but the fact that the Cramers were forthcoming with the information spoke well as another indicator of their innocence in the case. "Yes, that would be great. Thank you. I'll get that from you before I leave. So, are these girls your sister's children?"

"No," Darlene said, "she has no children, poor thing. She has been caring for these girls for a couple of years as a favor to Dave's brother. As I understand it, the brother's wife — I don't know his name but he's Dave's brother — the wife, or maybe girlfriend, was killed in a car wreck. These girls were the children of the brother and the woman who got killed, but I understood from Joyce that he wasn't very well equipped to care for them on his own."

Hayes nodded and noted the comments on a report form.

"He sounds a lot like Dave in that regard," Darlene said. "I don't think Dave could boil a hot dog without help. It's been a little bit of a strain on Joyce. Personally, I would love to have these girls in my house all the time, but she never loved children like I did.

"My other sister, Kathy, and I have helped her out by taking them for a while from time to time. Actually, I think Kathy only had them once because she lives in Arizona and it's pretty far away for Dave and Joyce to take them there."

"Is there anything else you can tell me about the girls or about your sister and her husband?" He phrased the question almost as an afterthought.

"No, not really," Darlene said. "The older one, Stacy, always seemed kind of sad and is really protective of her sister. They played well with my kids and the kids in my daycare, but Stacy never let Jennifer far from her sight. I just took it as the sadness of losing her mother, and really, her father at such a young age."

"I noticed that too," Alan said. "I tried to get her to open up a couple of times, but she would just shake her head and hang back. I also had a feeling that she's terrified of men, but I don't know why."

"I noticed that too," Darlene said. "She's pretty withdrawn around Dave, but I don't know the reason. I'm sure Dave wouldn't do anything wrong to a child, and I've seen abused children before. Stacy didn't show any of the signs that I recognize as abuse, but she just seemed to be a little afraid around all men.

"Come to think of it, I've noticed her kind of pushing Jennifer behind her when, for instance, a man comes to the daycare to pick up his children. But she never shared anything that would give me a clue to a reason why she would do that. I also have to stress that it's not really an obvious reaction. It's more of a subtle thing you probably wouldn't notice unless you've been around her a lot."

Hayes was happy to gain the couple's insight into the psyche of the girls. In addition, the wealth of information volunteered by the couple, especially Darlene, further contributed to the theory that the Cramers were not knowing parties to the crime being investigated by Detective Masters.

"One more thing," Hayes said. "Would you mind if I take a look around your house? It's just a base I have to cover to put in my report that the girls aren't here."

"Not at all," Alan said. He led Hayes through every part of the house, including the back yard. Two young boys were nestled in their twin beds, pretending to be asleep as their father entered, but there was no sign of other children being on the premises.

It was 9:15 p.m. when Hayes returned to his office. He dialed the number that Angi had given him.

"This is Detective Joe Hayes in Salem, Oregon ..." He was interrupted in mid-sentence by the dispatcher.

"We've been expecting your call, Detective Hayes. I'll transfer you to Detective Masters' home phone right away. Hold on, please."

A second later, another telephone rang just once before being picked up. "Masters," said the female voice on the other end of the line.

Not the usual way to answer your home phone, Hayes thought. *She was really anticipating this call.*

"Detective Masters, this is Joe Hayes in Salem."

"Please, call me Angi. How did it go? Did you find them?"

"Well, if by 'them' you mean the girls, no, but I did talk to the Cramers. They were very cooperative, and my gut feeling is that your theory about their involvement being innocent is correct. The girls have been there, but David Chamberlain left with them just this morning, presumably headed back to California." Hayes then filled Angi in on the rest of the interview, including the information about Stacy's reported aversion to men.

"Well, that makes sense. She was taken by a man she had never met, even though he is her natural father. She may have even seen that man stab her mother to death. Then she was with a rough character in Roy Chamberlain, and from there handed off to his brother, Dave.

"She probably has little trust in any man right now. Anyway, thanks for your quick work. I agree with your assessment of the Cramers' involvement. Since you've determined the girls aren't there now, we'll leave them alone for the moment. I'll let you know if we need you to go back there."

Joe gave Angi his office and home numbers before hanging up the call, and leaving for home. His wife would be interested to hear about this call, even though his part in the investigation had been minimal. This type of crime rarely touched a city like Salem. Thankfully, it appeared that this one had only tiptoed through their jurisdiction.

Chapter Thirty-Three

July 6, 1983

Six hundred miles to the south, the phone on Devon Anderson's kitchen counter rang. He answered it to hear an angry Angi Masters on the other end. "Devon, Joyce Chamberlain lied to us. Her husband was picking up the girls in Oregon as we were talking to her. Meet me at the station at 7:00 and let's head back to Benicia. We might just surprise them and find the girls." She filled Devon in on the rest of the findings of the Salem detective and they agreed to meet early the next morning.

Angi thought about driving to Benicia that night, but decided against it. They hadn't left Joyce with any reason to think they doubted her story about the girls being in Oregon. So even if she believed the detectives would check on the girls, she probably wouldn't think it would happen so quickly.

Also, it was a ten to eleven hour drive from Salem—longer with the typical road construction on I-5 during the summer. Angi don't want to show up at the house too soon and risk scaring Dave off if he would drive up with the girls. No. Early in the morning would be best—before they start moving around.

Angi laid back on her bed, still dressed in Cal State-Northridge warm-ups. She habitually bought a new one every year, in support of her alma mater. She thought for a moment and then dialed the 24-hour number for the Santa Rosa FBI Resident Agency. It was a courtesy call to let them know that she now had confirmation that the girls had been taken across state lines. Even after leaving a message with the clerk on duty, she doubted that the feds would offer much direct help. She fell into a fitful sleep while mulling a plan for what she hoped would be a great day tomorrow.

* * *

Angi and Devon were both at the Santa Rosa police station by 7:00 the next morning. Before leaving, Angi placed a call to the Benicia Police Department and asked to speak to the watch commander. To her relief, Lieutenant Miles Scott answered the phone. *Good! At least he's familiar with the situation and it would save time not having to explain the whole case to someone new.* "Lieutenant, this is Angi Masters in Santa Rosa. We are on our way back to your city and this time I think we could use some help from your guys." She explained the situation to Scott, including her feeling that the chances were good they might find the girls. "I feel a whole lot better knowing that Stacy and Jennifer are still alive—as recently as a couple of days ago. It's time to bring them home."

"I'll have at least a couple of cars, maybe more, waiting for you when you arrive. And I'll have an unmarked car sitting down the block to watch the house until then. That car can be in place in the next ten minutes," Scott said.

"Thank you, El-Tee," Angi said, using the nickname derived from the abbreviation for 'lieutenant.' "We're on our way."

Traffic at that time of morning would be a bear on Highway 101 headed south toward San Francisco. So, unlike the last time they had gone to Benicia less than twenty-four hours before, Angi and Devon left their unmarked detective cars in the parking lot. After a brief explanation to their own watch commander, Devon had the keys to a marked Santa Rosa Police patrol car, which he drove out of the motor pool.

As soon as Angi climbed into the passenger seat, they were on the road toward Benicia. With the rotating red lights activated and the electronic siren wailing, the detectives made the sixty mile trip in fifty-three minutes, half the time the trip would have taken if they had been mired in the flow of traffic in an unmarked car.

After a brief meeting in the parking lot with the Benicia officers assigned by Lieutenant Scott to assist them, Angi and Devon joined a procession of four marked Benicia Police cars, containing six officers, to the Chamberlain's neighborhood. Two of the officers assigned by the lieutenant were members of the

Solano County Combined SWAT team, dressed in their tactical gear. They would be the primary cover team for the initial approach to the Chamberlain house.

Following the plan agreed upon in the parking lot, two Benicia officers moved to a position behind the Chamberlain house. They remained concealed but ready to apprehend anyone who might flee out of the back of the house. Two additional officers deployed to either side of the house, taking up concealed positions in adjoining yards, in case a suspect would attempt to leave through a side window.

The SWAT officers covered the front, taking positions to either side of the front door but slightly out from the house. They could effectively cover anyone coming to the front door. The consensus was that Masters, as a woman, might have the best chance to make the first contact with the occupants without raising alarm inside the house. Devon would stand back across the street, armed with an M-1 carbine retrieved from the trunk of the borrowed patrol car. His job was to provide overall visual coverage of the scene.

Wearing a Kevlar vest, the first one she had been issued which was actually tailored for a woman, Angi approached the front door. She knocked sharply and then stepped to the side to avoid the dangers which might be present if whoever opened the door was armed. After a few seconds of no response, she knocked again sharply and this time announced, "Joyce! This is Detective Masters. I need to talk to you. Please come to the door." Again there was no response.

Just as she moved from the side of the door to make a third attempt, a man across the street stepped onto his front porch. "There's no one there," the man yelled. "They left about 9:30 or so last night and I'm pretty sure they moved out."

Chapter Thirty-Four

8:40 a.m.

Thirty-two-year old Detective Mike Allison arrived at work at the Salem Police Department with no inkling of what had happened in the past sixteen hours. His partner, Detective Joe Hayes, saw no urgency to inform Allison of the Cramer interview, since it seemed their involvement was finished, at least for the foreseeable future. Hayes was describing the events of the night before to his younger partner when their office phone rang. Allison, sitting closest to his phone, picked up the receiver, and pressed the button for their joint line.

"Ummm, yeah, can I talk to Detective Hayes, please?" said the halting male voice on the other end of the line.

"Sure, hold on, sir," Allison said, nodding to Hayes to pick up the call.

"Umm, Detective Hayes? This is Alan Cramer."

"Yes, Mr. Cramer. What can I do for you?" At the mention of the name 'Cramer,' Allison turned his attention to Hayes.

"I'm sorry, Detective, but my wife and I were wrong last night," Cramer said. Hayes pursed his lips, peaking Allison's interest even more.

"How so, Mr. Cramer?" Hayes mind raced. *What could they have been 'wrong' about? It all seemed so straight-forward during the interview.*

"Well, we've actually never seen those girls, and we don't know anything about them," Cramer said in a halting voice. "We were thinking of someone else when we talked to you."

This has got to be one of the strangest phone calls I've ever received, Hayes thought. Only twelve hours ago, Darlene Cramer identified the missing girls correctly by name without prompting and Alan Cramer agreed. They also identified Dave and Joyce Chamberlain as being involved with the girls. Now, Cramer was telling him that their identifications had been mistaken. It was so ludicrous as to be almost laughable, but in one way, it made sense. The Cramers had been threatened in some way.

"Mr. Cramer — Alan. I hear what you are saying but I'm a little puzzled. You seemed pretty sure last night. Has someone talked to you? Suggested you change your story?"

"No, no, nothing like that."

He answered almost too quickly, Hayes thought.

"We were just mistaken, that's all. We've never seen them and we can't help you so please don't call us again." Then, Cramer hung up.

"OK, that was weird," Hayes said as he slowly replaced the handset on its cradle. After he described to his partner what had just happened, Allison also agreed that someone had gotten to the couple.

"Maybe someone threatened the Cramers' kids. From what you just told me, they love kids and liked the missing girls. Sounds to me like the only thing that would cause them to turn against the missing girls would be a threat to their own children."

Hayes immediately picked up the telephone handset and dialed the direct number for the Santa Rosa detective office. Angi — Detective Masters — needed to know about this development right away. The detective who answered the phone, upon learning the call was for Masters from an out-of-state detective, immediately transferred the call to Sergeant Garrison.

Although Angi and Devon left before their supervisor arrived for work that morning, Angi left him a note outlining the developments in Salem and their plan to try to intercept the girls in Benicia. From the note, Garrison knew that the caller was the

Salem detective who had interviewed the Cramers. "Angi is headed to Benicia to try to intercept the girls," Garrison said."

"OK, Sarge. Let me tell you about last night's interview and the phone call I just received."

"Now that's completely strange," Garrison said with a low whistle. "There's definitely something hinky going on there."

"Yeah, my partner and I said the same thing. How would you like us to proceed?"

"Let me try to reach Masters or Detective Anderson in Benicia and let them know what's happened. Our radios don't reach that far but I might be able to connect with them through Benicia PD. Does Masters have your number?"

"Yes, she does. We'll sit tight here until we hear from your department."

* * *

When Dave got home the night before, Joyce told him about the visit from the Santa Rosa detectives earlier that day. When she told him she had mentioned that the girls were at her sister's house in Oregon, he had flown into a rage. *Who knows how much information those idiot Cramers will spill to the cops. They're probably on their way to Salem right now.*

After venting his anger at Joyce for her stupidity in telling the cops so much, he realized what had to be done. "If we want to stay out of jail, we have to get out of here! Tonight!"

Joyce was stunned that jail would be a possibility for helping the girls. Unless Roy did something illegal involving the girls and he could drag Dave down with him.

Dave also made a preemptive phone call to Alan Cramer that night. Detective Hayes had been gone from the Cramer house less than an hour when their phone rang. "Alan! Have you heard anything from the cops lately?"

"Yeah, Dave," Cramer said. *What is with this anger?* "A Salem detective was here a while ago asking some questions about the girls."

"And just what did you tell him? Don't lie to me!"

"Dave, I wouldn't. What's up?"

"Damn it! I said tell me what you told him!" Dave's heart was racing now. *Salem detectives are involved, so that means the Santa Rosa cops aren't driving north to check on the girls themselves. We have even less time than I thought. A phone call from the Salem cop could have the Santa Rosa cops, or even worse, Benicia cops at my door at any time.*

"We just told him that the girls were here but that you had already picked them up." Alan tried to downplay the encounter with Hayes, even though the detective had given him no indication that anything was really amiss.

"What else?"

"That's all, Dave. Honest. The detective didn't say that anything was wrong at all. He just said that detectives in California had asked him to check with us. He never said anything about any trouble, so we didn't think anything of it. I just thought maybe it might have something to do with your brother's custody or something. No big deal."

"Alan, listen to me good! You don't know nothing about those kids. Nothing! You hear me? Tomorrow, you call that cop and tell him you were mistaken. You've never seen those girls before. You thought he was talking about some of the brats Darlene babysits. You got that?"

Alan had not told Dave about the couple's identification of the photographs Hayes showed them. *Damn. No reason to make Dave any madder than he already is. But why?*

Had Dave known about the identification, he most certainly would have realized how truly idiotic was his demand that Alan and Darlene recant their story. "Call them tomorrow, first thing, Alan! You were mistaken about seeing those girls, ever."

"OK, Dave, whatever you say."

"And, Alan," Dave said, his voice calmer. "Convince that cop that you don't know nothing about those girls, or your kids will be dead in a week! If the cops come after me because of something you told them, those boys will get a bullet and you and Darlene will know it was all your fault!" Dave slammed down the phone and began grabbing clothes from the closets.

Cramer slumped into a chair, the blood draining from his face.

"Who was that, Alan?" Darlene asked.

"Dave. We're in deep trouble — and I have no idea why."

Chapter Thirty-Five

9:20 a.m. - Benicia, California

In Benicia, word was passed by radio to the perimeter officers. "Neighbor reports that the subjects have left. Maintain your positions while we confirm," the senior Benicia officer on the scene broadcast. Then he switched radio channels and called his dispatch center. "Have records find out who owns the property at our location. Contact the owner and have him get down here with a key. We'd like to preserve as much evidence as possible and need to get into that house. But we'll break in if we have to unless he gets here with a key soon." Three minutes later, the radio crackled with a message from the dispatcher. The owner was on his way with a key.

Angi and Devon, accompanied by one of the SWAT-clad Benicia officers, approached the neighbor. Martin Brady wasn't one to get involved, particularly when it came to cooperating with the police. But there was a more practical matter at stake. Brady knew from watching television that the SWAT cops would hold nothing back if they decided to batter down the door of the house across the street.

The man who owned that house was also Brady's landlord. The skinflint landlord, a humorless downtown banker, would probably raise Brady's rent in addition to the rent across the street if he had to replace a door frame. In this case, helping the cops seemed a better option to Brady than having the landlord raise his rent.

"OK," Masters said. "You said they moved out last night? Are you sure about that? Could they have just gone away for a while?"

"Nah, they're gone for good. The guy came home about 8:30 or so. I think he had been gone for a couple of days because I

143

hadn't seen him out on his porch slugging down beers like he usually does in the evening. Anyway, he drove up and he had their little girls with him. He must have been picking them up from camp or relatives or something because I haven't seen them around for a couple of weeks, maybe more."

Brady eyed the SWAT officer who was standing a few feet to the right of the detectives. The SWAT guy hadn't spoken since being introduced to Brady by the detectives, but Brady could feel the man's cold eyes staring at him the whole time.

"Go on, Mr. Brady." Angi made eye contact and moved to distract Brady from his concentration on the SWAT officer.

"Like I said, the guy and the girls came home and walked in like nothing was wrong. I was just sitting out here on my porch like I do in the evenings if it's not too hot. The guy had been inside about two minutes when all of a sudden he just started screaming. It sounded like he was really unloading on the wife. I couldn't make out what he was saying but there was a whole bunch of swearing going on. My wife even heard it inside the house."

Brady didn't mention that his wife had been so alarmed at the vitriol coming from across the street that she wanted to call the police. But calling the cops was something that was rarely done in this neighborhood, and Brady was not about to do it then, especially over a guy just arguing with his wife. After all, he had unloaded a few tirades on his own wife before, and thankfully no one had called the cops on him.

"After a little while, maybe ten minutes or so, the guy calmed down and things seemed to get quiet," Brady said. "Then about twenty minutes later, he came out hauling a bunch of clothes to their car. He wasn't using suitcases or even plastic bags. He just brought out arm loads of clothes like they had just come out of a drawer or the closet and stuffed them into the trunk of the car."

Brady paused for a moment and eyed the detectives, and especially the unmoving SWAT guy. The male detective had been taking notes but the female just seemed to be taking it all in. She nodded to Brady to continue with his story.

"So after he stuffed about everything he possibly could into the trunk, the wife and the girls came out and got in the car and they just drove off. Another thing, the guy was looking around the whole time he was loading the car, like he was afraid someone was going to show up. I thought maybe a loan shark or someone like that might be after him. And then today you guys showed up and that's it."

Chapter Thirty-Six

10:05 a.m.

Angi had barely finished talking to Brady when a man in a new silver BMW 5-series pulled up in front of the house across the street. Almost immediately behind that car, an unmarked police car stopped at the curb. Angi recognized Lieutenant Miles Scott as he stepped from the car and walked toward her and Devon.

Charles Edward Richards III slid from the driver's seat of the BMW. The man was obviously irritated at having been summoned to the area. He certainly looked out of place in the neighborhood where few had ever seen an Armani suit and Gucci loafers, let alone owned such clothing. But then Richards perfectly fit the description of a 'slumlord.' He owned the two shabby properties there but this was the first time he had ever personally visited the area. He rarely left his luxurious office in the state bank he owned in downtown Benicia, and preferred to send a lackey to deal with the people who rented his hovels. But today, there had been no one immediately available to deliver the key that the cops wanted.

Richards hadn't intended to bring a key, but then a police captain came on the line and told him to either bring the key immediately, or he would send officers to Richards' office to get it. The last thing the slumlord banker wanted was to have some flatfoot marching into his office in front of his customers and giving him orders. Richards couldn't know that the captain had no intention of sending officers to fetch a key. He was only asking for a key in deference to Richards' position in the community. Had Richards still refused, the officers would have merely battered down the front door of the house.

Now, Richards' attention was drawn to a cop in full SWAT regalia walking towards him from the front of the now-abandoned house. Richards thought he looked like a friggin' storm trooper.

"Good morning, sir," the officer said. "Thank you for coming down so quickly. Do you have the key for this house?"

"That's why you called me down here, isn't it?" The slumlord felt to need to show any respect to a public servant, particularly one dressed like a wannabe G.I. Joe. "I don't know what the damn rush was."

Lieutenant Scott heard the exchange as he was passing. Before another word could be uttered, the six foot three former linebacker abruptly changed direction and was beside the SWAT officer.

"The 'damn rush' as you call it is because this piece of shit house that *you* own has been used as a holding place for two kidnapped kids and maybe a murder suspect!" Scott said, his face only inches from the haughty banker's. "Now lose the damned attitude and give him the key, or I might begin to wonder how much you might be involved in the crimes done in your house. In fact, I still might send some city inspectors over here to see how many code violations they can find." Lieutenant Scott was not one to be intimidated, even by one of the city's 'elite.'

Richards wordlessly handed over the key and climbed back into his car, squealing tires as he drove away.

As the Benicia officers went about the task of clearing the house, Scott approached Angi and Devon, smiling. "I thought it might be a good idea for me to drop by. I kind of feel sorry for any bank customers who might have to deal with him for the rest of the day." Angi and Devon both grinned and nodded. "What's the status, Devon?"

"Well, El-Tee, it's not good. The girls weren't there yesterday and the woman was fairly cooperative as I told you before. It looks like the guy and the girls came home last night but news of our visit must have spooked him. According to a neighbor, they jetted out of here last night and are in the wind now."

Scott nodded.

"We had a detective in Salem check the house the woman told me about, in hopes of finding the kids, but they weren't there."

"The detective up there thinks the people were just being used to watch the kids," Angi said. "They probably had no idea about the kidnapping or murder. I tend to agree with him on that, so it looks like a dead end."

"Speaking of that," Scott said, "our dispatch got a call from your sergeant a little while ago. He wants you to call him before you leave Benicia. It has something to do with Salem."

"Thanks, Boss," Angi said. "We'll call him from your station as soon as we're done here."

"It looks like things are calm here now," Scott said. "I'll be on my way. But if you need anything, anything at all, have one of my guys get me on the radio."

The search of Dave and Joyce Chamberlain's residence yielded nothing to indicate where they might have gone. But then, the detectives had not expected it would. All indications were that their departure was both hurried and unplanned. Most likely, their goal was merely to put distance between themselves and the police. Where they were now was anyone's guess. Still, the detectives were puzzled why these two, who weren't involved in the kidnapping, were risking hard time by keeping the kids hidden.

"This is the part about investigations that I hate," Angi said. "Promising leads yesterday and not a single clue to go on today."

* * *

Back at the Benicia Police headquarters, Angi dialed the direct number to the phone on Sergeant Mike Garrison's desk in Santa Rosa. "We're done in Benicia, Mike. The Chamberlains were gone when we got here and now they're in the wind with the kids. We've got nothing to go on at this point."

"Well, we might have something," Garrison said. He then relayed the information Joe Hayes had given him about the strange phone call from Alan Cramer.

Angi's face brightened. "Thanks, Sarge. We're on our way back to the office." She hung up the phone and turned to Devon. "Looks like we might still be in business, partner. Let's go home."

Chapter Thirty-Seven

10:20 a.m. - Salt Lake City, Utah

At that moment, the gray Toyota driven by Dave Chamberlain was cruising east on I-80 just outside Salt Lake City. Their only goal was to get far away from the California cops, as Angi and Devon suspected.

During the night, Dave jumped the fence at a wrecking yard outside Auburn and stole a set of Illinois license plates from a junked car in the lot. He replaced the California plates on his car, registered to the Toyota in his name, with the stolen plates. He shoved the California plates in the trunk. Even if the Santa Rosa detectives broadcast his license plate number throughout the West, cops would be looking for a California plate. There were probably thousands of gray Toyotas in the country. A family of four from Illinois in their Toyota would likely be ignored by most cops.

They spent part of the night in a flea-bag motel somewhere near Fernley, Nevada. The girls had slept in the back seat most of the time since leaving Benicia and continued to sleep in the motel. While there, Dave finally told Joyce the whole true story of the kids, including the murder of their mother by a guy named Agenbroad whom Roy had known in San Sebastian.

Well, now it all makes more sense, Joyce thought. But the truth also filled her with a sense of dread. *I hate what's happened to these girls, and their mother, but Dave is my first priority. He says Roy roped him into this, and I believe him. But why don't we just turn the kids over to the cops?*

But before she could ask the question, Dave revealed his sense of desperation to protect his own safety. "When you told me about telling the cops about the girls being at your sister's house last night, I really thought about just getting rid of them."

Oh, my God. I would never have believed that Dave, criminal past or not, would even think about cold-blooded murder of children.

"I decided against it, though," Dave said. "That would only bring more heat on us. If the cops try to make us accessories to the murder, it could mean life — or maybe the gas chamber. So we might be able to use them as a bargaining chip some day. Besides, I kind of like them."

The last admission both surprised and relieved Joyce. They managed a couple of hours of fitful sleep before again hitting the road into the rising sun. Dave paid for the room in cash and signed the register as 'Bruce Alcott' from DeKalb, Illinois. He actually had no idea where DeKalb, Illinois was. He had only read the name in a magazine once and liked the way it sounded. Besides, it went along with the license plates now on the Toyota.

The bored clerk neither noticed nor cared what he had written down.

* * *

Angi and Devon arrived back in Santa Rosa shortly after 3:00 p.m. She immediately called the number Detective Hayes had given her.

"I was expecting your call, Angi," Hayes said. "Did your sergeant tell you what happened this morning?"

"Yes, he gave me the overview, but I'd like to hear the whole thing from you."

Hayes detailed the phone call from Alan Cramer, and shared his speculation about motive.

"Wow, that really is strange," Angi said. "I can't disagree with you on motive from what I've heard about the sister. Do you think they might be persuaded that we can protect them if they will talk to us?"

"I really don't know. The guy isn't stupid. He had to know that recanting the way he did would never fly with us. It was like he had been told what to say and he was so scared that he

151

parroted exactly what he was told, no matter how ridiculous it sounded."

Angi then filled Hayes in on what had happened in Benicia that morning. "Thanks for your help, Joe. I think my partner and I would like to meet these people for ourselves. Let me see if my sergeant will let us come up there. I'm pretty sure he will. I'm guessing we will drive so it will probably be tomorrow at the earliest."

"We'll keep a discrete eye on the Cramer house in case your Toyota shows up here. Keep me posted on your plans and we can meet you anytime you can get here."

Angi hung up the phone and relayed the conversation to Anderson.

"I agree with you, Angi. Go ahead and put it together with Garrison, but I can't go tomorrow. Remember I told you I am taking a vacation day. I promised to take Holly on a father/daughter shopping trip in downtown San Francisco for her birthday. I'd skip it if we had a hot lead but …"

"Nonsense, Devon. You have told me a dozen times that, in the end, family are all we have. A twelfth birthday only comes along once, so take your daughter shopping and put all this out of your mind for a day. I feel good that Hayes is on top of things up there in Oregon. I think I could use an R&R day too. I'll talk to the sarge about us going up there day after tomorrow and I'll let Hayes know. Now, why don't you get out of here a little early today? Give Holly and Christina a kiss for me. I'll clean up the paperwork from this morning and see you on Friday."

"Thanks, Angi. You're the best." Of course, there was no way Devon could put this case out of his mind, even while enjoying time with his daughter. But a rested detective has a better chance of not missing important clues and ultimately solving a case than one who tries to work non-stop for more than a few hours. The case was taking a natural pause and the detectives needed to take advantage of it. Things could really start rolling without warning.

* * *

Sergeant Garrison readily agreed to Angi's travel request. "I'll take care of getting everything through the finance people to get the authorization for you to go out of state. I'll have it for you Friday morning. In the meantime, wrap up your report from this morning and then take the rest of the day off yourself. You need some down time just as much as Devon does. And don't show your face in this office tomorrow. That's an order. We can take care of things here. If something does come in about the kids, I'll call you right away. Otherwise, Angela, relax!" Garrison could say that but the Angela Masters he knew would never truly relax until she solved this case.

While Angi was not one to relax easily, she thought of a way to take her mind off the intensity of the case, if not off the case itself. She reached for the phone and dialed a number she had not called in a long time.

"Muller's Shoes. Roger speaking," the voice on the other end of the line said.

"Roger, this is Angi. If you have time tonight, how about having dinner and taking in a movie with me," Angi said to her ex-husband.

"That sounds great, Angi. I'd like that!"

"Pick me up at 7:00 and we'll figure out what to see then." *Roger is the one person I can count on not to want to talk about police work. Right now, I need that.*

Chapter Thirty-Eight

July 7-8, 1983

That night, Angi enjoyed her time with her ex-husband, largely because neither of them harbored any delusion that they would ever again be a couple. They were just two old friends enjoying an evening together. And they were well aware of the issues that had pushed them apart. Neither the strains of retail sales nor the pressures of crime fighting ever entered the discussion.

Early the following morning, Angi capped the time off with a visit to another of her favorite relaxation places. The city-owned Chevy Caprice would remain at home today. She pulled her green Saab convertible out of her garage and headed north on Highway 101. With the top down and the cool morning air blowing her hair, she turned on to the meandering Mark West Springs Road. She followed it as it became the Porter Creek Road on an exhilarating fifteen mile drive to Calistoga.

From there, she turned south on Highway 29, through St. Helena, to her destination, the V. Sattui Winery. She arrived just as the winery shop was opening, a schedule she knew well. She bought a bottle of the winery's famous Gamay Rouge wine and some brie and gruyere cheeses and crackers from the shop. Then she settled into one of the familiar picnic seats on the wooded grounds. There she spent a relaxing three hours enjoying John Grisham's latest book.

In the early afternoon, she packed the bottle of wine, still two-thirds full, safely in her trunk. Nibbling on the remaining snacks, she drove south. After stopping in Yountville for a light afternoon meal, she did a little window shopping at the quaint Vintage 1870 Marketplace. Then she returned home back across the mountains on the more sedate Highway 12.

Devon, too, had renewed energy from his quiet time with Holly. Christina had come along on the shopping trip to San Francisco, which was followed by an impromptu dinner in Chinatown. For her part, Holly was thrilled with the time spent with her parents, an attitude sometimes waning in a child her age. She especially savored the time with her dad, who often worked long hours to 'catch the bad guys.'

* * *

The following morning, both Angi and Devon were in the office by 6:45 a.m. The break of the previous thirty-eight hours was revitalizing for both of them.

Angi had called Hayes the previous afternoon from St. Helena and told him they would be in Salem by mid-afternoon on Friday.

As he promised, Sergeant Garrison secured the needed authorizations and financial draws for the detectives to make the out-of-state trip. He left the package on Angi's desk with a handwritten note saying, 'I know there is no way either of you will be able to wait for a send-off from me at 8:00. Good luck on your trip and keep me posted on progress.'

Devon and Angi flipped a coin for whose car they would take, even though they drove almost identical Chevrolet Caprices. "I'm driving, too, Old Man," she said. "Get your stuff and let's go."

After a quick breakfast stop at McDonalds in Vacaville and gas stops in Redding and Roseburg, the detectives arrived at the Salem Police Department at 5:00 p.m. They had hardly parked the car in the 'police only' lot, as Hayes had instructed them, when they were met by a forty-something, jovial man sporting a goatee.

"Joe Hayes," the man said as he thrust out his hand. "Devon?, and you must be Angi? Welcome to Salem."

Before Hayes led the California investigators inside the building through a secure door, he told them, "Just leave your stuff in the car. We've arranged rooms for you at the Red Lion Hotel, right over there, pointing to a hotel a block from the police station. They have good food in the restaurant there, but tonight, Mike—that's my partner—and I want to take you to one of our city's signature places.

"Sounds great," Devon said, "but it will be our treat. Our case and all."

"Fair enough."

Hayes led them down a hall and stopped at a cross hallway. "Our office is down this hall on the left," he motioned, "but it's a bit small for all of us to work. So the chief has given us his conference room while you're here." They entered a glass-walled area with a stenciled sign on the glass beside the door—'Administration.'

As they walked into the conference room, Hayes said, "Our chief was born and raised in Salem and came up through the ranks. He was my sergeant for a few months when I first started. I've worked for him off and on several times and he's a great guy. But he doesn't tolerate criminal activity in 'his' city, especially if it's brought in from somewhere else. That might explain his attitude towards our participation. The way he looks at it, if your crime bled over into our city and you are willing to come here yourselves to deal with it, then it's up to us to help you however we can."

"Roger that," Angi said. "Our chief is exactly the same. Great to work for a guy like that."

The conference room featured glass walls, over which blinds were drawn for the privacy of their investigation. As they entered, a man seated at the conference table poring over some papers rose to greet them.

"Hi. I'm Mike Allison, Joe's younger and better looking partner," the man said as he extended his hand. The California detectives made their own introductions and then the four investigators spent the next forty-five minutes discussing aspects of the case which had not been publicly released. They also talked about each one's impression of Alan Cramer's strange phone call to Hayes.

All were in agreement that it was likely some type of threat had been made to the Cramers, most likely to their children — the center of their lives. However, the California detectives could not let that factor, even if true, give the Cramers a free pass on revealing any information they had on the case. They would have to try to persuade the Cramers to share whatever information they might know, especially if it might lead them to Dave and Joyce Chamberlain and the missing girls.

When they finished their discussion, Hayes said, "I'd suggest we wait until tomorrow morning to confront them. From our observations, we know they have kids at the daycare until at least 8:00 p.m. and I think the kids' presence would create a distraction. At very least, the need to look after her clients' kids could give Darlene a ready excuse to disengage from an interview."

"That makes sense, Joe," Angi said, "but do we know if they might have kids there tomorrow too?"

"We don't think so," Allison said. "The sign they have out in the front lawn says 'Monday to Friday', so I think she caters primarily to working mothers during the week."

The Oregon detectives made some good strategic points. Beyond that, Angi and Devon were both tired from the 600 mile drive. They could benefit from some rest before confronting the people who represented their best current lead.

Also, there was nothing to indicate that meeting with the Cramers immediately would result in a miraculous outcome for the case. Better to be alert and fresh to detect any nuance from either of the subjects, which might provide a window to more information.

"Sounds good," said Devon. "Angi, how about we get checked in and then we can meet Joe and Mike for some dinner. We'll get a fresh start in the morning."

Chapter Thirty-Nine

July 9, 1983 - 8:30 a.m. - Salem, Oregon

At 8:30 the following morning, the four met for a breakfast and strategy meeting in the restaurant of the Red Lion. Then they drove to the Cramers' neighborhood in Hayes' city issue Ford Crown Victoria. They agreed that all four would approach the house as a demonstration that they were on a serious mission, serious enough to get four detectives out on a Saturday morning.

Joe had already met the Cramers face-to-face so he would take the initial lead. Joe pulled his car to the curb in front of a house next door to the Cramers' house. "That's Alan in the yard," Joe said, pointing to a man in front of the house.

"Good morning, Alan," Joe said as the four approached the house. *No formal 'Mr. Cramer' now. I want this contact to be on a personal level.*

"Hello, Detective Hayes," Cramer said as he looked up from weeding around the trimmed base of an arborvitae tree. Alan knew Hayes hadn't believed his lame story. He wouldn't have believed it if he had been on the other end of the line that day, and he wasn't even a detective. This visit was just a matter of time.

But, damn, four people—all detectives by their look. Alan realized he was probably in big trouble. But could it be worse than what he might expect from Dave if he told them the truth? Nothing the cops could say or do would make him put his kids in danger. He'd rot in jail first! Alan dropped his small spade on the front lawn and crossed his arms.

"Is Darlene here, Alan?" Hayes asked. "We need to talk to both of you."

"Sure. Come on in."

158

"Darlene," he called as he entered the front door. "Detective Hayes is back and wants to talk to us."

Darlene Cramer was no more surprised by the visit than her husband. They had even discussed how long they thought it would be before the detective returned. Still, they both dreaded the inevitable. Now, the question was, how would they handle talking to him, to seem cooperative but not saying anything that might ultimately cause Dave to come after them, or their boys.

She shuttled the youngsters off to their room, with a promise of a treat later if they would play quietly in their room while she and Daddy talked to some visitors. Her sons didn't object. They were used to strangers coming to talk to their parents, their mother usually, about enrolling their children in her daycare.

After sending the boys to their room on the opposite side of the kitchen, Darlene took a second to compose herself. She knew she had to project an air of sincerity to the detective but to maintain the story Dave had ordered Alan to tell. *We have never seen or heard of Stacy and Jennifer and we mistakenly thought Detective Hayes was asking about two other little girls who used to be at the daycare center.*

She went over the fiction four or five times to get it fixed in her mind. Then, with a sigh, Darlene put on a smile and walked into the living room. What she saw there—four detectives standing in her living room—caused her to lose all pretenses of confidence and sincerity. *Why so many?*

"Please sit down," Alan said, motioning the detectives to a couch and love seat positioned at right angles to one another. Alan took a seat in an overstuffed chair opposite them.

Darlene stood at the doorway and, in the calmest voice she could muster, asked, "Can I get anyone something to drink?"

"No, thank you, Darlene," Hayes said. "This won't take long. Please join us." Darlene sat on the arm of Alan's chair.

"Alan, Darlene," Hayes said, "this is my partner, Detective Mike Allison. And this is Detective Masters and Detective

Anderson. They have come here from the Santa Rosa, California Police Department to talk with you."

The introductions sent the Cramers into an internal panic. Four Salem detectives was cause enough for concern, but two of the investigators in their living room had traveled from California just to talk to them. How much trouble were they in? Surely, this was more than a routine interview. They were part of some investigation, but why?

Honest people at heart, Alan and Darlene each felt deep down that they best thing to do was to tell the truth — the truth about everything, including the phone call from Dave. Yes, it might be best to tell the truth, but that would also be the most dangerous route for them and especially, their sons. If these officers knew where Dave was, or where Stacy and Jennifer were, it was highly unlikely they would all be here asking questions.

Dave might be watching their house right now, just waiting to see how they reacted to the police being there. Alan repeated in his mind the same conclusion he had reached as he saw the detectives approaching. They would have to stick to the story Dave directed, no matter what pressure was brought to bear. After all, they had done nothing wrong.

"I think it would be good for you both to understand the gravity of the situation here," Hayes said. "Detective Masters will explain what's happened with the girls and why we need your cooperation."

When Masters had concluded her explanation of the murder and kidnapping, Hayes said, "Now, I have to tell you that I have really been puzzled by your phone call the other day, Alan. I sat here with you earlier in the week and you both were very clear in your identifications of Stacy and Jennifer. In fact, Darlene, you knew their names before I told you anything about them.

"But the fact — and we know it's a fact — that these girls were here doesn't mean you are in any trouble. We just want to know the truth about how the girls got here and where they are now." He then paused and fixed his gaze on Alan, wondering if the man, or his wife, would come clean with whatever information they had.

For what seemed like long minutes, Alan met the detective's gaze. Options were spinning through his head. He knew he should cooperate. But then the vitriol in Dave's voice during that terrifying phone call would crash back into his mind. No matter what, he would protect his boys first.

"I'm sorry, Detective Hayes," he said with a lump in his throat. "We are sorry we wasted your time the other day, and wasted your time in coming up here, detectives. But we just made a mistake when we said we knew them. It's just a coincidence, I guess, that the girls we were thinking about, ones who used to be in the daycare before their parents moved away, just happened to have the same names as the girls you want. That's really all we can tell you."

Masters leaned forward and slowly shook her head. "Alan, do you really expect anyone to believe this bullshit story?"

"Alan," Hayes said, "we both know that's not the truth. You can't make an identification in the way both of you did and then claim it was someone else. If someone has gotten to you, threatened you, threatened your kids, we can help you. But we need to know the truth."

Angi thought he detected a flicker of change in Darlene's eyes. Maybe by showing Alan that he and Darlene weren't just witnesses to the officers, but people with real concerns, they might open up.

"Darlene," she said, "Stacy and Jennifer have a father who loves them very much. He's in agony waiting for them to come home. You know that if your boys were missing and someone knew something that would help find them, you would want that person to tell the police what he knew. That's all the girls' father is asking, for you to tell us what you know and let him have his daughters back."

Tears welled in Darlene's eyes and she started to speak, but Alan cut her off. "We've told you we don't know those girls and we can't help you. Now we have work to do, so please leave and don't call us again."

Chapter Forty

10:05 a.m.

Devon was through playing games and decided to play the 'bad cop' role. The detectives had discussed such a response that morning at the Red Lion. Now, Devon felt it was time. To add to the effect, people in general had come to expect a 'no-nonsense' attitude of law enforcement from California police officers, the result of years of indoctrination with television shows such as 'Dragnet', 'CHiPs', and 'Adam-12.'

Devon suddenly banged his fist on the coffee table. "Do you really expect us to believe that shit? We don't have time to play around here. The lives of those girls are at stake. You could help us find them, but no! You want to play bullshit games and sit here and lie to us."

Alan and Darlene both reeled from the anger in Devon's voice. Even Mike and Joe were unprepared for the ferocity of his attack.

"You know," Devon said, his voice more measured, "we could just have these detectives arrest you right now and hold you for forty-eight hours while we investigate you, your daycare, and everything else about you. Of course, your kids would probably wind up in state custody, but that would be a choice you brought on yourselves!"

Joe tried to maintain a supportive position, but Devon's threats were empty. There would be no arrests and no state custody for the Cramer boys. With the information they had, that wouldn't even be legal in Oregon.

Alan paled, and Darlene began to sob. Neither of them had ever been in trouble with the law and certainly had never been in jail. The thought terrified both of them. The thought of their sons being handed over to someone else was even worse. Still, either, or both, of those outcomes was preferable to losing the boys forever.

That possibility seemed even more real to them now that they knew the truth about the girls' plight. Dave was more than a gruff and distant brother-in-law. He was at least involved in a kidnapping and who knew what else. And what about Darlene's sister? How was Joyce involved in this? Was she a criminal who would harbor two little kidnap victims?

Anderson's ploy only made matters worse. The Cramers shut down completely.

"OK," Hayes said, "we're going to leave you two alone now. But think about what we said. All we want is your help in finding Stacy and Jennifer. No one wants to see you or your boys hurt. We can protect you, but you have to tell us the truth. I want you to think about that and give me a call on Monday."

* * *

"What was all that about arresting them, Devon?" Hayes asked as soon as they were off the Cramers' property. "We don't have enough probable cause to arrest them. That should be pretty obvious."

"I just wanted to shake them up a little," Devon said. "In California, we can jail anybody for up to forty-eight hours without charges on an investigative hold. It often works pretty well on people who have information but don't want to get involved."

"Well, that's not the law here," Allison said. "So let me get this straight. You were hoping to get them past a threat to their kids by threatening their kids?"

Even Angi thought Devon had overstepped, although she would never admit it to these detectives. "OK, guys," she said. "Joe, you can drop us off at the hotel and we'll be heading back to Santa Rosa. We've seen the Cramers' reaction, which is what we wanted to do. We hoped that they would give us a lead on Chamberlain, but I don't think there's any more we can do here now. We'd appreciate it if you would keep an eye on them and perhaps follow-up with some of their clients. Maybe a parent of a child they care for heard something."

* * *

The trip back to Santa Rosa seemed longer to Angi than it actually was. They hadn't anticipated that the trip would net the key lead which would break the case wide open. But Angi had hoped that their presence would convince the Cramers to give up some bit of information that they could build upon. But now, with the Cramers' steadfast denials of knowing Stacy and Jennifer, ridiculous as they were, meant there was noting on the investigative horizon.

Angi was also upset with Devon that he had played the 'bad cop' role so strongly. While she had seen him successfully use the ploy with witnesses who had their own criminal issues, everything pointed to the probable innocent involvement of the Cramers. This time, the ploy had backfired. Not only had it shut down further dialog with Alan and Darlene, the move also had a visibly negative effect on Detective Allison, possibly compromising his further cooperation.

It had also been obvious to Angi that Hayes, while more circumspect in his reaction, was also put off by Devon's approach. She could only hope that the Oregon detectives could move past any dislike of Devon and continue to assist with the case.

At that moment, the Cramers and their daycare clients represented the only hope for some piece of information that might move the case forward.

Chapter Forty-One

July - November 1983

Cramer's fears were unfounded. Dave Chamberlain was nowhere near Salem and hadn't been since he left with the girls. In fact, Dave had forgotten about threatening his wife's brother-in-law. Even if Alan talked now, it wouldn't make any difference. The threat had served its purpose — to buy the Chamberlains a few days to put distance between themselves and the only place Cramer could link to them, the Benicia house.

Once Dave and Joyce had left California, it didn't matter if Alan told the cops about the Benicia house. They already knew about it.

But Alan couldn't know the threat was moot in Dave's mind, and it would continue to haunt him.

Dave knew they had left no clues in the house about where they might be going. He knew because he, himself, didn't really know. He was concentrating on presenting the appearance of a couple and their young children on a vacation from Illinois. He didn't call attention to himself by speeding or any other actions which might bring police scrutiny. He and Joyce decided their route day by day, with no destination in mind. The only criteria was to avoid returning to California. He also avoided Joyce's sister Kathy's house in Arizona. He couldn't guess how much the cops might know about her.

Dave decided to only use cash for whatever the four travelers needed. He had seen an episode of *Columbo* in which the wily detective tracked down a crook by following a trail of credit card expenditures. Dave was not about to fall into that trap.

In fact, Angi had already asked the major credit card issuers to put a trace on any credit cards linked to Dave or Joyce.

However, there was no nationwide tracking system for credit cards, such as would exist later. So, while the premise in the *Columbo* episode was technically feasible, in truth the system contained so many delays that it was virtually useless in apprehending someone like Dave, who was constantly on the move and had no discernible pattern to his movements.

The decision to use only cash was not without its own pitfalls. Dave was not going to put down roots and actually work at a job. While employers who would pay in cash were not known for asking too many questions about their employees, their pay scale would not support much of a travel stash.

But Dave had a plan he had used before and which also better suited his personality. In Provo, Utah, he noticed a young manager of a local fast food restaurant walking to a bank with the day's deposits. Most fast food receipts would be in cash, he knew. Dave followed the manager until he was sure no one was watching, and then waylaid the unfortunate teenager. The heist netted Dave almost $900 and the teen-aged manager suffered a concussion. The scenario would be repeated in four other small towns from Colby, Kansas to Ruston, Louisiana in the next few weeks.

Dave and Joyce would stop for a few days in other remote towns, staying in cheap motels. If asked, they always told people that they were out to see the country and educate their young children to the variety of culture it contained. If someone inquired too closely, as when one woman asked whether the older girl should be in school, the pair and their young victims quickly moved on.

* * *

As summer turned to fall and on into the early stages of winter, Angi and Devon were having no luck turning up new leads. They had been notified that Joyce Chamberlain made a credit card purchase of children's clothes at a K-Mart store in Salina, Kansas. However, that information didn't come to them until three weeks after the purchase. Salina Police were cooperative in interviewing store employees, but no one could recall anything about the purchaser or whether any children had been with her at the time.

Dave was furious when Joyce told him of her mistake, but to his relief they encountered no roadblocks or other indicators that police were on their trail as they headed south into Texas. *Good thing those damn California detectives aren't as savvy as Columbo,* he thought.

Salem detectives Hayes and Allison also interviewed several clients of Darlene Cramer's daycare center. A few, including Mike Allison's neighbor, who took her four-year-old to Darlene's center, remembered seeing the girls in the detectives' photos at the daycare. However, to a person they reported that the little girls had played with other children and that Darlene had not seemed untowardly concerned about them interacting with others.

Hayes often reminded patrol officers who worked the area of the Cramers' house to keep an eye out for any out-of-state cars in the area. That effort also proved fruitless. Two cars with California license plates were seen parked on the street at night near the Cramers' home. In each case, Hayes responded to the area from home to investigate. However, the owners of both cars turned out to be people visiting friends who just happened to live in the same general area as the daycare center.

As Thanksgiving approached, Masters and Anderson had several meetings with Sergeant Garrison and the district attorney, Anson Krupp. Krupp was one of the younger district attorneys in California and had followed the case closely since his election to the post the previous year. The officers and the prosecutor agreed that they needed to try a new tact to resuscitate the case. The only potential lead still unresolved was Alan Cramer.

Krupp agreed that a more decisive action was needed. The next monthly session of the grand jury was scheduled for December 15th. Krupp would subpoena Alan Cramer and, if necessary, Detective Hayes to testify.

Cramer would be questioned under oath about his knowledge of the welfare and whereabouts of Stacy and Jennifer as part of the ongoing inquiry into the kidnapping and the murder of Sharon McElroy. Hayes would be on hand to testify about his encounters with Cramer if the man continued to deny knowledge of the girls.

Cramer would likely be jailed for contempt or perjury if he maintained his improbable story before the grand jury. If that happened, he would then probably spend Christmas in the Sonoma County Jail. The psychological bonus of that possibility was not lost on the investigators.

But a mere seven months remained before Agenbroad would be released after serving time for the assault on Celeste in Idaho. If they didn't have some way to hold him at that time, he would disappear. Worse, he might regard the girls as expendable witnesses against him and react accordingly.

* * *

Had Masters been privy to Dave Chamberlain's thoughts at that moment, her concerns for the girls would have been exponentially higher. Dave was coming to the same conclusion that Angi feared would be in Agenbroad's mind—the girls were becoming more of a liability as they grew older, and they were expendable. Still, he had never harmed a child in any of his jobs. And he actually liked these girls. No matter what challenges the four had faced in their cross-country flight, Stacy and Jennifer adapted without complaint.

Chamberlain didn't know, however, that Stacy's young mind was constantly searching, within her narrow view of the world, for a way to get away and get back to her father, Doug McElroy. She hoped that the story about the traffic accident had been a lie. If she and her sister could get free, maybe her mother would be there too. The only thing maintaining her cooperation with her captors was her overriding devotion to her sister. No matter what happened, Stacy would never leave Jennifer.

Chapter Forty-Two

November 30, 1983

Alan Cramer had never really relaxed since the encounter with the California detectives a few months before. Of course, he had lied to the police, even in the face of the obvious and sheer idiocy of his contentions. But he had done it for the best of reasons, to protect his children and his wife. He knew Darlene had nearly broken down and told the detectives everything that day, but he had effectively cut her off.

Both sets of detectives seemed competent and would eventually find the missing girls, he hoped. He really wanted to help, but the threat to his own children was always at the forefront of his mind. His fears were heightened when the detectives told them about what had really happened, about the murder and the kidnapping.

His fear of Dave's threat was overwhelming before, and with the new knowledge from the detectives, his fears reached dizzying heights. Alan parried the questions from Detective Hayes, even though he was certain Hayes knew, or at least strongly suspected, the reason for his reluctance to cooperate.

Then the totally unexpected had happened. Alan had never contemplated the possibility that police officers whose sworn duty it was to protect all citizens, would threaten the very children he was most trying to protect. But that was precisely what Anderson had done. In Alan's mind, Anderson was no better than Dave, threatening his children to achieve his own ends.

Many sleepless nights followed.

Alan thought he had seen more police cars on this street than ever before, but maybe he was just being paranoid. Once, when he was awake in the early morning hours, he looked out to see a police car stopped in the street next to a parked car a few houses away from his. As he watched through the window in the darkness, an unmarked police car drove up. A man he thought was Detective Hayes got out and both officers when to the door of the house where the car was parked.

A few minutes later, the two police cars left, but the next morning, Alan noticed that the car in front of his neighbor's house had a California license plate. Did the police think that Dave was visiting the Cramers? His fears that Dave would show up in his neighborhood returned. He began to obsessively watch the street for any car displaying a California license plate.

Some of Darlene's clients told her that police had questioned them about seeing the girls at the daycare. Several innocently said that they had identified Stacy and Jennifer, although they hadn't known their names, as girls being in Darlene's care.

Alan couldn't blame those people for telling the truth, but that had put his family in even more danger. Alan and Darlene might get arrested for obstructing the investigation now that other people had told the police more than enough for them to be sure the Cramers were lying about the girls.

With the heat being turned up, Darlene tried to convince her husband that they should call Detective Hayes and tell him the truth about everything they knew. "We don't actually know that much, and Hayes seems to know that we weren't involved in the murder or kidnapping. I'm sure he also knows, or is pretty sure, that we didn't know anything about it until they told us."

"You didn't hear Dave's voice," Alan said. "I never dreamed he could do something like that, kill his own nephews. But that voice convinced me that he not only could, but he would if he was cornered. We can't take that chance, Darlene. Our boys' lives depend on it."

Darlene uneasily maintained her silence.

* * *

A further blow to Alan's world arrived when a Marion County Sheriff's deputy knocked on their door one Wednesday evening, the last day of November.

"Alan Cramer?" the deputy asked when Alan opened the door.

The deputy handed Alan a folded piece of paper with an official looking seal on it. "Sir, you are ordered to testify before the Sonoma County grand jury in Santa Rosa, California on December 15. This is the summons. It's been countersigned by a Marion County judge, which means it's a legal document here in Oregon. California will pay for the cost of your trip down there. This paper tells you how to claim expenses for that. Any questions?"

Alan just stared at the paper. After a few seconds, he realized the deputy was still standing there and shook his head.

"Thank you, sir." The deputy returned to his car, leaving Alan standing on his doorstep with tears flowing down his cheeks. He had never felt so trapped and so alone in his life.

* * *

Two days later, the phone rang on Detective Allison's desk. "Mike, this is Angi Masters." Angi made up her mind on the trip back to California from Salem that she wasn't going to let Devon contact the Oregon investigators. They were all professionals, but the case was too important to risk interference of personality conflicts from Devon's handling of the Cramer interview. "Is Joe available?"

Allison had no beef with Detective Masters. In fact, he felt that day that she was almost as taken aback by Anderson's outburst as he and Hayes were. "No, he's off today. His anniversary is tomorrow and he's taking his wife on a little vacation over to the coast. Can I help you?"

"I just wanted him to know that we've subpoenaed Alan Cramer to testify before the grand jury about the girls and about David Chamberlain picking them up from his house. We would like Joe to come down in case Cramer holds on to his BS story in his testimony before the grand jury. We would need Joe to testify about the identification if that's the case."

"I'm sure it will be no problem. I'll let him and our sergeant know about it on Monday. When is the hearing?"

"Great," Angi was delighted to hear that Allison still seemed to be fully involved. She had only spoken to Hayes in the time since the interview. "It's December 15th here in Santa Rosa. Will he need a subpoena?"

"No, I don't think so, Angi. I'm sure our bosses will be happy to let him come down without a subpoena. I guess you can serve him down there if your process requires it."

"No. That's great. We'll just see him here on the 15th at 9:00 a.m. I would imagine that he will want to come down the night before. Have him call me and I'll arrange a place for him to stay — on our dime of course."

Chapter Forty-Three

December 5, 1983 - Salem, Oregon

Hilary Wintershank was making her mark as an intrepid young reporter for the Salem Post Sentinel. Wintershank, or Hilary Winters as her more compact byline read, never complained about the routine and sometimes inane stories she was assigned. At 24, the Valparaiso University journalism graduate was learning the ropes of reporting the news for a capitol city newspaper. On this day, she was poring over recent judicial records for information on a land-use dispute when a document caught her eye.

The document was a subpoena for one Alan Cramer with a Salem address. Cramer was being summoned to appear before a grand jury in California. The document was signed by a California judge but just below that was the signature of a Marion County Circuit Court judge with a notation below the signature in longhand which said 'Approved for Service in Oregon.' It seemed strange, even to a young reporter, and Hilary knew she needed to look into it.

After some calls to a reporter in Santa Rosa, where the subpoena originated, Hilary nearly sprinted to her editor's office.

* * *

"Harry! What do you make of this?"

Harry Beauchamp was a veteran newsman with two overriding peeves. He hated reporters who jumped to conclusions and reported information that was not backed up with fact, or at least with sound research. Even more, he detested reporters who jeopardized criminal cases in a headlong quest for the 'big story.'

He always told his reporters, "The successful prosecution of a criminal is the 'big story.' A 'scoop' that the police are about to arrest a specific person, or revealing evidence that they haven't released to the public is not, and never will be to me, the 'big story.' "

In this case, Harry looked at the document Hilary laid on his desk. What could it all mean?

He staunchly believed that journalism was a profession, with standards of conduct. Journalism was supposed to inform the public, not be springboard to fame for the reporter, he believed. But he was part of a dying breed.

"Well," he said after what seemed to Hilary to be hours. "It could be something—or it could be nothing. It certainly could look like a big case and it obviously has a Salem connection. But the subpoena? They aren't all that common—not all that unusual either. Maybe this Cramer guy is just a simple witness. And maybe he's a major player. And maybe it's something in between.

"The answer, Miss Winters, is that you have nothing—nothing but a starting point. See if the local cops know anything about it. See what you can find out about this Cramer guy. And make sure you have a source locked down in Santa Rosa to let you know what happens after this guy testifies. Then, maybe, just maybe, you'll have a story."

Hilary knew that was the right answer, but she had a gut feeling that this could be something big. She wanted to make sure Harry wouldn't pull it from her if it did turn out to be the 'big story.'

* * *

A thousand miles to the south, Roy Chamberlain was also wondering about the case. Since moving from the Richmond house during the Thanksgiving week after the murder, he had taken refuge in a run-down neighborhood in Exeter, California. There he lived a quiet life, avoiding his neighbors and getting by performing odd jobs for businesses in the small town.

He feared that any day the police might knock on his door to arrest him for his part in the kidnapping. So far, the knock had not come. He might have maintained that lifestyle until the day he died but for one thing—he could not get three images out of his head.

Try as he might, Roy Chamberlain could not forget the faces of Stacy and Jennifer—the fear in the young eyes, coupled with the glint of defiance in Stacy's eyes anytime he had come near Jennifer.

The other face that haunted his dreams was Tooey O'Banion's. 'You need to tell the police what you know, Roy,' the ghostly voice of Officer O'Banion would whisper from Roy's tortured brain. 'It's the right thing to do, Lad. You're not a bad lad. You made some bad choices in the prison but you didn't hurt anyone yourself. And you took care of those girls as best you could. Call the police and tell them everything you know, everything Agenbroad told you, and clear your conscience.'

But even if he followed the sage advice from his long dead mentor, would it do any good? For all Roy knew, the girls were already dead. Certainly his brother was capable of murder, even though Roy hoped Dave could not harm children any more than he would.

If something did happen to the girls, could he be blamed for not doing more when he had them? Could he even be considered an accessory to the kidnapping, or maybe even the murder? If so, it could mean spending the rest of what could be the very short life of an ex-guard turned inmate.

The moment he would decide it was less risky to just keep quiet, Stacy's cherubic face would well up in the back of his brain. The tortured mental cycle would begin again.

Chapter Forty-Four

December 15, 1983

Since the deputy's visit, Alan Cramer had thought about contacting a lawyer. But he decided against it. It would only be a waste of money. Besides, what would a lawyer tell him? Cooperate with the police and the lawyer would ensure that the family would not be impacted? That might be reasonable advice if it weren't for the looming threat that no lawyer could prevent.

Alan could never tell anyone, not even a lawyer, about Dave's threat. No, the police could not protect his kids and certainly no lawyer could. The only choice Alan saw was to go to California, stick to his story, and hope for the best.

* * *

At 8:30 a.m. on December 15th, a nervous Cramer walked into the outer office of the Sonoma County District Attorney. "I'm Alan Cramer from Salem, Oregon, and I received this," he told the receptionist as he handed her the subpoena.

"Yes, Mr. Cramer. Do you have an attorney?"

"No, ma'am, I don't. I'm okay." He hoped his voice showed some confidence that he certainly didn't feel.

"Please have a seat then." The receptionist indicated a chair near a low table holding several magazines. "Mr. Krupp will be with you in a moment."

Krupp! That was the name on the glass outer door, the district attorney himself. If he was personally involved, did that signal that things were even worse for Alan? A fleeting thought that maybe he should have an attorney passed through his mind, but he quickly dismissed the idea for the same reasons he had before.

A few minutes later, the door to the inner office opened. The detective who had threatened to jail Alan and Darlene and to take their kids emerged, followed by the female detective who had also been at his house. They brushed past Alan and out the front door without acknowledging or even looking at him. The detective from Salem followed a short distance behind them. Detective Hayes acknowledged Cramer's presence with a slight nod but also walked out without speaking to him.

Close behind Detective Hayes was an impeccably dressed man wearing the most expensive-looking tailored suit Alan had ever seen. A dark mustache gave the man a slightly older look than his probable thirty-five years. The look was all confidence. Alan cringed.

"Good morning, Mr. Cramer," the man said, extending his hand. "My name is Anson Krupp. I'm the District Attorney and I'll be asking you a few questions this morning." He gripped Alan's hand in a firm handshake. "Please follow me," he said as he held the outer door open for Alan.

Cramer followed Krupp down a wide hallway a pace or so behind.

"So, you don't have an attorney with you?" Krupp asked over his shoulder.

"No, I don't but I'm ready." *Yeah, I'm anything but ready for this.*

Krupp stopped, opened a door and held it for Alan to enter. 'Grand Jury In Session' said an engraved plastic sign on the door, which closed behind the men.

A stifling feeling of being totally alone and defenseless swept over Alan Cramer.

* * *

"Please take a seat there, Mr. Cramer," Krupp said, indicating the witness chair.

Cramer looked around the room. It was completely different from what he had expected. Alan's only exposure to a courtroom was through television shows such as 'Matlock' and 'LA Law.' Here, there was no judge's bench, no jury box to the side of the witness stand, and no attorney tables facing the judge. Neither was there a spectators' section.

Instead, Cramer was directed to an elevated stand which held a single leather-covered chair. The witness stand was partially surrounded by a long semi-circular bench. Twenty-three people, appearing to be from all walks of life, sat in high-backed leather chairs behind the bench. Krupp moved to a podium in front of and at the center of the jurors' bench, facing Alan. To Cramer's left sat a court reporter, her stenotype machine ready.

"Please stand and raise your right hand and repeat after me," Krupp said.

It was like being in a dream—a bad dream—where Alan heard his voice say, "I, Alan Cramer, swear to tell the truth, the whole truth, and nothing but the truth ..."

Cramer repeated the oath mechanically as it was stated by Krupp in short segments. It was almost as if he were looking at himself from the outside.

Then Krupp completed the last segment of the oath, "... so help me God."

Suddenly, Alan's mouth was as dry as the Mojave. After a few long seconds, he repeated, "...so help me ...... God."

Several grand jury members took mental note of the unusual pause in the oath. This panel was nearing the end of their thirty-month term of service and they had become accustomed to the way the oath was recited, both by the innocent and by the guilty.

Cramer's time on the witness stand was short. Krupp showed him photos of Stacy and Jennifer, of Dave and Joyce, of Agenbroad, and a crime scene photo of the murdered Sharon McElroy. Alan readily identified Dave and Joyce, although he only framed them as his sister-in-law and her husband. He did not mention the threat from Dave. He truthfully testified that he did not recognize the man Krupp identified as Elmont Agenbroad in the photo. He was visibly and genuinely repulsed by the photo of Sharon.

But when it came to the photos of Stacy and Jennifer, Alan said, "No, Mr. Krupp. I've never seen either of those girls before."

"Mr. Cramer, did you in fact identify these girls to Detective Hayes of the Salem, Oregon Police Department when he came to your home in July of this year?"

"Well, I think I did, but it was a mistake. I wasn't used to having the police come around to ask questions and I thought they were asking about two other girls who my wife used to care for." Alan had told the story a hundred times and it still sounded like bullshit, even to him. But he had to pray that the jurors believed him.

"You're excused, Mr. Cramer—for now," Krupp said. "Please wait across the hall. That deputy will escort you."

No defense attorney had provided a witty cross-examination. Not one of the grand jurors had asked a question of him.

As Alan approached the door from the hearing room, he was met by the deputy Krupp had indicated. "Please come with me, Mr. Cramer," the deputy said, and led Alan to a small waiting room across the hall from the grand jury room. The deputy offered Alan a bottle of water, which he readily accepted and chugged in two gulps. As Alan finished the water, he looked out the window of the waiting room and saw Detective Joe Hayes entering the grand jury room.

Chapter Forty-Five

December 15 - 1:45 p.m.

Twenty minutes after Alan saw him go into the grand jury room, Joe Hayes left by the same door he had entered. As he walked into the wide hallway, his gaze drifted to Alan Cramer standing behind the glassed waiting room wall. Hayes looked at Cramer and slowly shook his head.

Why was this man, by all indicators an innocent party to the whole affair, willing to put himself through what he had, and what would soon be coming? Hayes was sure he knew but still he regretted that Cramer couldn't or wouldn't put enough trust in the police that they would protect him and his family. It was one of the saddest days of Hayes' long career, simply because of the unnecessary waste and hurt this was causing.

A few seconds later, Anson Krupp emerged and walked straight across the hall to the waiting room. As he entered and closed the door, he asked, "Mr. Cramer, Alan, would you like to go back in and reconsider your testimony before the grand jury?"

"No, sir." Alan choked out the words. His throat was tightening, constricting his breathing. "I've said all I can say."

"Then, Alan Cramer, you are under arrest on a charge of perjury before the grand jury. This is a felony in this state since the subject case before the jurors is a felony," Krupp said to the unsurprised Cramer. "Deputy, take him to a cell."

* * *

Within an hour, a local reporter placed a phone call to Hilary Winters in Salem. "Your guy Cramer was just jailed for perjury before the grand jury." Now, maybe Hilary had a story for the local readers.

With Harry Beauchamp's blessing, a story by Hilary Winters appeared the next day on the second page of the local section of the Post Sentinel. It was headlined 'Salem Man Jailed for Perjury in Murder/Kidnapping Case.'

The story identified the man as Alan Cramer of Salem, whose wife operated a daycare center out of their home. It also outlined the basic facts of the brutal killing and the abduction of two small girls. The story went on to say that sources were unsure of Cramer's role in the case, but that Salem Police had been assisting with the case for some time. More information would be forthcoming, the article ended.

* * *

The following day, nine people withdrew their children from 'Darlene's Day Dream for Kids' daycare. Two days later, the owner of the electronics firm that had employed Alan for several years called the Cramer house. Darlene answered the phone, afraid that it was another daycare cancellation. It wasn't.

"Mrs. Cramer, I really hate to do this, but we are terminating Alan's employment, effective immediately. We're a small company and this is a small town. We simply can't deal with the notoriety of being associated with Alan so long as he's got this trouble. I wish both of you well."

How could this be happening? Darlene asked herself through anguished tears. Only a few months before, their life could not have been happier. Now, there was nothing but despair in every direction she looked. And it all began with her taking care of two beautiful children for her sister, something she would do again without hesitation.

* * *

Krupp had approached Cramer twice in the previous two weeks, asking if he would reconsider his testimony before the grand jury. Each time, Cramer gave the same practiced response, "I've told you what I can."

"Do you think he'll talk?" Krupp asked the detectives assembled in his conference room. Krupp had called a meeting of

Sergeant Garrison and Detectives Masters and Anderson to discuss the issue of Alan Cramer.

All felt that Cramer had some type of useful information, information the detectives needed now that the case seemed to have gone cold again. However, the consensus also was that Cramer was deathly afraid of something and preferred to go to jail rather than reveal whatever information he might have.

The detectives agreed with Detective Hayes that the threat was probably against Cramer's children and probably came from either David Chamberlain or Butch Agenbroad. "I don't think anything is going to change, Anson," Masters said for the group. "He won't tell us anything if you keep him in jail for a year."

On December 28th, Krupp presented a motion to a Superior Court Judge, dropping all charges against Alan Cramer. The gambit to force Cramer's hand had failed. The judge ordered him released that day.

He had missed Christmas with his sons for the first time in their lives. He made his way back to Salem and was never contacted by police again. A pretty young reporter knocked on his door once, but he refused to speak to her.

Cramer's life had been turned upside down. His job and most of Darlene's income were gone. Sonoma County never paid for his travel expenses to testify before the grand jury, because he never filed the paperwork for the reimbursement. Cramer was alive, his wife was alive, and most of all, his children were safe. Alan Cramer was ready to move on with his life.

Chapter Forty-Six

December 20, 1983 - Exeter, California

Louis Lasky had enjoyed a long career as a criminal defense attorney. He had worked in such hotbeds as Chicago's South Side, San Francisco's Tenderloin, and South Central Los Angeles. Four years earlier, he had retired to the small picturesque town of Exeter, at the foot of the Sierra Nevada mountains and only thirty minutes from Sequoia National Park. A Chicago native and honor graduate of the prestigious University of Chicago Law School, Lasky maintained a small office on North E Street.

He kept the space mostly to relieve the need to 'go to the office' even though he had no staff and the door has shuttered most of the time. Lasky occasionally defended someone charged with some minor infraction or advised friends and family, often working pro-bono. Usually, though, he spent his time golfing or reminiscing about his high-profile cases from years past.

On this day, a few days before Christmas, Lasky stopped by his one-room office next door to a flower shop. He was collecting an envelope containing a gift for his wife, tickets for the two of them to spend the Christmas holiday at the luxurious CasaMagna Marriott hotel in Puerto Vallarta. Laurel Lasky would be thrilled to spend ten days in the beautiful resort city in the company of her beloved husband of forty-five years. Lasky smiled as he placed the envelope in his jacket pocket and opened the door to leave. His smile was interrupted by an unkempt man standing in his doorway, his fist poised to knock on the door that suddenly opened.

"Mr. Lasky," the man said, "my name is Roy Chamberlain and I need your help."

For a moment, Lasky considered sending the man to one of the younger attorneys who practiced law in the small town. But there was something in this man's face that piqued Lasky's curiosity. *I guess I can give him a few minutes of my time.* "Come in, Mr. Chamberlain. Please have a seat and tell me what's on your mind."

Chamberlain sat on a straight-backed wooden chair across an aged but well-crafted oak desk from the attorney. He didn't say a word, but reached into his pocket and extracted a weathered newspaper clipping, handing it to the lawyer. Lasky carefully unfolded the paper and read the clipped story. The news source was unclear but the headline was unmistakable: "Woman Brutally Murdered — Children Taken." The dateline on the story was Santa Rosa, almost three years previously.

* * *

"Ok, Mr. Chamberlain," Lasky said. "Tell me what's on your mind."

Lasky had a tee time in two hours with three other retirees but he was intrigued by this man's possible involvement in the brutal crime depicted in the news story. Lasky remembered hearing some courthouse scuttlebutt of the crime because of its raw brutality but he had no real knowledge of the details. Could this man be the killer or is he an accessory of some type?

"Are you going to help me?"

Lasky nodded. He would take the man as a client even before hearing his story.

Chamberlain hesitated for a minute but then Tooey O'Banion spoke in his head. 'Tell him, Lad. Tell him everything and it will all be okay.'

Chamberlain spilled out the whole story of Agenbroad bringing the girls to his house, Agenbroad's story about kidnapping them for ransom, his meager attempts to care for them before turning them over to the care of his brother, Dave, and his wife.

Chamberlain told the attorney about subsequently reading about the Santa Rosa kidnapping and murder, the clipping he had handed to Lasky. From that, Chamberlain put two and two together. He remembered Butch talking about how much he hated his ex-wife, a woman he called Sharon, the name usually punctuated with several choice expletives. The article also listed the missing girls' names, Stacy Agenbroad and Jennifer McElroy, even though they were juveniles, because they were kidnap victims.

"Why didn't you come forward sooner, Roy? What kept you from sharing this with an attorney when it was still fresh information? It would have helped cast you as an unwilling accessory. Now, it could be said that you have kept your silence to further the concealment of the children." Lasky wasn't pulling any punches with his client.

"Well, I was afraid I might be charged, especially since Agenbroad had disappeared. The cops might need someone to pin it on."

"I'm not buying that one, Roy. I can tell you that the cops rarely just grab someone out of thin air to charge with a crime, especially one like that. That's especially true of someone who gives them useful information. I can't help you if you don't tell me the whole story."

Chamberlain took a deep breath and unburdened himself of the entire sordid affair inside San Sebastian, in concert with both Gomez and Agenbroad. Yes, he was afraid of being arrested for his role with the girls. But more than that, he feared that calling attention to himself would lead prison authorities to him, if they had been able to connect him to the prison assaults.

"OK," Lasky said. "We can work with that. Did you ever personally injure anyone in the prison?"

"No, not once, and that's God's truth."

"Good. Let me give it some thought and I'll give you a call after the New Year."

"I don't have a phone"

"Not a problem." Lasky was used to his clients not having access to electronic communications. "Come back here at 10:00 a.m. on January 6. In the meantime, stay low and don't talk to anyone about this."

"Thank you, Mr. Lasky. Thank you," Chamberlain pumped the lawyer's hand. He was more at ease than he had been in years. Maybe all of this could be worked out after all.

Chapter Forty-Seven

February 7, 1984

Following his January 6th meeting with Roy Chamberlain, Attorney Louis Lasky was optimistic that the man had information which would be valuable in the right hands. He spent the next few weeks in discrete research to determine how much trouble Chamberlain might be in with either the San Sebastian administration or the Santa Rosa police.

He did not contact anyone in Santa Rosa directly, but his review of media coverage and the legal documents which were part of the public record in Sonoma County convinced him that the investigators were not focusing on his client as a primary suspect.

Likewise, a friend in the California State Attorney General's office told him that no inquiries had been made regarding any involvement in criminal activity Chamberlain may have had inside the prison during his tenure as a guard.

* * *

"OK, Roy. I think we're on good ground. With your permission, I'll make a call to Santa Rosa authorities." Chamberlain nodded, and Lasky dialed the number of the Sonoma County District Attorney's Office.

"Mr. Krupp, my name is Louis Lasky and I represent a party who may have information regarding the murder of a Sharon McElroy in your jurisdiction."

Krupp had heard of Louis Lasky, although he had never met the man. The lawyer was a legend in California criminal defense circles. If Lasky was representing someone that was somehow involved with the McElroy case, his information was probably significant.

"I'm listening, Mr. Lasky," Krupp said.

Lasky outlined Chamberlain's involvement. "Also, Mr. Krupp, although Agenbroad never admitted to Roy that he killed the woman, Roy knew from prison conversations that Agenbroad loathed an ex-wife named Sharon. Agenbroad had also mentioned once that he had a daughter with this Sharon. But when Agenbroad dropped the girls at Roy's house, he never mentioned that one of them was his own daughter."

"And what does your client want in exchange for this information?" Krupp asked. Something like this — information which tied Butch Agenbroad directly to the kidnapping and circumstantially to the murder — wouldn't come without a price.

"He wants to avoid any charges."

"I'll bet he would! But I don't know about that. After all, Mr. Lasky, you've told me he would be admitting to being an accessory after the fact to kidnapping, and knew it at the time. He will have to serve some time for that. You know I can't just let him walk."

In the back of his mind, though, Krupp was already mulling the consequences of that exact action. Such a bargain would generate negative publicity, but that would likely be more than offset by the positive aspects of building a pretty solid case against Agenbroad. And if the information led to the safe return of the girls, then it would be worth it.

"Ok, I'll talk to my client. Would you consider perhaps a guilty plea to a misdemeanor and some county time for what he has to say?"

Krupp was surprised at how easily Lasky caved in on jail time for his client. Maybe this Chamberlain had a conscience and really wanted to tell authorities what he knew. The DA suspected that the informant had already told his lawyer he would go to jail if it meant he could atone for his part in the girls' nightmare.

"There's just one other thing, Mr. Krupp," Lasky said, with a tone of an afterthought. He told Krupp about Chamberlain's activities while he was a guard at San Sebastian. "My client never actually hurt anyone himself. In fact, my sources tell me that the people at San Sebastian might not even know that he was involved. In any case, we feel the information he has to share with you merits him avoiding any charges out of anything that might have happened at San Sebastian as well."

He didn't mention that Chamberlain was also willing to accept some type of punishment for his actions at San Sebastian but was afraid of being sent to prison. Ex-guards were instant targets if they became inmates.

"That's a pretty tall order, Mr. Lasky. I'll get back to you."

* * *

As much as he would have liked to share the news with Masters and the other detectives, Krupp decided this revelation needed to stay within the realm of attorneys for the moment. There were several legal decisions which would have to be made, decisions which could be compromised if he was too quick to involve the detectives now.

Krupp pressed a button on his intercom. "Melissa, please get the deputy attorney general assigned to prisons on the phone. San Sebastian specifically if they divide the workload in their office. And would you get me the file on the McElroy murder and kidnapping?"

Within a few minutes, the intercom on Krupp's desk buzzed. "Deputy AG John Boomsma on four," his assistant said. Krupp gave the state's attorney an outline of their case and the news that a former San Sebastian guard was an informant.

"It sounds like he may have info that could break this case open for us, John, but there could be a problem." Krupp explained Chamberlain's involvement in the retribution beatings of inmates inside San Sebastian.

"This informant, Chamberlain, wants immunity from prosecution from anything that happened inside the prison in exchange for helping us on this case. I know it's a tall order and a dilemma. On one hand, we may be able to save two little girls. At the very least, with Chamberlain's help, we may be able to put away the guy who took them and perhaps some of the people who have concealed them. On the other hand, you may have had a prison guard involved in some pretty serious behavior. Would you look into it discretely and let me know what the State would be interesting in doing?"

"Absolutely," Boomsma said. "I'll call you back, hopefully sometime today, but tomorrow at the latest."

Krupp turned his attention to the McElroy file. He was most interested in any information the detectives had developed about Chamberlain during their investigation. What he learned concerned him.

While the detectives had identified Roy Chamberlain as a person with possible involvement, they had been unable to locate him. They had located his former residence and Anderson had interviewed a witness who positively placed Stacy Agenbroad at that house.

The witness had also identified the man who dropped the girls off with Chamberlain as Butch Agenbroad. That identification would frame a strong case for charging Agenbroad with the kidnapping. However, only Roy Chamberlain had information linking Agenbroad to the murder and Butch could not be convicted solely on the testimony of a co-conspirator. Krupp would need additional evidence linking Agenbroad with the murder itself to obtain a conviction for that crime.

One positive report in the file indicated that Masters had interviewed the warden at San Sebastian about links between Agenbroad and Chamberlain. That interview established that both men were in the prison at the same time, one as an inmate and the other as a guard.

Masters' report also mentioned the retribution attacks in the prison during the time Agenbroad was incarcerated and the fact that prison officials felt that a guard might have been involved.

However, she reported that there was nothing to point to Chamberlain or Agenbroad as specifically being involved in those crimes, although both names had come up as individuals to look at. If that held true, particularly in the case of Chamberlain, then the Attorney General would not likely have a reason to arrest the informant. The decision on any mitigation of charges in exchange for his testimony would be left solely to Krupp.

* * *

The next afternoon, Boomsma called back. "We don't have anything on our end regarding Roy Chamberlain. He was under some suspicion as perhaps being involved in some assaults on prisoners. I should clarify that he was suspected of directing prisoners to locations where they were subsequently assaulted by other inmates, but the warden hasn't developed enough information for us to proceed with any type of action. In fact the warden told me that Chamberlain had been mostly discounted as being involved until he got a call from a Detective Angela Masters regarding Agenbroad and Chamberlain."

Damn! I hope Angi's call didn't alert them too much. Of course, Krupp's prosecutorial instinct was that if Chamberlain was involved in prisoners being assaulted, he should be held accountable. However, the kidnapping case, and perhaps even the lives of Stacy and Jennifer, might very well depend on gaining Chamberlain's cooperation. The fewer hurdles there were toward that end, the better for the moment.

Chapter Forty-Eight

February 10, 1984

Television detective shows feature investigators in tailored wardrobes and only one case assigned to them. They solve that case in forty minutes, often making one or two false arrests in the process. In contrast, real investigations are often stymied by long droughts of information, false leads and dead ends. Adding to that is the inevitable pressure of new cases demanding attention.

So it was with Masters' investigation of the Sharon McElroy murder and the snatching of her children. Once the decision was made to release Alan Cramer, Masters was at another complete dead end in the case.

Angi maintained monthly contact with Doug McElroy. She assured him that she and Devon would move immediately on any lead that came in. "But I have to be honest with you, Doug. It's not looking good for a solution to this case."

In nearly three years, they had nothing more to tie Butch Agenbroad to the murder of his ex-wife than a child's toy found in the back of a car he had been driving and a tentative identification of him in a similar car dropping off the girls with Roy Chamberlain. Even some of that information probably could not be used to prosecute Agenbroad because of the hypnosis issues.

While Angi liked Butch Agenbroad for the murder, she and Devon had investigated other possibilities. They researched Doug and Sharon McElroy's backgrounds, financial situation, and friends and associates to determine if there could be another viable suspect in the murder. That investigation revealed nothing and the focus for the murder sharpened on Agenbroad.

The girls were a different story. "I'm still very hopeful, though, that we will find Stacy and Jennifer," she told McElroy. It seemed that if Butch were the killer and kidnapper, he had acted alone. However, the detectives learned of several people who had custody of the young girls at various times throughout the past three years.

How many were innocent people merely trying to help the girls or a friend without any knowledge of the California crimes, as the Cramers likely were? And how many were true accessories to the abduction and continued concealment of Stacy and Jennifer? The answers to those questions continually eluded the detectives.

* * *

As the third anniversary of the crimes approached, Angi and Devon were busy working on other cases, new cases involving other victims and suspects, cases that never stopped coming into the detective division. They were both alert to any new information on the McElroy case, as was Sergeant Garrison. But the reality was that many of those other cases would be solved long before they might see success in the McElroy case.

Angi had just completed an interview of a suspect in an attempted murder case when Garrison summoned her to his office. "You'll have to finish that report later, Angi. Come with me," the supervisor said as he grabbed his suit jacket.

With Angi matching his quick pace, Garrison led the way to the office of the District Attorney two blocks away.

"Go right in," the receptionist said as Michael and Angi burst through the glass doors. "He's waiting for you."

* * *

Three other people were already seated in the room at Krupp's conference table. Angi recognized one of the two men present from an old driver's license photo she kept in the front of her case file—Roy Chamberlain. She also recognized a female court reporter who regularly worked in the Sonoma County Court system. Could this be a badly needed break in the case?

Krupp opened the discussion with introductions and a statement about the current state of negotiations regarding Chamberlain's information. "Mr. Chamberlain has agreed to tell us everything he knows about Butch Agenbroad, the kidnapping of Stacy and Jennifer, and what he knows about their current whereabouts. If it all checks out and he is telling us the complete story about what he knows, my office has agreed that he will be charged with two counts of custodial interference. Those are misdemeanor charges and he will be sentenced to incarceration in the Sonoma County Jail.

"We have agreed with Mr. Lasky and Mr. Chamberlain that the District Attorney's office will recommend a sentence of three months for each count, to be served concurrently. However, should Mr. Chamberlain be untruthful in any of the statements made to either me or the investigators here, the deal is off and he will be charged with accessory to kidnapping, two felony counts. Is that your understanding and your client's understanding, Mr. Lasky?"

"It is, Mr. Krupp."

At Lasky's urging, Chamberlain leaned toward one of the microphones on the table and said, "Yeah, that's what I'm agreeing to."

Chamberlain spent the next forty-five minutes recounting the events surrounding his initial custody of the girls, his conversation with Agenbroad, and his decision to turn the girls over to Joyce and Dave Chamberlain. He did not mention the events in San Sebastian involving himself with either Agenbroad or Gomez, as Lasky had instructed him.

"Do you have any questions, detectives?" Krupp asked when Chamberlain finished his monologue.

"I have a couple," Angi said. "For the record, Mr. Chamberlain, I am Detective Angela Masters, the lead detective on this case. Do you know where Stacy and Jennifer are now?"

"No, I'm sorry, I haven't seen them since that day when Dave and Joyce drove off with them."

I think there's some remorse there, but I'd still like to strangle you, you son of a bitch. "Have you spoken to Dave since then, or had any type of communication with him at all since that day?"

"I talked to him once and he told me the girls were with Joyce's sister. I don't know anything about her family so I can't tell you anything about where they might have been at that time."

Garrison started to speak, but Angi cut him off. "Do you think your brother or his wife would harm the girls?"

"Joyce, no. My brother? Well, I don't think he would. He likes kids usually but if he was cornered, then I don't know. He's been in some trouble before and if it was a choice between the girls and going back to prison ... I'd like to think he wouldn't harm them, but I honestly don't know for sure. We haven't really been close since we were teenagers and I can't guess how he thinks."

"Do you know where Dave is now?

"No, I don't. I know he had a place in Benicia but I've never been there. I tried to call the number listed for him in the phone book, but it was disconnected and the operator said there was no forwarding number. That was several months ago and I've just been keeping to myself lately."

"One more question," Angi said after a long pause, "Do you know Alan or Darlene Cramer?"

"Cramer?" Chamberlain said without thinking about an answer. "No. Never heard of them."

Angi believed his answer.

"Thank you, Mr. Lasky, Mr. Chamberlain," Krupp said when the detective was finished. "As we agreed, I have a deputy sheriff waiting in the outer office. He will take Mr. Chamberlain to the county jail and book him on the custodial interference charges. Mr. Chamberlain will remain in jail overnight and at the arraignment tomorrow morning, he will enter his guilty pleas and I'll present a sentencing recommendation right then, unless I hear objections from the detectives in the meantime."

"Very well, Mr. Krupp," Lasky said. "Roy, go with the deputy and cooperate. But don't say anything to anyone, including these detectives, about the case unless I'm with you. I'll see you in the morning."

* * *

"Well, what do you think?" Krupp asked the detectives when Lasky and Chamberlain were gone.

"It pretty well fits what we knew or suspected," Angi said. "At least now we have Agenbroad on the kidnapping charges. Maybe we can leverage that to find the girls. As for the murder, it doesn't look to me like we're any closer."

"Unfortunately, Angi, you're not much closer on the kidnapping either," Krupp said. "At least, you can be pretty sure you have the right guy, but you still have a long way to go before you can make a case on anything."

Angi's eyes opened wide. Garrison, who had remained quiet up to that point, said, "What he means, Angi, is that he can't get a conviction solely on the testimony of a co-conspirator. That's what Chamberlain is, based on charging him with a related crime, even if it's just a misdemeanor."

"Mike is right, Angi. I can get a warrant for Agenbroad on probable cause based on the statements we have here today and the identification by the witness in Richmond. But I can't possibly get a conviction on that alone. The witness can place him with the girls but she has no knowledge that he was involved in the kidnapping directly. Only Chamberlain can provide that testimony from Agenbroad's admissions."

"Then why do you have to charge him?"

"I charged him because we need some positive publicity to report to the public. There is still a lot of interest in this case and we would all be under intense criticism if we just let him walk. Also, I don't think his credibility would be good enough in front of a jury, even if he weren't charged. You'll just have to get more."

Angi knew he was right. "OK. Sarge, do you think we can get that reporter for *Real Detectives* magazine to do a follow-up story on the girls. He could report that someone has been arrested. Maybe that would get someone's attention that hasn't come forward before."

"It's certainly worth a try. Thanks for your help, Anson," Garrison said as he and Angi rose. "Now, we've got more work to do."

Chapter Forty-Nine

Spring 1984

The arrest of an accessory in the McElroy murder and kidnapping generated a short burst of media interest in the Sonoma and Napa valleys, but otherwise reporters paid little attention. Certainly, the fact that this suspect, one Roy Chamberlain, was arrested in connection with the kidnapping of the two young girls was newsworthy. But the resulting misdemeanor charges signaled the media that nothing truly significant had happened in the case.

The *Real Detectives* reporter promised to do a follow-up piece in his magazine, using Chamberlain's arrest as a hook to bring readers' attention back to the case. However, magazine publishing schedules being what they were, and with more current cases to report, the story wouldn't appear for two more months.

Masters and Anderson made the rounds of witnesses again, with little change. Helen Bernstein identified the Sonoma County booking photo of Roy Chamberlain as the 'awful' man that once lived across the street from her in Richmond. She again identified Butch Agenbroad as the man who dropped off the young girls.

Martin Brady, the neighbor of Dave and Joyce Chamberlain in Benicia, stated that he had never seen either man in his neighborhood and especially not at the house across the street.

Martita Sandoval identified the photo of Roy Chamberlain as a one-time guard at San Sebastian. She had met him while she was a social worker there. However, she was unaware of any connection between him and her now ex-husband, Butch Agenbroad.

This meeting with Martita carried an extra element of frustration for Angi. It occurred three years to the day after

Sharon's murder. Now, the energy which had roiled immediately after the meeting in Krupp's office subsided. It now seemed the detectives were entering another of the case's maddening droughts of information.

By the middle of May, the case remained bogged down. In the past six weeks, the detectives had come up empty in their attempts to locate Dave and Joyce Chamberlain and the girls. Only one lead had come in in that time. On May 1, the latest issue of *Real Detectives* had hit the newsstands. A woman in Anniston, Alabama, who saw the story called to say she was certain she had seen the girls at a food store there a couple of weeks before. She told Masters that her attention was drawn to the girls by the close attention the older one, a girl of about eight, paid to the younger girl. The older girl seemed very protective of the younger one and very wary of those around her. This was despite the fact that the girls were in the company of a woman who appeared to be in her mid-thirties.

The caller described the woman and Masters noted that the description fit that of Joyce Chamberlain. *Well, if that's the case, then at least they are still alive and being cared for.* Angi thanked the caller for her information and immediately placed a call to the Anniston Police Department. A detective interviewed store employees, but none could recall the girls or the woman.

"We'll keep our patrols alert for them," the Anniston detective said, "but this is a small town and likely they've moved on by now." Angi had to agree, but that didn't make her feel any relief.

* * *

Angi was in her car following a lead on yet another case when the radio crackled. "Detective 74, call Sergeant Garrison ASAP." Angi acknowledged the call, and pulled into the parking lot of a 7-Eleven two blocks away. 7-Eleven stores nationwide had a policy of allowing emergency personnel to use the phone in the back of the store for official business. Angi entered the store and discretely flashed her badge to the kid with curly red hair behind the counter. The kid smiled and slightly jerked his head toward the back room, a sign of 'go on back.'

"Angi, I just got a call from a jail deputy in Ada County, Idaho. I think that's Boise," Garrison told her. "Anyway, he had a note to call us when Butch Agenbroad was about to be released on the assault charge up there. Agenbroad got credit for some good time in the jail, if you can believe that. He will be released a week from today."

"Thanks, Sarge. Of course, Devon and I would like to be there to greet him."

"I never doubted that for a minute. I faxed them the warrant that Krupp got, charging Agenbroad with two counts of kidnapping. That will let us hold him for a while. I also faxed a copy to their prosecuting attorney up there and they promised they will get to work on the extradition order. Krupp called and said that the California Board of Parole will defer action on Agenbroad's parole status pending the outcome of any criminal trial. He's all ours for now."

"Great, Sarge. Thank you." Maybe with Agenbroad in jail back in California, they might have a chance at getting him to open up with more information. At least they would have to try. It was all they had.

Chapter Fifty

May 23, 1984 - Boise, Idaho

Six days later, Angi and Devon boarded a commuter shuttle flight from Santa Rosa to San Francisco. Angi hated the small, noisy and cramped shuttles. But even more, she hated the wait in the terminal that inevitably occurred between the arrival of the shuttle and the departure of the larger commercial jets.

However, if all went according to plan, they would be returning with a handcuffed prisoner, and neither Devon nor Angi wanted to make the 67 mile drive from San Francisco International Airport to Santa Rosa with a violent fugitive like Agenbroad in the car. So a shuttle flight seemed the best choice.

Angi's preference, the Oakland International Airport, was virtually the same distance from Santa Rosa. However, the flight choices to Boise were more numerous to and from San Francisco and the shuttle choices from Santa Rosa to and from Oakland were fewer. So, San Francisco it was.

Both detectives had only packed a single carry-on bag for the trip. The flight to Boise was uneventful and gave Angi and Devon time for last minute strategizing regarding the return flight. It would be a trip neither looked forward to.

Traveling on a commercial airliner with a prisoner required daunting preparation and coordination with the airport police and the flight crew. Flight crews generally did their best to be accommodating, within the confines of passenger safety, but it was still a stressful experience for officers.

Alternatively, the thought of driving 675 miles, much of it across the deserts of Nevada with limited radio communication, was even less appealing. So Angi and Devon set their sights on the preparation for an eighty-minute commercial flight and a short shuttle flight back to Santa Rosa.

A young Boise Police uniformed officer met them at the gate in Boise. "Detectives, I'm Officer Bengoa, Mark. The chief assigned me to pick you up and take you to your hotel. Your prisoner will be released into your custody in the morning. I'll pick you up from the hotel and take you to the jail, then bring you and your prisoner back out to the airport. Is all that okay with you?"

"Of course, Officer Bengoa," Angi said, "that would be great." Angi could not believe the cooperation they were receiving in Idaho. They had planned to rent a car, which of course would further complicate their prisoner transport during the check-in of the car. This turn of events not only eliminates that as a possible problem area, but Bengoa would likely take them right to the plane via the tarmac. That will eliminate having to parade Agenbroad through the terminal.

"I assume, then, that your governor signed the extradition warrant," Devon said.

"Oh, yes, sir. I'm sorry I forgot to mention that. The chief told me to tell you that the governor signed it immediately upon being told about your case. The chief also said that the governor himself asked the chief to do all he could to assist you in—the governor's words—'getting this SOB out of our state as soon as possible'."

Angi smiled. "Well, your chief was very helpful to me when I was here last year. He's a great guy and we really appreciate his help."

* * *

The next morning, Bengoa picked up the two California detectives at the Holiday Inn and drove them to the jail. "We share a building with the sheriff. It makes it pretty handy for us, since the jail is right there. For the most part, our guys and the deputies get along really well." Bengoa anticipated a question that always seemed to come up in any discussion of relations between city officers and county deputies.

He drove through a security gate at the back of the building and into a closed garage connected to the jail. The 'sally port,' as it was called, allowed officers to move prisoners to or from a car within an enclosed area, which limited escape attempts.

"Nice facility," Angi said as they left the car after the overhead door to the sally port closed behind them.

"We like it," a male voice said from somewhere off to the right of the car. Then a man in the brown uniform of a deputy sheriff approached.

"Hello, Detectives, I'm Lieutenant John Bengoa, the day shift jail supervisor. I'm here to help you with the transfer of your prisoner."

"Bengoa?" Devon said, as Officer Mark Bengoa interrupted his thought. "My older brother. He went to the *dark side*, the sheriff's department." Both brothers grinned at the detectives.

"We like to spread it around, Detective," the lieutenant said before Angi could introduce herself. "Our other brother, Matthew, is an Idaho State Trooper."

"Interesting family, El-Tee," Angi said as she extended her hand. "I'm Angela Masters—call me Angi—and this is Devon Anderson."

"Nice to meet you. Please follow me."

"I'll wait here for you in case I have to move the car for an incoming prisoner," Mark Bengoa said.

Only an hour before, Agenbroad was informed that he would not become a free man today. Yes, his sentence was up on the charge in Carlisle, but two detectives from Santa Rosa, California were waiting to arrest him on a kidnapping warrant. They would be transporting him to California to answer to those charges right away. Butch stood at the jail release station wearing something besides an orange jumpsuit for the first time in almost nine months.

He turned to see a familiar face walking toward him, the female cop from California that he had already thwarted twice in her attempts to get information from him. Maybe this wouldn't be so bad after all. He might not walk free immediately, but it was a long trip to the Bay Area. His chances to escape were numerous. No doubt—he would be a free man by this time tonight.

One thought nagged at Butch. Someone must have dropped a dime. How else could these cops have a warrant for him for the kidnapping? His mind rolled over the events surrounding the long-ago crimes. It had to have been Chamberlain. The cops didn't have a warrant for Sharon's murder, only for kidnapping. That probably meant that no one had seen him at Sharon's house, as he hoped had been the case.

And the only person he had told about kidnapping the girls was Roy Chamberlain, the day he left the girls at Chamberlain's house. *I'll take care of that witness easy enough.* He smiled at the approaching detectives. *If he doesn't want the shit at San Sebastian spilled to the cops, he'll forget that he ever saw me with those girls.*

"Hello, Butch," Angi said. Then as she got a little closer, she looked at the scar above his right eye and said, "Oooooo. What's that? Four or five stitches? No, it looks like it just healed on its own. Does it still hurt?"

Bitch! Butch's grin abruptly changed to a scowl, remembering the deputy slamming his head into the concrete floor the last time he saw this female cop. *Calm down. You'll have the last laugh on her and her dippy looking partner when you've left them wondering how you got away so easy.* His crooked smile returned and he said nothing.

"Butch, we're going to be taking you back to California today."

"And what if I don't want to go?" Butch said. "I kind of like this hick state."

"Well, it seems that the governor would rather you didn't stay here. He's already signed the extradition warrant."

Woman, you talk pretty big right now, but I'll show you who's the smart one before I ever see your lousy California jail. You have no idea who you're dealing with. Hell, I might even jump out of the car somewhere around here, just to show you and that asshole governor.

Angi sensed Butch's defiance behind his forced smile. *This is going to be a real challenge. There's no way this guy will let us take him back without a fight.*

Devon Anderson was thinking exactly the same thing, but the arrangements had been made. But maybe they could get a few extra cops from Boise to help until they were on the plane. Then they could call ahead and have additional Santa Rosa officers meet them at SFO.

After Angi signed the Ada County Jail paperwork accepting custody of the prisoner, the three, escorted by Lt. Bengoa, walked to the sally port. Agenbroad was in handcuffs and leg irons. "It's going to be a long drive, lady," he growled in a whisper to Angi as they walked, her hand on his elbow.

"That's why we think we should just fly, Butch." She hoped her voice didn't betray her concerns.

Lieutenant Bengoa pulled Angi aside as she was getting into the patrol car. "Watch him every step of the way, Angi. He's probably one of the worst we've ever seen here."

Chapter Fifty-One

May 24, 1984

Butch would now have to think of another plan. There wouldn't be as many opportunities for escape if most of the trip was by air. Still, he was sure they would have to take him through either San Francisco or Oakland, since he didn't know of any commercial flights between Boise and Santa Rosa. Maybe it would be best to just wait for the car trip from whichever California airport they went to.

It would be even better for him to escape in the Bay Area. He had connections there and the huge population would serve to mask his escape. It seemed far better than running into the desolate, treeless sagebrush around Boise.

The three entered Mark Bengoa's marked patrol car, Angi in the right front seat, Devon behind the driver, and the trussed Agenbroad in the right rear seat. The front overhead door of the sally port opened and Officer Bengoa drove through the security gate. Almost immediately, two Boise Police Kawasaki motorcycles fell in behind his patrol car. "Just a little maneuverable insurance in case Mr. Agenbroad should decide he doesn't like our company," Bengoa said over his shoulder.

Devon looked to his right at Agenbroad and smiled. His smile was not returned.

As they approached the airport, Angi was going over in her mind the steps that needed to occur to get Agenbroad aboard the flight to San Francisco. It was scheduled to depart in 55 minutes. As she processed the checklist, she noticed that Bengoa drove past the entrance marked 'Emergency Vehicle Field Access.' She looked over at the driver but he merely smiled and said nothing. *Perhaps he's taking us a better way out onto the field,* she thought, although the unexpected change in plans momentarily alarmed her.

Moments later, Bengoa turned into another gated area, several hundred yards beyond the emergency vehicle entrance. The sign on the security gate, which was electronically opened by some unseen hand immediately upon their approach, read 'Private Access—Emmett McCall Corporation.'

Before Angi could speak, Bengoa smiled again. "Our chief wanted me to tell you that it seems that there is an Emmett McCall executive who is needed for an urgent corporate meeting here. He just happens to be in the Santa Rosa area and they are sending that plane down to pick him up."

The three looked to their right to see a shiny Gates Learjet 55 emblazoned with the Emmett McCall logo. The access stairway was down and Bengoa drove up to within a few feet of the aircraft.

Bengoa overheard his older brother's cautionary advice to Angi in the sally port, but even John Bengoa did not know about this arrangement.

"The governor asked to have Mr. Agenbroad removed from our state as quickly as possible," the officer said. "So, the Chief made a couple of calls and said to tell you that his friend and the Mayor's, the president of Emmett McCall, offered to let you and your *guest* ride down since the plane will be empty. It should be easier than all that commercial airline hassle."

Angi was impressed. This was the second time the private company boss had come to their aid in this case.

Agenbroad swore under his breath. The flight would be directly from Boise to Santa Rosa, with no stops in between. There would be no civilian passengers who might be used as hostages to affect an escape. There would also be no protracted car travel through the metropolitan San Francisco area where he might leap from a car and fade into a crowd. Butch Agenbroad now found himself on a 500 mile per hour fast track to the Sonoma County jail.

The pilots and the detectives exchanged introductions and the three passengers boarded the aircraft. The co-pilot closed the door and then took her seat on the right side of the cockpit. Angi, Devon, and Agenbroad sat toward the center of the plane in the custom designed conference style seating arrangement.

"Help yourselves to snacks in the refrigerator or pantry there," the co-pilot called back, as the two Garrett turbofan engines spooled up.

An hour later, they touched down in Santa Rosa. As he had promised, Officer Bengoa had called Sergeant Garrison with their anticipated arrival time. Four Santa Rosa patrol cars were waiting as the corporate jet engines shut down in front of the private aircraft terminal. The detectives handed their prisoner over to the uniformed police officers.

As the convoy of patrol vehicles left the airport for the county jail, Devon turned to Angi. "Well, this has been some surprise, but a very welcome relief."

Angi nodded and said to the pilots, "The uniformed officers can take care of getting our prisoner booked into jail. I don't see anyone who looks like they're waiting for you right now and we'd really like to thank you. We have a car here and we'd be happy to take you for a quick bite to eat while you wait for your executive."

"No, thank you, Detective Masters," the pilot said. "We really have to get back."

The proverbial light came on for Angi. "There never was an executive to pick up in Santa Rosa, was there?"

The co-pilot merely smiled. She handed Angi an impressively engraved business card and said, "Here's the boss's card, Angi. Send him a Christmas card and a news clipping from when you put this bastard away for life."

Chapter Fifty-Two

May 24, 1984 - Memphis, Tennessee

For more than ten months, Dave and Joyce Chamberlain had been on the run. There were a couple of close calls, but so far no one had identified the two girls traveling with the family 'on vacation.'

A few times, Joyce was asked by neighbors in one of the tenement neighborhoods where they had taken refuge why the older girl wasn't in school. Joyce always replied that she was a teacher and was home schooling her daughter while they were traveling. No one asked the obvious question: If these people had money to travel around the country, why did they stay in $15 motels and $125 a month flop houses?

Dave had successfully stayed off everyone's radar, paying cash for everything as they went. He couldn't remember how many robberies he had pulled off, but each netted only a few hundred dollars to continue their meandering flight. Twice, Dave had stolen license plates from cars in junk yards, always careful to keep the old plates he had been using so as not to tip anyone who might find them and report the number to police.

Dave spent a great deal of time pondering his next move. The problem was that the girls were getting older. Stacy was now eight and seemed to be developing more courage to approach other people. It would only be a matter of time before she told someone what had happened to them. That information, given to the wrong people – say someone in a shopping mall – could bring the police knocking on the Chamberlains' door. That would mean a long time in the slammer for both of them.

Dave had considered dropping the girls off somewhere, maybe a fire station or television station, and just driving away. He discounted that idea. Even though they had eluded police scrutiny thus far, the girls knew about their car and some of their contacts. For all Dave knew, Stacy might even have written down the latest license number for their car.

No, the only way for me and Joyce to avoid jail is for the girls to disappear permanently. That was easy to think—even to say—but Dave still felt some compassion for the girls. Besides, Joyce would never cooperate in harming them.

* * *

The thought became academic one day in early June, 1984. The foursome had spent the past week in a cheap motel in Memphis. Dave took the girls to Graceland, Elvis Presley's home, although the landmark meant nothing to the bewildered youngsters. Otherwise, they just laid low, watching television on the ancient color set in the motel room.

Joyce had gone out alone to get a few groceries. She returned to the room with panic in her eyes. She motioned Dave to the bathroom and closed the door, leaving only a crack to observe the girls. With a shaking hand, Joyce passed the latest issue of *Real Detectives* magazine to Dave.

She often looked for the magazine on the shelves, but this time, another woman brought the publication to her attention. Joyce was in the checkout line and a woman behind her was flipping through a magazine. Joyce had not paid much attention until the woman behind her said, "Honey, this picture looks just like you!" There in the woman's hands was a copy of *Real Detectives* magazine.

The teaser headline on the front cover read, 'Murder and Kidnap in California. Are Detectives Closing in on the Culprits?' The cover featured photos of Stacy and Jennifer, of Roy Chamberlain, of another man identified as Elmont Agenbroad, and worst of all, photos of Dave and Joyce.

Joyce had stared for a moment at the photo on the magazine cover, the same picture as on the California's driver's license in her purse at that very moment. Then she managed a laugh and told the woman, "No, of course not. I don't see the resemblance, but they say everyone has a twin somewhere." Joyce had hurried through the check-out process. On her way out the door, she shoplifted a copy of the magazine.

When Dave saw the magazine cover, it was all he could do to contain his rage. It boiled over as he sat on the closed toilet seat, reading the article inside. The reporter noted that the arrest of a man called Roy Chamberlain on charges of custody interference had been covered by the magazine in its previous issue. In a box at one side of the article, under a bold tagline of 'Update' there was a notation that the previously mentioned Roy Chamberlain had pled guilty to the misdemeanor charges. He was currently serving time in the Sonoma County (CA) jail. The update also noted that Chamberlain had received a reduced sentence in exchange for his cooperation with police.

To Dave, that could mean only one thing. Roy had named names and Dave had no doubt those names included him and Joyce. *I don't know how much Roy knows about the murder, but he definitely knows that I like to hold up night managers of fast food joints for cash whenever I'm on the run.* All police would have to do to track Dave would be to put together information on such robberies across the country. Dave knew they could do this from similar cases he had seen on TV cop shows.

Dave didn't realize the vast difference between what information TV cops could amass and what was feasible for real life police, even in a murder case. Tracking him by his robberies would be virtually impossible. It would be difficult for Masters to even learn about such robberies, and if she did, the information likely would not be timely. In any case, the idea was moot, since Roy had not mentioned Dave's pattern to investigators.

The article further went on to talk about the arrest of Elmont Agenbroad for the kidnapping. It said that Stacy, the older of the girls, was the suspect's daughter by a previous marriage. The article stated that on the day of the kidnapping, Sharon McElroy, the mother of the kidnap victims, was found murdered in her house. The writer speculated that Sharon McElroy might be the ex-wife of Elmont Agenbroad, but didn't offer any speculation as to whether Agenbroad was also a suspect in the murder. He left that to the reader.

"Pack up, Joyce! We've got to go now!" At any moment, the Memphis Police might be surrounding their squalid room.

* * *

He wasn't far from wrong. The woman who identified Joyce in the store check-out line was perplexed by the reaction of the woman in front of her. She was sure it was the woman in the photo. She completed her grocery purchase and walked to her car. *I should tell my husband about this, and maybe call the police.*

The decision was simplified when, as she was loading the purchases in her car, a Memphis Police car pulled into the lot and parked two cars away from hers. The officer had no idea about the cloud of intrigue swirling over the area. He had merely pulled into the lot with the intent of buying a pack of cigarettes from the store. But at the woman's urging, he looked at the photo on the magazine cover and listened to the excited woman's description of what had happened in the check-out line.

"Definitely sounds suspicious," the officer said. "Let's take a drive around the parking lot and nearby streets and see if you can spot her." The witness stared intently out the patrol car window for any sign of the woman from the check-out line, but she was nowhere to be found.

The officer radioed a request for detectives to respond to the store. After unsuccessfully canvassing the area, he returned to the store lot and briefed the two just-arrived detectives on what had happened and the actions he had taken. The detectives took a statement from the witness and interviewed store personnel. The clerk who had checked out the witness and Joyce reported that the blonde woman paid cash for her purchases.

Police also interviewed a couple of people who were walking in the area. No one had ever seen the woman in the magazine photo in the area before. Another potential lead had produced a maddening dead end.

As detectives stood in the lot interviewing a man who was also in the checkout line, a gray Toyota with North Carolina license plates drove down the four-lane street in front of the store.

Chapter Fifty-Three

June 6, 1984 - Bluefield, West Virginia

Two days later, Dave, Joyce, and the girls, were settled into a seedy tourist cabin on a side road just off US 19, east of Bluefield, West Virginia. They were the only guests. From the looks of the place, they were the only guests in quite some time.

The place had been developed as a tourist camp in 1933, but over the years, the main highways had bypassed the camp. This would be the perfect place to carry out his long-delayed and unfortunate but necessary plan.

The leather-faced, chain-smoking proprietor took Dave's cash in payment for a room. No registration form was needed, he told Dave. The proprietor offered Dave a draw of the clear liquid in an old gallon vinegar jar. This was the heart of Appalachia, and known for its 'white lightening.' Dave shook his head.

That night, after the girls were asleep, Dave pulled Joyce to a small storage room off the postage-stamp living room. "Joyce, I've made a decision and I know it's not what you want to hear."

Joyce had a very good idea of what her husband was about to say. She wished she could just close her ears and her mind to the thought and will it to vanish. She could not.

"Joyce, Honey, we've got to get rid of them. It's only a matter of time before the cops catch up with us. Stacy, especially, can implicate too many people. If we get rid of them, we can just tell the cops that we dropped them off at some police station months ago when we found out who they were. We can claim we never knew and wanted no part of any crime when we found out about them."

Joyce understood the twisted logic of the denial. But logic had no place beside what had to happen to the girls in order to make that denial plausible. It was more than she could stand to think about.

"The cops will never be able to put them with us for long. Nobody is going to be able to tie us to them, even if the cops do stumble across one or two places we've been. We would also be protecting your sisters. The cops don't know about Kathy, at least as far as we know. And the magazine just mentions a couple in Oregon who haven't been charged."

She'd better buy this. Dave was really looking out for himself, but he needed Joyce's cooperation. Unless he was ready to kill her, too. He wasn't—at least not yet.

"I can't get a gun without attracting attention, so I'm thinking I'll just get a baseball bat, or maybe a knife." Dave was putting together a plan as he spoke. "I promise you I'll make it quick and they won't suffer. Then we can dump the bodies in a coal shaft. There must be hundreds of them around here. Then we'll put some distance between us and this place and maybe turn ourselves in. We can say we saw the magazine cover and want to set the record straight that we don't have the girls."

If the plan sounded plausible to Dave, the thought horrified Joyce. *I would never have believed Dave would be capable of cold-blooded murder, but there it is.* Her husband was discussing murder as easily as a man might discuss his plans to play golf the next day. Dave said he would wait until the first light to search the tourist cabins and a nearby tool shed for something he could use for his grisly mission.

Joyce nodded almost imperceptibly in acquiescence. But her mind screamed, *I have to do something drastic in the next few hours, and it will almost certainly land me in jail right along with Dave.* But she couldn't accept the alternative that he was describing.

* * *

That night, Joyce feigned sleep, waiting for her chance, but it seemed like hours before Dave drifted off to sleep next to her. As Dave snored beside her, Joyce left the squeaky bed. Dave moved a little, but remained sound asleep. Joyce held her hand over Stacy's mouth as she woke the girl. After signaling Stacy to remain quiet, Joyce woke Jennifer the same way.

She then picked up the car keys from a rickety night table and quietly ushered the girls out the door. Joyce drove silently away from the cabin. She left the car headlights turned off until she was a hundred feet away—insurance that Dave wouldn't be awakened by the bright light.

As the car rolled away, a man moved stealthily toward the cabin. Moments later, Dave Chamberlain was rudely awakened by a twelve-gauge double-barreled shotgun being jabbed into his ribs.

* * *

Joyce raced to Bluefield, the closest town. As she entered the town, she spotted a lone police car driving slowly down the street. The driver was shining the vehicle spotlight on the doors and windows of local businesses. There wasn't much crime in Bluefield and Officer Nathan Puckett, the lone officer on duty on the night shift, busied himself checking the doors and windows of businesses for signs of a break-in. He had found such a break-in a few months earlier and had single-handedly caught the teenaged burglar inside the business. In his mind, that validated the spotlight checks.

Joyce pulled the Toyota in front of the police car and screeched to a stop. Puckett, intent on watching the lighted glass for signs of breakage, nearly ran into the gray car. He was about to berate the crazy driver when she came running toward him, a young girl holding each of her hands.

When Joyce finished her story, in which she cast herself as a guiltless guardian, Puckett notified his chief. Chief Oliver Westcott had been an officer in Morgantown before being named as chief of police in Bluefield only six months earlier. As Puckett was briefing the chief on the woman's story, Westcott recalled seeing a bulletin about a murder and kidnapping out west. The bulletin had been circulated to Morgantown and other cities by the state police.

Westcott's sergeant read the bulletin in the roll call meeting, but few, if any of the officers paid much attention. After all, the crime had happened on the other side of the country — California. Now, the chief struggled to recall the details.

Westcott asked Joyce a few questions, and then turned to Puckett. "OK. Let's take Mrs. Chamberlain and the girls to my house. They'll be safe there." Puckett parked the gray Toyota in a nearby alley, locked the doors, and followed the chief as he drove the woman and the girls to his residence.

Mrs. Westcott, on hearing her husband's brief description of what was going on, welcomed the trio inside. "I'll take care of them, Ollie. Now you and Nathan go do your thing."

* * *

Since the old tourist camp was outside the Bluefield city limits, the chief called the Mercer County Sheriff's Office. "Have a deputy meet me in Bluefield ASAP."

A short time later, Deputy Lonnie Ackerman, one of four deputies on duty in Mercer County, rolled up in front of the Bluefield police station. Minutes later, Deputy Ackerman called his sergeant on the radio. "Sarge, Chief Westcott may have something here. Could you meet us at the turnout on 19 just before the old tourist camp. I'll brief you there."

Thirty minutes later, the four law enforcement officers idled their cars toward the tourist camp with headlights extinguished. They left their vehicles and moved as quietly as they could to the cabin Joyce had described. Suddenly, a man shouted from the shadows, "He's over here!"

Westcott and Ackerman drew down on the man, before Ackerman recognized the eccentric proprietor.

The sight greeting the four lawmen would become a story each of them would tell for years. There, lashed spread-eagle to a split rail fence, was Dave Chamberlain. He was bound hand and foot and a dirty rag was stuffed in his mouth as a gag.

"I don't usually have much doin' with the po-lice," the proprietor said, "but this ole boy, he done gone too far, keepin' them girls from their daddy and their kin. I knowed who he was the minute he drove up. At first, I was gonna get him drunked up on 'shine, so's you could pick him up. But he refused. You believe that? So, when I sees the woman drive off with the girls, I decided y'all could use a little help afore this polecat got away. You might find a couple of bruises on him, deputy. I kind of had to jab him a little with my shotgun to get him cooperatin'. But I never shot him — not that the yellow bellied varmit don't deserve it."

"Cut him loose, Elmer," Ackerman told the proprietor, a broad grin on his face.

Chamberlain was cut from the rope bonds and placed in handcuffs. As he was being led away, he heard Elmer's mountain voice, "Ya see, Boy, even us mountain folks read *Real Detectives*. And ya never refuse a sip of a man's 'shine if'n it's offered."

Chapter Fifty-Four

June 7, 1984

Four hours later, the phone jangled on Angi's desk. As she listened, her face showed no expression, except for a faint smile that crept across her lips. "Thank you very much," she told the caller and placed the receiver back on its cradle.

Then, she stood up, raised both arms and shouted to the room, "We got them! Stacy and Jennifer are safe in West Virginia and the Chamberlains are in custody. The girls are coming home!"

Then, as the pandemonium of cheers and high-fives broke out in the normally staid investigative workroom, Angi sank into her chair and sobbed as relief washed over her.

* * *

"It's yours if you want it," Garrison said to Angi a few minutes later.

"Is there any doubt, Sarge?" She dabbed away the tears and her face lit up as it hadn't in a long time. Hurrying from the building, she drove to an address across the city. Her face was still beaming when she entered the office of Sonoma Valley Data Partners. The receptionist sensed from the detective's smile that she had good news. She electronically opened a connecting door, allowing Angi into the back offices.

Angi approached a familiar office in the corner. Seeing the man sitting at his desk, she quickened her step.

Doug McElroy saw the detective approaching from the corner of his eye and turned to see the wide grin on her face. "Angi?" he said with an edge of hope when the detective was still twenty feet away.

"Yes, Doug! Your girls are safe! They are at an FBI office in West Virginia at this moment."

Doug McElroy dropped back into his chair as tears streamed down his cheeks. The reaction of his co-workers was even more ecstatic than the response of the detective office. Angi continued into Doug's office and hugged him. "You never stopped believing, Doug, and neither did I. Now it's paid off and I'm so happy for you."

* * *

When Angi returned to the station, she went directly to Sergeant Garrison's office. "How's he doing?" Garrison asked before she could sit down.

"Doug is doing great. I've never seen a man so relieved and so happy. It was even greater for me to see him now because I've seen him so down in the past."

"I've seen you gutted by this case, too, Angi. But at least this part of it is looking up now."

"I just got off the phone with Agent Shearn," Garrison said, indicating the FBI senior resident agent in the Santa Rosa office. "The girls are being medically checked out this afternoon. Assuming they are cleared, and Shearn thinks they will be, an FBI plane will bring them home tomorrow."

Angi beamed at the news. "Doug will be thrilled beyond belief to hear that."

"Of course, they will probably need some counseling to get back into their life here," Garrison said, "but from what I've seen, Doug is strong and a good parental figure. That will help the girls, I'm sure."

"Absolutely," Angi said. "I'll let him know as soon as we're done here."

"Dave and Joyce Chamberlain are being held on a federal unlawful flight warrant in Beckley, West Virginia. Krupp will be filing paperwork to have them extradited here. He's going to charge both of them with felony accessory to kidnapping under the state penal code. I think the plan is for the feds to drop charges once they are charged here to allow us to prosecute them."

"Yesss!" Angi pumped her fist. It would be gratifying to see the people primarily responsible for keeping Stacy and Jennifer from their family for so long behind bars, no matter what jurisdiction put them there. But it would be doubly gratifying for the Sonoma County District Attorney to be the prosecutor that convicted them.

* * *

The following afternoon, Angi and Devon sat with Doug in the general aviation terminal at the Santa Rosa Airport. With them was RuthEllen Grimes, a child psychologist employed by the California Department of Social Services. Dr. Grimes would be responsible for monitoring Stacy and Jennifer as they were re-integrated into normal family life with Doug and their little sister. Or, at least as normal a family life as could be expected in the aftermath of the loss of the strong and loving mother they had once known.

Shortly after 1:30 p.m., a Cessna Citation jet bearing no markings except the tail number taxied to a parking space in front of the terminal. The airstair door opened and folded down, creating an exit stairway from the plane. Almost immediately, a man in a crisp business suit appeared at the plane's doorway, a young girl to either side of him. The man, an FBI agent from the Beckley resident agency, escorted Jennifer down the stairs. Stacy descended on her own. At the first sign of the girls, Doug was out the door like a shot from a Howitzer.

For the first time in three years, Stacy left Jennifer's side. She ran to the man she knew as her father and leaped into his arms, tears streaming down her cheeks. Jennifer stayed back with the agent. She thought she knew this man, but she had been very young when she was abducted. She wasn't sure.

Sensing her sister's bewilderment, Stacy kissed Doug on the cheek and jumped from his arms. She ran to her sister, the sister she had protected for so very long.

"It's okay, Jenni," Stacy said as she took the younger girl's hand from the agent. "It's really okay. That man is our daddy, our real daddy, *your* real daddy, and we're home!"

Now Jennifer began to cry and ran to Doug, with Stacy right behind her. As he knelt on the tarmac embracing his daughters, Dr. Grimes turned to Angi and whispered, "A good start, a very good start indeed."

* * *

Three days later, Dave and Joyce Chamberlain arrived in San Francisco aboard a U.S. Marshal's transport plane. Marshals transported them to the San Francisco County jail, which served as a contract federal holding facility. Three hours later, a San Francisco County judge ordered that the pair also be held without bond on a state kidnapping warrant issued in Sonoma County.

The following day, a federal magistrate dismissed the federal charges against Dave and Joyce without prejudice, meaning that the charges could be re-filed at any time in the future. The way was clear for their prosecution by the State of California.

* * *

Now that all the major players to the McElroy case were incarcerated in California, Anson Krupp's workload increased exponentially. He would be preparing for an aggravated kidnapping trial against Butch Agenbroad for the original kidnapping, as well as prosecuting Dave and Joyce Chamberlain as accessories after the fact of aggravated kidnapping.

The charges were quite clear, since one of the aggravating factors under the California Penal Code was the use of force or fear to detain a child under the age of 14, an obvious fact when it came to Stacy and Jennifer. Making the cases more difficult was the apparent fact that Agenbroad and the Chamberlains had never met and the transfer of the children had taken place through Roy Chamberlain.

The easiest to convict was Joyce Chamberlain. The girls were in her custody when she stopped the Bluefield officer. The officer could also be brought to California to testify not only about witnessing the girls in Joyce's custody but also about statements Joyce voluntarily made to him regarding the girls' custody status.

Faced with that possibility and plagued by her own guilt, Joyce, with the support of her court-appointed defense attorney, pled guilty to one count of being an accessory to kidnapping. In exchange for being allowed to plead to only one count and without the 'aggravated' enhancement, Joyce agreed to testify to the extent she could at any other trials. The judge accepted the district attorney's recommendation and sentenced her to four to six years imprisonment.

While Joyce could not testify against her husband directly, she did provide information about places she had been with the girls during the past three years. "It's a simple thing for the cops," Dave's court-appointed attorney told him. "If they find people in only a few places who can put with the girls, that's it for you."

In the end, Dave Chamberlain also entered a guilty plea. He was sentenced to a fixed term of sixteen years in a California prison, eight years for each count of being an accessory to kidnapping.

Two down, three if Roy Chamberlain was included in the count of involved parties, and one to go. But that one would be the most difficult. Anson Krupp knew he faced an uphill battle in convicting Elmont Agenbroad of anything. Only Roy Chamberlain could link Agenbroad directly to the kidnapping, and his testimony would require corroboration. That corroboration was still frustratingly lacking.

Chapter Fifty-Five

June 21, 1984

No one was smiling as they entered Anson Krupp's conference room. Krupp had called a meeting of two of his senior prosecutors and included Detectives Masters and Anderson, and Sergeant Garrison. The purpose of the meeting was to discuss how to proceed in the prosecution of Elmont Agenbroad. The question looming before everyone was whether he could be successfully prosecuted for anything.

Krupp reiterated the problems. "The only witness to the actual kidnapping, Chelsea Leedy, is barred from testifying because she had been hypnotized. In any case, she was unable to positively identify the man that she had seen as Agenbroad."

When Deputy District Attorney Elisa Montgomery started to speak, Krupp interrupted her. He knew what she was going to say but he didn't need any finger-pointing now.

"The detectives were operating within accepted practice at the time that they had the girl hypnotized. Under hypnosis, she was able to give them information about the license plate of the suspect car. That led them to Agenbroad's mother-in-law and ultimately placed him in the car at the time of the murder. It's not the detectives' fault that the Supreme Court later decided to change their view on admissibility. But we have to deal with the reality that the court decision has had an adverse impact on our case."

Montgomery nodded and leaned back in her chair.

"The only other link we have between Agenbroad and the girls are three witnesses near Roy Chamberlain's house in Richmond. And if I'm correct, Angi, only one of them can positively identify Agenbroad."

"That's correct, Anson. Helen Bernstein also identified Dave Chamberlain with the girls, but that's a moot point now."

Angi was as dejected as she had been in a long time. She and Devon, not to mention many other investigators, put in thousands of hours on this case. Now, with the primary suspect only a few hundred yards away in the county lockup, it seemed that he might very well walk on everything.

"What about Stacy?" Angi asked. "I've talked to her with Dr. Grimes present and she has a lot to say. She can talk about being taken from the house by Agenbroad, of being left with a man who likely was Roy Chamberlain although she can't be sure from his picture.

"She can talk about being taken from that place by Dave and Joyce Chamberlain, people she came to know well since she spent most of the three years with them. And, although it's still a delicate subject with her that we haven't fully explored, she can talk about seeing her mother naked and bloody and tied to a kitchen chair as she was being led out of the house by Agenbroad. In short, she can give us the entire case."

Elisa Montgomery was renowned for her expertise in prosecuting criminals. A career prosecutor with more than fifteen years experience in the Sonoma County District Attorney's Office, Montgomery was a civil service employee rather than an elected official like Anson Krupp. She was now the senior deputy district attorney, having served three elected district attorneys, including her current boss, Krupp. Her opinions carried a great deal of weight in the district attorney's office.

"In short, *Detective* Masters," Montgomery said. "In short, Stacy Agenbroad is nine years old. You can't seriously expect us to stake a case of this magnitude on the testimony of a nine-year-old. The court might not even let her testify because of her age, and then where would we be?"

"Even with the girl's testimony, I have to tell you that this case is pretty weak, Angi," Krupp said. "We have a better chance of getting Agenbroad convicted on the kidnapping now. But the murder ... it's not looking good. Not even Stacy can testify to actually witnessing the murder, thank God for her sake."

Angi nodded and then turned to Montgomery. "Well, yes, and she is eight years old, but she's also very articulate for her age and a very intelligent young lady." *So there, you sarcastic bitch!* "I think we owe it to her, to her little sisters, to Doug, and to Sharon to let her have a chance to tell her story. I believe we can convince a judge that she knows the difference between the truth and fiction, which is the basic requirement as I understand it. If she's not allowed to testify, at least we tried.

"And in answer to your question, *Ms.* Montgomery, if she is not allowed to testify, we would probably be right where we are at this moment, which if I'm not mistaken is nowhere. But at least we would have tried."

* * *

One issue surfaced in Angi's mind and became more acute after she heard Joyce's story of their time on the run. Why had the girls stayed with them? Surely there was opportunity in those three years for them to run to an authority figure. At the least, they might have caused a commotion that would have attracted enough attention that Dave and Joyce might have fled without them.

"Angi," Dr. Grimes asked when Masters approached her for an answer, "have you ever heard of the Stockholm Syndrome?"

"Of course, I have. The name came from the way some bank robbery hostages bonded with their captors over several days in the early 70s. But I thought that was a defense mechanism for people who were being threatened with bodily harm, like Patty Hearst when she was assaulted and locked in a closet by the SLA."

"Yes, it is a response to a threat, but a threat can mean different things to different people. In this case, Stacy was told during the first week that her parents and sister had died in an automobile accident.

"So in her mind, she had nowhere to go. She was still under that belief until she was told the truth by an FBI agent and a psychologist in West Virginia after she was safe. Also, there was the matter of Jennifer. Stacy felt that if her parents were gone, it was up to her to protect her little sister. Stacy would never have run away and left Jennifer, even for a few minutes, to get help.

"Finally, there is the matter that they were not mistreated by the Chamberlains. They were concealed, certainly, and kept from their family, which is the issue for the courts. But from what I've learned from Stacy, the Chamberlains often referred to her and Jennifer as their daughters. They did try to take care of them, even though they didn't have much money most of the time. Stacy simply bonded with them because the alternatives, being alone and taking care of her sister, were simply too terrifying for her to comprehend."

Angi nodded. Dr. Grimes' explanation only elevated her admiration of the bravery of little Stacy Agenbroad.

Chapter Fifty-Six

June 27, 1984

Charles Cotesworth Teska IV was an imposing figure in California legal circles. His great grand-father, Charles Cotesworth Teska, had been named in honor of Charles Cotesworth Pinckney, the South Carolina statesman, Revolutionary War hero, and Constitutional Convention delegate, who was also a life-long confidant of George Washington. Teska IV — Chuck to his friends and associates — carried himself with an aristocratic bearing that never seemed to conflict with his dedicated belief in the defense of the underdog.

Chuck Teska had paid his dues in the legal community, serving as a deputy district attorney and as a defense attorney in private practice. Unlike the elected District Attorney, the county public defenders of California were appointed to their position by the various Boards of Supervisors of the counties.

Three years previously, Teska had been approached by a friend to consider accepting the appointment for Sonoma County. He accepted the invitation and was readily appointed by the supervisors. The position of Public Defender fit perfectly with Teska's belief that even those accused of the worst crimes deserved a vigorous and expert defense.

Teska was meeting for the fourth time with his assigned client, Elmont Jacob Agenbroad, in the attorney visiting room at the Sonoma County Jail. During their first meeting, Teska, in trying to establish rapport with his client, made the mistake of casually calling the man 'Elmont.'

Agenbroad had flown into an immediate rage and snarled at his legal representative, "The name is Butch, and don't you ever call me that other name again if you care about your ass!"

We are sunk if he displays that kind of rage in the courtroom, Teska thought. But he apologized to his hair-triggered client, who immediately calmed down. *This one is going to be a real shit show.*

"We have an issue," Teska said when the guard closed the door, leaving the lawyer and client alone. "The judge is going to allow Stacy to testify."

"How can they do that? "She's a little brat, and a girl. No little girl—no damned woman for that matter—should ever be allowed to testify against a man."

"Well, the judge has talked to her and to the psychologist who's been seeing her since she was found. He feels she knows right from wrong and has information pertinent to the case. And, Butch, be careful with your comments about women. You can think whatever you want, but right now is not the time to be telling the world you hate women."

"Yeah, yeah. Whatever you say."

"I can't really attack Stacy on the stand. That could really backfire on us in front of a jury if I were to be too hard on a child in cross-examination. We will just have to talk about the complete lack of evidence and paint the use of Stacy as a desperate move on the part of the DA."

"I could get on the stand and tell everybody how much I love my little girl and how I would never hurt her."

"Not a good idea. If you get on the stand and make some statement about being a loving guy, the DA will be able to bring your ex-wives to testify in rebuttal. Right now, he can't call them because your prior incidents aren't related to this crime, but if you open the door with some statement like that ..." the defender's voice trailed off. He had almost said 'some asinine statement like that' but thought better of it at the last second.

Chapter Fifty-Seven

August 9, 1984

Six weeks passed with no progress in the case against Butch Agenbroad. Angi and Devon re-interviewed every witness, showing them the most recent photo of Agenbroad in a photo line-up. No one could provide any more information than they already had, and no one other than Roy Chamberlain and Helen Bernstein could identify the photo of Agenbroad.

Hoping that somehow, Krupp might find a way to get around the issue of hypnosis, the detectives even re-interviewed Chelsea Leedy, the girl who witnessed Agenbroad leaving the house with the girls on the day of the murder. This time, she tentatively picked Agenbroad's photo from the lineup, but her identification was less than certain. It would be useless if the ban on her testimony remained.

Masters and Anderson also re-interviewed Elena Sandoval and her daughter. Martita had re-taken her maiden name after receiving a divorce from Agenbroad on grounds of abandonment. Not surprisingly, they both readily identified Butch.

However, a cloud remained over any testimony Elena might give, since the investigators only found her as a result of the license number obtained from Chelsea during the hypnotic session. While Martita could technically testify, she actually could testify to very little, apart from conversations with her husband, Butch. The content of those conversations would be barred by law.

Masters noted that the yellow Honda Civic still sat in the driveway, but its very existence was not admissible in a court because of the hypnosis ban. "I'm thinking about trading it in," Elena said when she caught Masters' gaze. "My good memories in that car are mixed with bad ones of how it might have been used."

* * *

Ten days before Butch's scheduled trial date, the fatigued investigators sank into overstuffed chairs in Krupp's office. "No good news, Anson," Masters said. "We've been over every rock—hell, even under every rock—and we have nothing more than we had before."

Krupp shook his head. "We are all doing the best we can. Sometimes, no matter what we do, the bad guy gets away."

Angi's eyes opened wide and her jaw clenched. "Well, not on this one! Are you sure there's no way we can use any of the information we got from Chelsea Leedy? We could argue that we might have found Elena Sandoval eventually. After all, we did interview her daughter when we first talked to Butch. Checking on her mother might not have been in our first line of investigation but I think I can say that we probably would have gone that direction eventually."

Angi was searching for anything that would allow the DA to enter the information about the fake trip to Reno or the mileage on the borrowed Honda nearly matching the round trip distance from Soquel to Santa Rosa.

"I'm certainly willing to give it a try, but it will be an uphill battle. The defense will probably argue that we might not have made the connection between Elena's car and the drop off of the kids in Richmond had we found the car in the way you suggest. I think we would have to admit, Angi, that finding Martita would not necessarily have led you to Elena and the car."

"Are you sure you're on our side, Anson?"

"Angi, yes he is. We all are with you on this," Devon said. "This is just a lot tougher case than normal, in a lot of ways, and we're all on edge. We also all know that a conviction is no good if it gets overturned because of improper evidence."

Angi sank back in the overstuffed leather chair. "I know, Devon, and I'm sorry for going off on you, Anson. I know you're doing your best with what we have to work with."

Krupp nodded. "We're in pretty good shape on the kidnapping, so I plan to try that one first. We haven't charged Agenbroad with anything connected to the murder, so the defense can't force us to try that part of the case along with the kidnapping. Roy Chamberlain has been consistent with his story and it's backed up by the witness, Helen ..?"

"Bernstein," Devon said.

"Yes, Helen Bernstein. Who knows, maybe something will come out in testimony in the kidnapping trial that will be useful in the murder trial."

"You didn't mention Stacy," Angi said. "Are you going to call her as a witness? You said the judge cleared her for that."

"Yes, I know. I'm going to hold her until last. I'll see how things are going at the trial. Perhaps we can get a plea to a decent lesser charge from Agenbroad after he hears Chamberlain and Bernstein's testimony. He might decide to cut a deal to avoid a life sentence that comes with a conviction to agg kidnapping, and accept a plea to something that we can still lock him away for a long time."

Chapter Fifty-Eight

August 15, 1984

A week later, Angi was at her desk reviewing reports on another new case. This one involved the severe beating of a woman by her live-in boyfriend. She was so engrossed in the vivid descriptions of the scene that she didn't hear her phone ring the first two times. "Masters, wake up and answer your phone," another detective yelled across the work room.

Oh, shit. I hope this isn't another new case. The upcoming trial of Agenbroad for the kidnapping was on her mind constantly. She worried that she and Devon had not done enough, had not found enough evidence to put the monster away for a long time.

"Detective Masters, this is Agent Jayne Andrews in the San Jose DOJ office."

Uh oh. Why is a California Department of Justice investigator calling from San Jose, a hundred miles away? The DOJ had agents stationed in Santa Rosa to help with state investigations in the area. *Must be something involving a local perp who got out of line in the South Bay and the DOJ wants to dump it off to us. Not important enough for the Staties, probably.*

"Yes, Agent, how can I help you?" Angi did her best to remain pleasant.

"I should have called you a couple of weeks ago when this first came in, but we have been so busy around here," Andrews said.

Angi said nothing.

"About three weeks ago, the Santa Cruz PD got a call from a local car dealer. It seems that the car dealer had taken a car in on a trade. While the car was being cleaned before being put up for sale, one of the detailers found a knife wedged into the seat track of the driver's seat."

Angi sat up in her chair. "OK." *I'm not sure what this has to do with me – us – but Santa Cruz?*

"It was strange in that it appeared the knife had become wedged when someone moved the seat forward to allow a shorter person to drive the car. Apparently, the driver never moved the seat again, because it couldn't move with that thing stuck in the track."

Oh, great! The seat won't move with something stuck in the track. I need to know this because ...

"Anyway," Andrews said, "SCPD responded and recovered the knife from the car dealer. The knife appeared to be bloody, although the blood was obviously old and thoroughly dried. What caught their attention was a fingerprint in the dried blood on the handle."

"Hm. OK." Now it was getting interesting.

"SCPD processed the print and it is the right thumbprint of one Elmont Jacob Agenbroad."

"OK, Agent Andrews. You have my full attention. But why am I just hearing about this now, and why not from Santa Cruz PD?"

"From what I understand, SCPD didn't put it together with any outstanding case. The blood was very old and degraded. However, on the off chance that something might come of it, they sent the knife to the Freedom BFS for testing."

The Freedom Bureau of Forensic Services lab in nearby Watsonville was one of several forensic labs operated by the State of California. "The lab techs at first didn't think they could do anything with it because of the state of the substance on the knife. However, it seems that one of the old techs decided to use something called .... Hold on a minute ..."

Angi was on the edge of her seat, but listened as Andrews shuffled some papers. *I don't need the scientific mumbo jumbo. Just tell me what the damn conclusion is.*

"I guess it's just called a crystal test. Anyway, it's a blood test developed about fifty years ago that's not used much anymore. The thing about it is that it works on really old blood samples, like fifteen or twenty year old samples. The lab couldn't determine an ABO type because of the age, but it's definitely human blood on that knife."

"OK."

"And I'm sorry for not getting back to you sooner, but after the lab notified the DOJ about the blood being human, things just got lost in the shuffle. We did see a bulletin where you were looking for this Agenbroad character for some pretty heavy stuff so I thought it best if I just called you rather than the usual notification letter. If you want the knife, I can have it shipped up to you or you can pick it up at the Freedom lab."

"So we have a knife found in a trade-in car with Agenbroad's thumbprint on it. There's blood on the knife that is human but it can't even be type-matched to anyone. So it could just be Agenbroad's blood when he cut himself sometime. Is that about right?"

"Yes, I'd say it is, Detective. Maybe that's why it wasn't given much of a priority. There isn't enough to tie it to any crime."

"Any idea how long it had been in the car?" *Don't get your hopes up too high, yet, Angi.*

"The lab people told me that they thought the blood was between three and five years old, but that's just a window. A lot would depend on where the car had been—heat, cold, sunlight—those kinds of things. Not only was the blood pretty old, and it's likely that the knife was in the car a long time.

"Both our agents and the SCPD detective checked out the previous owner. She is squeaky clean, not even a traffic ticket. So it seemed even more logical that the knife might just be part of someone accidentally cutting themselves."

"Who owned the car?"

"Umm, let's see. Oh, yes. It belonged to a woman named Sandoval, Elena Sandoval."

Chapter Fifty-Nine

11:20 a.m. - Watsonville, California

"Julie, cover for me," Angi yelled across the room to another detective. To the phone, she said with her now intense interest obvious, "I'm on my way down right now, Agent Andrews. Can you meet me at the BFS in about two hours?"

An hour and twenty minutes later, Angela Masters arrived at the Freedom BFS in Watsonville. Agent Andrews was waiting for her. "What's so urgent, Detective?"

"We are about to go to trial on this guy, Agenbroad. If this knife means what I hope it does, the whole scope of our prosecution could change."

Once the women's identification was checked by the guard at the reception desk and they signed the log stating their purpose for visiting the lab, they were escorted through a secure door to an evidence holding area. There they were greeted by Lab Technician Harlan Motichka.

"I performed all the tests on the knife myself, Detective," Motichka said. "Here is a copy of my complete report, but in essence, this is what I found. The knife is a six-inch Buck knife. They are extremely common and there's nothing that can be used to track down a purchaser or anything like that. There are no engravings or other identifying marks on the knife."

Get to the good part! Angi balled her hand into a fist.

"The blood, as I'm sure Agent Andrews has told you, is human. But beyond that we can't get enough of a viable sample to even determine ABO." ABO referred to the standard typing of the blood of any primate, including humans, into one of four types: A, B, AB, or O. The types were identified in 1900 and constituted the best method at the time for matching a blood sample to a person.

While it could not identify a single person, whether suspect or victim, it could be used in elimination in some cases, or as an element of a larger scheme of corroboration.

"The fingerprint, or thumbprint actually, was quite easily identified. The print is what we refer to as plastic, meaning the ridge detail is retained in a substance after the finger is removed, like mashing your finger into a piece of clay. In this case, I suspect the blood had dried somewhat on the handle and thus had thickened, causing it to be a good medium to retain the print."

Angi nodded. *I know this shit. Get to the good stuff!*

"Sometimes, technicians make the mistake of overlooking the possibility of other prints that aren't as readily seen when they have one that's so obvious," Motichka said. "I am more thorough than that. I also discovered a partial print on the blade. The print is much smaller, that of a woman perhaps. There is very little ridge detail for comparison, but enough to make an identification if the owner's print is on file somewhere. I checked that and came up empty on finding a match."

"This is all very interesting and helpful, Mr. Motichka," Angi said. "Is there anything else I need to know about it from an evidentiary standpoint? Any hairs, fibers, semen, or anything else found on the knife?

"There were a few fibers stuck to the blood, but I determined those came from the carpet in the Honda. Otherwise, nothing of that nature."

Very thorough. He'll make a good witness.

"Too bad we don't have DNA yet," Motichka said. There was a sadness in his voice.

Should I bite? What the hell. I'll humor him because we might be able to use this in court and need his testimony. "What's DNA?" *I hope this doesn't take too long.*

Motichka happily explained the concepts of deoxyribonucleic acid, first discovered in 1869 and its uniqueness in living things first postulated in 1953. "Someday soon, the way you conduct an investigation will be totally different, because you will be able to use something like blood or hair or even fingernail clippings to positively identify a single individual."

Identify a specific perp from a fingernail clipping? Science fiction if you ask me. "Sounds great, but I guess for now we have to go with what we have. I really appreciate your work, Mr. Motichka. I'm sure we'll be in touch." The trial would be starting in a few days if she didn't get this information to Krupp.

Angi signed for custody of the knife, still in the evidence envelope where it was first packaged by a Santa Cruz detective, and placed it in a leather attaché case in the back seat of her car.

"Thank you for your help, Agent Andrews. We just might get this guy after all."

* * *

The next morning, Angi and Devon were waiting in the hallway outside Krupp's office when the first clerk arrived. They were allowed into the outer office and offered seats in the waiting room. Thirty minutes later, Krupp walked through the door. Without a word, both detectives rose and followed him into his office.

"I take it you have something important to talk about," Krupp said over his shoulder as he unlocked the door to his private chamber and left the door open for the investigators to follow.

"More than important, I think." Angi said.

"Coffee?" Krupp asked as he poured himself a cup from the CoffeeMate in the small alcove to the right of his desk. Melissa always had the allowable four cups of coffee brewed each morning upon his arrival. Krupp allowed himself two or three cups in the morning, but never any after lunch.

The detectives both declined and Krupp poured himself a cup of java. "OK, What's up?"

Angi recounted the events of the day before. "Last night, I booked the knife and its packaging into our evidence locker. But I have the lab tech's report here," she said as she handed the document across the desk to Krupp.

The District Attorney read the document, twice letting out a low whistle as he read the findings. "Well, it's not conclusive but even if they had been able to get an ABO type on the blood, it still would have not been an iron-clad tie to Sharon McElroy."

The detectives said nothing but waited for the lawyer to finish his thoughts. Krupp re-read the report twice before laying it aside.

He closed his eyes briefly then punched a button on his intercom. "Melissa, please have Elisa come to my office right away."

He had barely punched the clear button on his intercom when there was a light knock on his door and the Senior Deputy District Attorney let herself into the office. Angi started to speak but Krupp held up his hand to signal her silence as he said, "Elisa, please join us. There's something I'd like you to read."

Montgomery read Harlan Motichka's report, going over it a second time.

"Well, what do you think?" Krupp asked as she laid the document back on his desk.

"I think this changes everything, Anson. Since this was an independent discovery by Santa Cruz detectives who had no part in the investigation and weren't privy to the info from the hypnosis, this information would independently lead us to Elena Sandoval and of course her knowledge of Agenbroad."

Angi smiled.

"We don't need to worry about putting Chelsea Leedy on the stand. My opinion is that everything Elena Sandoval told Angi and Devon would be admissible. You just lay the foundation to Sandoval based on connecting the bloody knife to her car. Then you let her talk about Agenbroad's strange trip. It should also let you bring in the stuffed toy, something that Elena herself said was not there previously. The judge might disagree, but at least it's an arguable position now. I think we have him!"

Chapter Sixty

August 18, 1984

Two days later, the telephone rang on Anson Krupp's desk. "Anson," Chuck Teska said, "my client would like me to discuss a deal on the kidnapping."

"Go on, Chuck."

"Well, to be frank, I've gone over the testimony I expect you'll present. I've advised my client that it would be a crap shoot."

"You're putting Roy Chamberlain on, first I would presume," Teska said. "He has some damaging information for your direct examination, but I could destroy his credibility on cross. I know a lot about what he did in San Sebastian and know that you haven't addressed those in your plea deal with him."

"OK." Krupp was not surprised at the revelation. Of course, Agenbroad would have told his attorney everything about his relationship with Chamberlain, including the assaults in the prison. *No worries and no commitments yet.*

"My problem, as we both know, is that I can't bring up Chamberlain's past without my client admitting to additional felony charges. The two are completely entwined."

Exactly how I read it, Chuckie boy. Agenbroad will have to admit to his crimes in prison, most of which were felony assaults, in order to discredit Chamberlain. Agenbroad and Teska had to realize that if no one had brought up those crimes yet, with Butch in custody as he was, it wasn't likely that he was going to be charged—unless he admitted his involvement. It was a classic Catch-22 and Agenbroad could see it.

"Next, and probably last from what I see in your discovery, you'll put Helen Bernstein on the stand. She'll be believable and

I'm sure you already know she has the background of a saint. The jury would eat up whatever she says."

Again, the defense assessment exactly matched Krupp's strategy. The defense attorney would find it almost impossible to discredit Bernstein, and could be perceived as desperately bullying an old lady if he tried. It was not the most solid case Krupp had brought to court in his short time as a district attorney, but it was solid enough for a jury to come back with a guilty verdict.

"You might put Stacy Agenbroad on the stand. You might, but I suspect you'll hold her back because you don't want her to be subject to a rigorous cross-examination, which I would have to do."

Bluster, and you know it, Chuck. You would never try to aggressively cross-examine an eight-year-old.

Teska was not required to reveal his defense strategy, but it didn't take a legal genius to know that he had nothing of substance to counter the prosecution's case. His only witness was Agenbroad himself. No defense lawyer in his right mind would put a convicted felon on the stand, especially to testify to nothing more substantial than, 'some other dude did it.'

Neither did Teska reveal his other concern, although he was certain that Krupp was thinking along the same lines. The Honorable Alistair M. 'Sonny' Compton had been assigned as the trial judge. At age 78, Judge Compton was not only the most senior active judge in the Sonoma County Superior Court, he was the most senior active Superior Court judge in any of the fifty-eight counties.

Judge Compton had a solid reputation for preserving decorum in his courtroom. As a result, he did not 'take kindly,' as he would often say, to courtroom antics and grandstanding from lawyers. Most importantly, Judge Compton was the epitome of fairness in the conduct of a trial. To Krupp, this meant that the judge did not go out of his way to slant his rulings in favor of the defendant, as Krupp and many other DAs felt was all too common among liberal California judges.

He didn't slant his rulings in support of the prosecution either, but Krupp could accept that. He believed strongly that a 'fair trial' meant a fair hearing for both sides and a judgment based on evidence. On that, the district attorney and the judge agreed.

To Teska, it meant he would have little leeway in any attempt to confuse or redirect a jury's attention away from the prosecution witnesses' damning testimony.

"What do you have in mind?" Krupp asked when Teska had finished.

"Mr. Agenbroad will plead to one count of kidnapping, without the 'aggravated' enhancement. That would put him in prison for four to eight years, and he would take whatever sentence you recommend."

Teska didn't reveal his concern that any admission by Agenbroad about taking the girls, even one artificially amended to only one count, could be introduced as corroboration of complicity in Sharon McElroy's murder. Agenbroad had not been charged in that crime but it was not a secret to anyone within two hundred miles of Santa Rosa that he was the prime suspect. He could only hope that Krupp had no other evidence linking Agenbroad to the murder. It was a reasonable hope since Krupp had never mentioned charging Butch with anything but kidnapping.

For his part, Krupp had no interest in accepting a plea bargain in the aggravated kidnapping case. He merely entertained Teska's offer and explanation as a means of gaining insight into the defense thinking and strategy.

"Well, it's an interesting offer, Chuck. However, we have some new information so I'm going to pass on your offer. In fact, I was about to call you this morning. Later today, I will be amending the complaint against Agenbroad to include one count of first-degree murder with special circumstances. I'm including a motion for the death penalty for the murder. I'll also notify Judge Compton's clerk of the new filing, since I would guess that you will want a new trial date."

What new information could have possibly come up this late in the game? "OK, thank you, Anson. I'll be looking for your amendment."

Shocked you, didn't I, Chuckie?

Charles Cotesworth Teska IV would not get much sleep that night.

Chapter Sixty-One

August 19, 1984

The following morning, Teska visited Krupp's office to discuss the new charges.

"Let me show you what we have now, Chuck." He handed a copy of Motichka's report to the defender.

Whether the newly discovered evidence would be admitted in court became a moot point that afternoon, when the public defender returned. "I've reviewed the additional information you gave me this morning—all this stuff from Santa Cruz—and I've discussed it with my client."

As Krupp was certain he would be, Teska was concerned that the unidentified print on the blade might be that of Sharon McElroy. She would have been fingerprinted as part of the autopsy, but those prints would not have been entered into the regular databases. They would still be available for comparison however. It was a chance the defense couldn't afford to take. "Take the death penalty off the table and reduce the kidnapping to one count without the 'aggravated' enhancement, and you've got a deal."

* * *

The defense attorney didn't know that his client at that moment was mentally kicking himself for the lapse. He had intended to throw the knife into San Francisco Bay on his way back to Santa Cruz, but had become distracted by the girls. *I should never have snatched those brats in the first place!*

Now it appeared that he had somehow dropped the knife in the car and it had become lodged in the seat track when he had moved the seat back to Elena's driving position. *I'm not sure how Sharon touched the blade, trussed up like she was, but maybe I bumped her hand with it. Anyway, I ain't gonna face the death penalty to find out.*

* * *

Krupp appeared to consider about the new plea offer for a moment, although he had already gone over every scenario he could think of for this situation. He was pretty certain what Teska would propose as soon as he heard that the defense counselor wanted to see him.

"No death penalty and two counts of non-aggravated kidnapping. No mitigation on sentencing." That meant sentencing would be left to the judge with no plea on the part of either attorney for enhancement or leniency.

"My client will accept that." Teska knew that Agenbroad was more at home inside the walls of a penitentiary anyway.

* * *

Three days later, the attorneys and Agenbroad appeared in Judge Compton's courtroom. Detectives Masters and Anderson, Sergeant Garrison, and Doug and Stacy were all present in the visitor's gallery. Across the hall, Jennifer and her younger sister, Kelsey, watched the court proceedings on a closed circuit television with a family friend.

"I understand the parties have reached an agreement," the judge said.

"Yes, Your Honor," Teska said. He stood and directed Agenbroad to stand as well.

"Mr. Agenbroad, do you understand that by pleading guilty you are giving up your right to a trial?" the judge asked.

"Yeah, I know. This ain't my first rodeo, judge."

"Very well. How do you plead to the count of first-degree murder?"

"Guilty, Your Honor." Butch also stated a 'guilty' plea to each of the kidnapping charges.

"The pleas of guilty to all charges are accepted by the Court as being knowingly and willingly given. ALE-mont Jacob Agenbroad," the judge said, his Southern accent dragging out the first syllable of the defendant's hated first name, "this Court sentences you to life imprisonment for the willful murder of Sharon Kelson McElroy.

"You are also sentenced to eight years imprisonment for the kidnapping of Stacy Agenbroad and an additional eight years imprisonment for the kidnapping of Jennifer McElroy. These sentences are to be served consecutively. It is also the recommendation of this Court that you shall never be considered for parole."

Teska jumped to his feet. He had counted on concurrent sentences and no judicial recommendation. That might have allowed Agenbroad to be released on parole one day. "I ob ..."

But before he could even complete the words, Judge Compton slammed his gavel. "Oh, stuff it, Counselor. You agreed to leave sentencing to me and this is my decision. Unless of course your client wants to withdraw his pleas and go to trial with the death penalty back on the table. We can start that today." The senior judge had his own way of making a point.

"Sit down and shut up, counselor," Agenbroad said, loud enough for the entire courtroom to hear.

"No, Your Honor," Teska said and sat back down. The exchange was reported in the official transcript as an objection by the defense which was denied by the Court.

Secretly, Teska was relieved at the outcome. He had done his professional duty to provide Agenbroad with the best defense possible. But personally he was happy that the monster would never again walk free.

It was over. Retribution, legally obtained, for the wanton taking of a beloved life and for three years of mental agony was long in coming for Doug and the girls. But now they could go on, knowing that Butch Agenbroad would never again hurt them. Sharon could at last rest in peace. The McElroys went outside, hand in hand, squinting in the bright California sunshine as they left this dark and tragic chapter of their lives behind.

"Do you want to get some ice cream?" Doug asked.

Stacy let go of her sister's hand. "Mommy loved strawberry ice cream. Can we get some strawberry?"

"I'm sure Mommy would think that's a great idea," Doug said as he picked up Jennifer and tossed her in the air. Jennifer let out a peal of laughter and Stacy felt a tremendous weight lifted from her tiny narrow shoulders.

Epilogue

Twenty years have passed since the sentencing. Butch Agenbroad died in prison eighteen years ago, the victim of his own brand of violence. While he was walking across the yard with a group of inmates, he suddenly fell out of the pack and his body thudded to the ground. In an act eerily similar to the death of his mother, a sharpened screwdriver had been jabbed between Agenbroad's third and fourth ribs, piercing his heart. No one was ever prosecuted for his murder.

Kelsey McElroy graduated from San Jose State University with a degree in Economics of Developing Countries. She is currently working on a Master's Degree at San Jose State and is planning on a career in the Foreign Service.

Jennifer McElroy Inman pursued a love of flying that she discovered in junior high school. During her pursuit of a flying career, she met and married Major David Inman, currently assigned as a B-1 bomber pilot at Edwards Air Force Base. Jennifer herself graduated with honors from Embry Riddle Aeronautical University. She is presently a First Officer flying Boeing 737 jets for United Airlines.

Stacy Agenbroad was adopted by Doug McElroy shortly after the sentencing and legally changed her last name to McElroy. Stacy had only one life goal in mind. After college, where she obtained a degree in history, Stacy started on a path to emulate her hero, Angela Masters. She became a police officer.

As part of the process to become an officer, Stacy was fingerprinted. A routine database check showed a match to a bloody print on a knife blade, evidence in a long closed murder case—the small print Harlan Motichka could not identify. While Butch was driving toward Chamberlain's house, Stacy had found the knife on the floor of the back seat where he had dropped it. She placed the knife under the car seat, fearing that the stinky man claiming to be her father would use it to hurt her or her sister. It had become lodged in the seat track until its discovery by the auto detailer.

Four months ago, Stacy attained a major step toward her goal in a police promotion ceremony. Today, she carries in her purse a black leather wallet, its surface stamped in a basket-weave pattern. On one side of the opened wallet is an official police identification card. On the other, nestled in an especially cutout section of leather, is a gold-colored metal badge inscribed with the words *Detective – Santa Rosa Police*.

Thank you

Thank you for your purchase. I hope you enjoyed this book.

I would sincerely appreciate your review on Amazon.com. Reviews help an author produce content that readers would like to see.

Are you on my mailing list yet? If not, please follow the link below (or type it into your browser) to sign up. You will hear about new releases, get the inside track on the development of each new book, and be eligible for occasional special offers such as giveaways, advance reader copies, and special pricing on individual books and sets only offered to subscribers.

www.mikeworleybooks.com/subscribe

Other Books in the Angela Masters Detective Novel Series

"Grand Jeté"
"Entitlement"
"Ghost"
"Fire Storm"

About the Author

Mike Worley is a veteran of 34 years in law enforcement, moving through the ranks from Police Officer to Captain with the Boise, ID Police Department. During his career, he served as an investigative commander in both criminal investigations and internal affairs. He then accepted a position as Chief of Police with the suburban Meridian, ID Police Department.

Following his retirement from active policing, he continued his law enforcement involvement as an instructor and course coordinator for a university-based police training facility. He has also consulted nationally on police policy issues.

He is retired and lives with his wife, Nancy, in Louisville, KY.

www.ingramcontent.com/pod-product-compliance
Lightning Source LLC
Chambersburg PA
CBHW061607170626
46811CB00001B/351